THE CHRIST TRILOGY

BOOK I

THE LOST CHRIST

SterlingHouse Publisher, Inc. Pittsburgh, PA

THE CHRIST TRILOGY
BOOK I

THE LOST CHRIST

ISBN 1-56315-463-3
978-1-56315-463-8

Trade Paperback
© Copyright 2009 Mike Difeo
All rights reserved
First Printing—2009
Library of Congress #2009922475

Request for information should be addressed to:
SterlingHouse Publisher, Inc.
3468 Babcock Boulevard
Pittsburgh, PA 15237
www.sterlinghousepublisher.com

Cambrian House
is an imprint of SterlingHouse Publisher, Inc.

SterlingHouse Publisher, Inc. is a company
of the CyntoMedia Corporation

Cover Design: Brandon M. Bittner
Interior Design: N. J. McBeth

All rights reserved. No part of this publication may be reproduced, stored in a retrieval system, or transmitted in any form or by any means—electronic, mechanical, photocopy, recording or any other, except for brief quotations in printed reviews—without prior permission of the publisher.

This is a work of fiction. Names, characters, incidents, and places, are the product of the author's imagination or are used fictitiously. Any resemblance to actual events or persons, living or dead is entirely coincidental.

Printed in the United States of America

Dedication

This writing is dedicated to those that are helping to keep the earth clean, the skies and oceans clear, and to those that are bringing the word of the Lord to the hearts and minds of mankind all over the world. And, "May the Lord always be with you."

INTRODUCTION

First imagine ... it's later in the 21st century and at a time when mankind finally blew it ... carbon pollution that led to climate warming and the violent winds, earthquakes and tsunamis that followed. And with the oceans rising the cities and lower lands perished, becoming a new ocean's floor. A time when millions ... No, when billions of animal, plant and human life was lost, extinct ....

Then imagine ... it's 2000 years later, *a new world* ... the seven continents are a maze of islands, each continent a country, the memory of the 21st century and before wiped from mankind's mind ... No carbon polluters of any kind ... A candlelight world ... A world that is somewhat like it was in the 15th century ... and a world with no God....

And then imagine ... a new mankind, *Formed In a Test Tube* mankind, a FITT. No romances, just pre-arranged, platonic, same sex civil unions ... Pairings. Their names fit their personality or profession to be. Everyone is dressed the same and living in communes. No wireless communications, only hand delivered messages. The only weapons ... are repeater rifles and sidearms, and only in the hands of the policing forces. The seven New World Governments thought it a utopia world ... But was it?

Now imagine ... what would happen if three educators would happen across a buried time capsule from the 21st century, and inside was a veritable treasure of photographs, newspaper articles, reference books, a Tanakh (written Torah) and a New Testament (Christian bible.)

The educators, confused, not knowing what to make of the two religious books ... hand scribed onto scrolls all of what was the same, and then added the differences ... One Holy Scroll ... and yes, one new belief emerged. Thus, a new underground society was born ... Pariahs, was what the government councils named the neophytes ... Enemies with a belief defying the social law could threaten all seven of the New World Government's existences. The movement had to be stopped and the governments would do anything to do so, no matter the cost in human life.

Mankind, for the first time in twenty centuries, was learning the meaning of new words. Words like — "Love" — "Marriage" — "Childbirth" — "Family" and "God" — But with the discovery will come another word — "WAR."

Chapter One
The Year 4050

The bay at Yeshiva Island was choppy, the small waves rushing to shore. It was the dark of night and just beginning to rain. On the shore was a shore boat with but a small mast at the center, its canvas sail reefed. Standing next to the shore boat were five men, all students. Off in the distance out over the ocean were the occasional flashes of light, each followed by the faint noise of its thunder.

The five were dressed in only a white cloth wrapped diaper-like around their waist and between their thighs, sandals and an ankle long, hooded, white, slip over robe. Hanging from a rope tied about the waist was a sheep skin pouch filled with water to drink. They had no food supplies. Nor could anyone navigate using the stars.

Three of the men; Jesus, John and Joseph were but twenty years old. The other two, Salient and Pathos, were much the older and had been learning at the school too long, so they thought. The best of friends they became those years, always at each other's side.

Jesus always had a gathering of students about him listening to the teachings of the Lord, of which he spoke. The teachings were often indifferent than what was being taught in the classes. Too often He spoke up in defiance of what was being taught. For speaking out He was considered rebellious by the teach master of the school, and marked as not ready to go forth unto the communes to teach the words from the Holy Scrolls Writings, the teachings of the one Jesus took the name of.

Pathos still had the scars from years earlier, scars that cut deep into his mind. The begging screams from his teacher Genial *"Please kill me, please. Dear God, please!"* woke him many a night. Through it all Salient was always there for Pathos, always there to comfort him. It was more than pity or sorrow, because Salient, too, had the memories. It was he that held Pathos back that awful night, saving him from the same fate as Genial, a sharp blade of a knife across his throat. But now Pathos also had Jesus. He loved Jesus and what Jesus spoke of. He would follow him to the ends of the world.

John was a big man with a long beard and much hair on his chest, arms and legs. Since birth his right eye was blinded and of a different color. His left leg was shorter than his right and, because, he walked with a limp and used a walking stick for balance. Smiling was difficult for him, but when he did laugh it was a roaring laughter. John was the smartest of the four that were following Jesus, and the most outspoken.

Joseph was a thin, wiry man. He too had a long beard. His hair was of a red color, and already at such a young age the hair was graying. Most likely, the early graying was because of his worrying. He worried about everything and almost didn't come along because so. Already, as the rain started falling harder, he was wishing he had stayed in his bedding this night.

"The water's cold," Pathos whispered to Salient when he stepped into the bay's edge, the bottom of his robe floating atop the water.

"Push!" shouted Salient. "Push hard!"

John and Joseph were on the other side of the shore boat helping push the boat out into the bay. Jesus was pushing from the rear, and He was the last one of the five to jump into the boat. They were finally on their way. On their way to teach the good words of the Lord.

It was three days and nights since they left Yeshiva Island, the sky cloudless and the wind still. Salient felt like his body was cooking, like that of a chicken over a fire pit. The sun's glare was strong, his stomach ached of hunger, his water pouch was almost empty, and it had been three days without a meal. What fools we are, he thought, too leave on such a journey and without food supplies.

Next to him sleeping was Pathos. The two were lying close to the lone mast, its sail up and without wind. Asleep at the rear of the boat were John and Joseph. Jesus was sitting near the hull.

Suddenly Jesus stood up and raised both his arms, extending his palms outward. Then Jesus began to pray, and having seen Jesus pray Salient rose to his knees and he, too, prayed. He prayed for his life, for all five's safety.

The wind got stronger, and stronger as Jesus raised his arms higher. Then, *Bang … Bang … Bang*, the sound as the sail filled quickly with wind and the boat began to move.

The excited Salient reached over, tapping Pathos on the shoulder awakening him. The two watched Jesus extend his arms yet higher, as if drawing the clouds closer.

The boat began to rock up and down onto the ocean's water. Yet Jesus stood unshaken by the wind, His robe tossing about his body snapping with each wind's gust, His hair soaked with rain brushing across His face.

A streak of lightning struck downward from the black clouds that rushed by overhead and hit upon the water nearby. The blast of loud thunder that followed woke John and Joseph. Confused, they too watched Jesus, they too began to pray, they too prayed for their lives.

"Look," shouted an excited Pathos, his mouth left open as he pointed toward Jesus. Jumping into the boat was a small fish and it landed at Jesus' feet, its fins and tail flapping up and down slapping the boats decking. Then, into the boat jumped a second small fish, a third, a fourth and fifth; each and every one of them lay at Jesus' feet. Sent by God, thought the other four.

"A miracle!" John cried out.

Jesus was the most common name chosen from the Holy Scrolls and given to Pariah children, and because, there were many young men at the school with the name of Jesus, John thought, but this Jesus before me is the son of God — The re-birth of Christ — **The Lost Christ** … lost and forgotten for two thousand years.

"He is the Messiah! He has come to show us the way, just as it is written in the Holy Scrolls; He has returned," John yelled out. Then he fell to his knees re-joining the others in prayer.

Jesus sat down, the storm had passed, and the sail was full of wind.

"Eat from the meal thy Father has given us," and then He rested His head between the palms of His hands. Hungry, and without hesitation the others ate from the fish brought unto them. And after, when they thirsted they lifted their pouches to find that the pouches were filled with fresh water.

It was the dawn of the next morning when Jesus and his retinue sighted land. It was the settlement of Harbinger. They sailed into the harbor and past the many supply and freedom ships that sat anchored. Their shore boat with its small mast and sail looked lost amongst the greatness of the sailing vessels. One of which they would board for the next leg of their journey, a journey that would take them to all the lands of the settlements and then to the United American Union of Communes.

Chapter Two
✠ Forty years earlier ✠

Ardent sat up in his bedding still half asleep from what was a sound night's sleep. The vociferous wakeup call from the intercom that hung on the wall nearby was still ringing in his ears, reminding him of how much he hated the thing. He wished he could just rip it off the wall.

"I hate you," he yelled out, as if the intercom had ears.

This was a special day for him. It was his 16th birthday. Today he would be finished with his Commune Office of Protective Services (COPS) training. The four years of tough enforcement training was finally over, all the pain, hard work, and studying that he hated.

Now all that was left of training was the 90 days of pairing preparedness and then he would finally, and with his civil union pairing-to-be, go out into the real world for the first time in his life. Once he was assigned a commune community, he knew he would make a real difference. He was ready. He was trained. He was strong. Today, however, he would get ready for the graduation celebration and worry about what commune community he would be assigned at another time.

The commune communities were divided into four separate areas. Each of the areas was called a cocoon. One cocoon was where all the trained males that were paired together quartered. Another cocoon was for all the trained women paired together. The third cocoon was for the Declared Incapable Public Servants (DIPS), which were not allowed to pair together. And the forth cocoon was where the mealing area, meeting area and working areas were. Having spent all his 16 years in area training schools Ardent had never seen a commune community. He knew only what he was taught of them.

All 236 Formed in a Test Tube (FITT) trainees in his group turned 16 years old on this 28th day of September, 160 men and 76 women. Two of the original group died in training accidents. Both of them were women.

Ardent, named so because of his passion, devotion, high emotions and because he also showed great enthusiasm for the people close to him, heard the water bubbling as it came to a boil. The steam was rising to the ceiling and forming a cloud-like resemblance from the coldness. The bath that he needed to fully wake up each morning would soon be ready.

He slipped onto his right hand the mitt that was hanging from the side of the wood burning stove. It felt hot, warming his hand. He rubbed it with the other hand to warm it also. Even with the wood burning stove blazing hot his quartering area was cool.

He picked up the pan of hot boiling water and carried it over to the wash tub. After adding the hot boiled water to the cold water in the tub he fetched the night before, he felt the water with his ungloved hand. "Just right," he said, as if someone else was there with him.

He quickly took off his wool robe. His naked body suddenly felt the coldness. "Burrrr," his head was shaking the word from his mouth. His long hair shook back and forth, hair that went all the way down to his shoulders.

With his body shivering, he hastily got into the wash tub. It was much too small for his body, but with a wiggle here and a wiggle there he managed to sink deep into the water, deep to his chest as he always did.

Bathing was the easy part, getting out of the tub was the hard part. To do so he had to put his right leg over one side and then his left over the other side. With his hands he lifted himself up, being careful not to tip over the thin wooden wash tub.

The only mirror in his living quarter was mounted next to the door. Space was very limited. From in front of the mirror he stared awhile at himself. His eyes were deep blue and his hair a golden yellow, unlike most the other FITT's with brown eyes and hair. His birthing tube, he had guessed, was one of the rarer ones.

He was running late, so he hastily put on his tan color, woolen lined, high neck, collarless and long sleeved shirt. It fit nice and tight to his virile body. Instantly he felt the warmth it provided. Then he stepped into his pants, also made of wool. The pants were a dark brown color, loose fitting and a bit baggy around the legs. After tying the waistline strap and ankle straps he put the heavy woolen socks and lined boots on over his pants, lifting each foot as he pulled onto the laces. *Thump* — the sound of each boot hitting the floor as he tied the laces good and tight.

Over his head he slipped a tan color, robe-like tunic that was also made of wool, covering his shirt and pants to below the knees. The tunic had a deep pocket on each side with a hood that could be tied tightly to the face, for the worst of weather.

After he got the tunic in place he slid a red dyed, wide leather belt through the loops. The belt was usually used to hold a revolver's holster, extra ammo and accessories.

Lastly, he put his left arm through the looped, red-braided rope — COPS insignia — sliding it up onto his shoulder and buttoning the shoulder flap that kept the insignia in place. Finally he was ready to leave.

On the way out he grabbed the mittens and hat that were hanging on the wall by the door next to the mirror. The hat was made of soft leather and wool lined with ear flaps that were usually tied up. Except for the color of the braided rope insignia and belt, which stood for the citizen's job classification, everyone, including the women, dressed the same.

⊂⊃⊂⊃⊂⊃

The Area #26 COP training school was located on a mountain in a small valley. The area around the school was of mostly willow trees and a modicum of pine trees. Even though it was only the month of September, at that high an altitude it was cold. This morning was no different.

When Ardent opened the door to exit his quartering area he felt a blast of cold air rush in and onto his exposed face. A dusting of snow snaked across the floor from the flurries of the night before, the first of the year.

He shivered the cold off, and then proceeded across the parade ground area. Coming from the other side of the parade ground area he saw Jewel. She, too, was a COP and a good shooter, both side arms and rifle. She had good steady hands and good aim. He was the best, but next to him she was probably the best shooter there, he thought. He liked being with Jewel, she wasn't all that bad a person to be with.

"It's sure cold today. I hope it gets warmer by the time the graduation celebration starts." Jewel remarked, having stopped to walk with him. The bounce in her step oscillated up and down her body making her long hair also bounce, that which hung below her hat. On this morning it shined and smelled of soap.

"I doubt that. It's cold here all the time." Ardent answered, while putting his gloves on, and then rubbing his hands together to get the blood running. "There will be plenty to eat, and for the first time in our lives we will get to drink rum."

"What is this drink they call rum?" Jewel asked.

"I really don't know, except that troopers and sailors are given a ration of rum every day, first thing in the morning."

"Slow down Ardent," he heard, and looking over to his left where the yelling came from, he saw Jejune rushing to catch up. His skinny and tall body looked awkward weaving side to side from the waist up, undulating because his hands were sunk deep into his tunic's pockets to keep them warm, restricting the movement of his really long skinny legs. Ardent thought Jejune was a bit dull, immature and lacking in insight.

"Watch out! You're going to fall." Ardent yelled out. But it was too late. To the ground Jejune started to fall. Unable to get his hands out of his pockets fast enough to break the fall he hit the ground very hard.

"Ouch … Ouch!" he yelled out, rolling over several times and looking like a gypsy clown, his tunic all dusted with snow.

"That was so funny. Could you do it again?" Jewel laughed, the wide smile showed a missing tooth.

After getting his hands out of his pockets he got up from the ground and very slowly he walked over to Ardent and Jewel. "Don't tell anyone else, please. I feel stupid enough," and the three shook hands. It was going to end right there. No one else would ever know how stupid Jejune looked. Ardent and Jejune being in a rush and hungry started to run, leaving Jewel standing still.

"Wait up, Ardent, Jejune. Wait for me!" Jewel yelled, but to deafened ears.

THE LOST CHRIST

By the time the two finally arrived at the graduation celebration Jewel had caught up with them, and approaching them from within a crowd of trainees was Bandy, known to exchange witticisms or insults.

Ardent thought Bandy looked like any one of the men. Even her insults were manly. Her hair was cut almost to the scalp. A small noticeable scar was just to the side and just under her right eye next to a broken, flattened out nose. But what stood out the most were her large, man-sized feet. Bandy, unlike he and Jewel, wasn't much of a shooter, but when it came to a hand to hand fight, she was good.

"Hey guys, I already had my rum ration, and boy did it taste good. Bovine didn't like his, so I drank it too. I feel a little dizzy though," a burp then a giggle followed Bandy's remark.

"Let's go get ours," and as soon as he got the words out of his mouth, Jejune started running straight for the tent area with the rum rations. Following close behind were Ardent and Jewel.

The three soon were sitting under a large willow tree, one of the very few types that survived the holocaust. Its branches hung low to the ground, the ground under was warm. It was a perfect shelter from the cool breeze that had reddened their faces.

"This here drink called rum tastes funny. It's too strong tasting and burns my throat," Ardent told the others.

"Give it to me, I think it's good," Jewel remarked, hastily grabbing Ardent's cup out of his hand spilling some.

"Who do you suppose they will pair you up with tomorrow, and what if it was me?" Jejune asked Ardent.

"Let's find Bandy and then get something to eat. She disappeared again. Tomorrow is going to be a long day." Ardent suggested. He avoided answering Jejune's question. Jejune incessantly asked questions, and usually Ardent would answer them, annoying as some of them were. But this was one of his stupidest yet, Ardent thought.

The mealing area was crowded with trainees. Apparently everyone decided to eat at the same time. The meal being served wasn't of the usual boiled vegetables and baked corn bread. Instead, they were being served fish from the ocean.

"They must have carted it up from the ocean just for our celebration," said Jejune, just before stuffing a heaping spoonful into his mouth. The others were too busy spooning the treat into their mouths to reply.

The DIPS were still running about wiping clean the tables and gathering up the dirty wooden bowls that everyone had eaten from, when the commander of the training school arrived. Rarely did the trainees get to see him. So this, their last night, must have been important enough for him to come, thought Ardent.

Right behind the commander were all of the instructors. In their lead was Tome, the head instructor and Ardent's favorite. When he was a young birthling, Tome was a voracious reader of large writings, the kind the others usually didn't like reading.

Tome stood very tall over the rest there. A squared chin with a dimple in its center gave him the look of a very stern person. Stern and to the point he usually was. His deep sounding voice always got everyone's attention.

⌒⌒⌒

Tome stepped forward to face the trainees, and with a couple quick claps of the hands he got their attention: "I personally will be accompanying all of you during your 90-day preparedness training." He spoke loud and clear. "Then I will pick 50 pairings for a new elite protection service force, of which I will be in command. My choices will be decided by your individual performance in the past and the performance of each pairing. The elite unit will be posted at a citadel being built near the Capital Commune where there is unrest amongst our citizens." Tome paused when he heard a buzzing of whispers spread throughout those gathered, much to his disliking. "Your group of trainees, however, will be paired with trainees from the United Communes of Europe. That is if enough make the journey here safely across the ocean." Then he dismissed the trainees, not taking questions.

"Wow, I guess we won't be paired after all," Jejune said to Ardent, a surprise look of disappointment on his face. He so much wanted to be paired with Ardent. After all, Ardent was his best friend. After the 90 day preparedness training we might never see each other again, he thought, unless he and his pairing-to-be were chosen by Tome. Ardent and his pairing surely would be.

"I hope Tome picks me," Ardent said.

"You're one of Tome's favorites. Of course he's going to pick you. It's me he probably won't pick," Jejune remarked. "Do you suppose he might pick me?"

Not unless you put more effort into your training," Ardent honestly answered. But it was probably too late now for Jejune to impress Tome, Ardent truly thought. "C'mon, let's go to our quartering area." Ardent, having put his hand on Jejune's shoulder, nudged him forward.

⊂⊁ ⊂⊁ ⊂⊁

Once inside his quartering area, Ardent took a long look. A last look, he thought. His quartering area was small and all he had in it was a little pot-bellied wood burning stove for heat, a small bedding area, the wash tub in the corner, a small round table with only one chair, his footlocker, an end table with a wash bowl, pitcher of water and a candle on it, and the mirror that was mounted next to the door.

Ardent blew out the candle, and then he pulled the bedding up over his shoulder tight to his neck. Lying there in the dark and before going off to sleep, Ardent thought about tomorrow and what it might bring.

⊂⊁ ⊂⊁ ⊂⊁

The sound from the intercom was deafening, causing Ardent to all of a sudden jump up from his bedding.

"Wow, the floor's cold," he said aloud, just as his bare feet hit the hard, cold, dirt floor. After turning around he reached for the bedding cover and wrapped it around his naked, shivering body. Coming from outside was the sound of the wind blowing against the door. He felt the cold draft entering and since he forgot to put a log in the stove before going to sleep he would have to suffer.

Because it was so cold he skipped taking a bath. Instead, he just washed his face and under his arms, brushed his teeth and then got dressed for morning meal. The mealing area, he knew, would be loud this morning, loud from all the talk of the pairing selections and the "guess who is getting picked" chatter from all the trainees.

⊂✕ ⊂✕ ⊂✕

When Ardent got outside it was warmer than it was inside his quartering area, but still cold. The dawn was just breaking, but the sun wasn't out yet. He could see that the sky was already getting its usual pinkish-gray, dirty-looking color, the color that was left after the holocaust of 2000 years earlier; the holocaust that almost wiped all mankind off the face of the Earth, but for the foresight of the then government to build a shelter deep into a mountain for but a few hundred influential citizens, and the foresight to build birthing tubes so that the Earth could be repopulated.

When Ardent got to the mealing area, Jejune and Bovine, a dull, unresponsive person and a bit slow since birthing, were waiting for him. What if, Ardent suddenly thought, my pairing was like Bovine? *Ouch! How horrible the thought.*

"Good morning." Ardent spoke first.

"Are you ready for this day?" Jejune asked.

"Yeah, about as ready as I could be," answered Ardent, who was ignoring Bovine whom he really didn't like one bit. He never understood why Jejune was friendly with him. He was a bit boring besides, thought Ardent.

⊂✕ ⊂✕ ⊂✕

When the three got inside heads turned their way and the chatter got louder.

"I think they're talking about you," Jejune joked.

"Why would they be talking about Ardent?" Bovine had to ask, a bit slow upstairs, as was the usual for him.

"Because, they all think Ardent is the teacher's pet," Jejune joked. The remark was ignored by Ardent, a bit of red started to blossom on his face.

"Eggs, and with fresh melon, wow, what a treat!" Jejune said when he saw what was being served. He was excited when he held out his tray to the DIP serving the morning meal, and said jokingly, "I'll take extra," to which the DIP just ignored him. In fact, everyone usually pretty much ignored Jejune.

The trainees, or anyone else for that matter, were not allowed to speak to the DIPS. If caught the punishment was harsh. But Ardent gave the DIP a smile anyway when he held out his tray.

Ardent spoke briefly with the very same DIP about a year or so earlier and thought he was a nice citizen. He knew he was in the wrong for having started a conversation, yet still several months later he spoke to the DIP again. He realized then that he was only feeling sorry for him. Since then he avoided any conversations. Weaknesses of that sort he knew he had to take better control of.

At the daily morning assembly the chatter was louder than usual until Head Instructor Tome arrived, and he wasn't smiling. Right away the gathering of trainees quieted down.

Tome wasted no time. Right to the front of the gathering he walked. He stood tall and a quick step was in his stride, his shoulders back. Under his right arm rested his hat. He stopped, turned to face his trainees and without hesitation he began to speak:

"A communication runner has brought word that the United Commune of Europe trainees have already arrived at Area #56. As was expected they encountered a tempest and some trainees didn't make it here. Fortunately, enough to pair everyone up did arrive safely."

Tome stopped speaking to scratch the back of his neck with his left hand. Quietness lingered over the gathering, not even a cough heard.

"The United Commune of Europe's trainees are moving their gear into their assigned quarters as I speak, so we will be departing in exactly one hour. Backpacks with your name and new quartering area number imprinted on them are being placed at your quartering area here."

Tome started walking up the aisle in amongst the trainees, slowly and deliberately was his pace. Turning, he headed back, speaking as he walked.

"When you arrive you will go to your civil union pairing who will be in your new quartering area waiting for you. Good luck and I'll see you all at the parade ground area in just one hour." Finished with what he had to say Head Instructor Tome immediately left the area. He was not the type to take questions, not from his trainees.

"We've got plenty of time to pack. What I have in my quartering area will only take a couple of minutes to throw into the backpack," Ardent said. Jejune's head was bobbing up and down in agreement.

The march to Area #56 had only taken six hours, but was downhill and tiring on the feet. At least for Jejune it was. His face lit up when he saw the entrance gate. Even Ardent, who usually liked the hikes, was glad to be there.

The DIPS had it the worst. Their backpacks were not only filled with all of their own gear, but also with Tome's office supplies. Hanging from their backpacks were also the extra meal preparing and eating utensils that would be needed, a much heavier load to carry. Ardent felt sorry for them, but he was glad to see that the DIP he spoke to on a couple occasions was also picked by Tome.

When the column reached the entrance gate, Instructor Tome raised his hand stopping the march to wait for someone from inside to open it, and he also wanted to give instructions before going any further.

"When you get into your living quarter and meet your pairing mate, the two of you must decide on a pairing name before the morning comes. Many other citizens will have the same first name as yours. So you can understand how important a pairing name is. The pairing name will stay with you the rest of your life. Therefore, I suggest you pick a good one," and as soon as Tome finished speaking the entry gate opened. Standing there holding the gate open was one of the instructors. He nodded his head, apparently over at Tome.

It didn't take long for Ardent to locate his quartering structure. The training compound was small in area and the structures were close to one another. Too close, he thought.

His new quartering structure was much the same as the one he had just left. A wide narrow structure with ten side by side quartering areas and each had its own entrance door. All the structures were old, built with cut tree trunks and there were no windows. The roofs were of wood covered with a clay-like dirt and wiry leaf mixture. They usually leaked when it rained. It was not unusual for the structures to rip apart in a strong wind, only to be hastily reconstructed again, and again.

Unsure what or who he would find inside, his anxiety rising, Ardent slowly entered his new quartering area. The door squeaked when he opened it, and again as it closed, an announcement of his arrival. His face reddened a bit.

"Hello mate," said the stranger inside. He was big and physically strong looking with the usual dark hair and the usual brown eyes. His hair was cut short along the top and sides, but was long in the back and reached to below his shoulders. An odd look, one Ardent had never seen before. It made him smile.

"Hello" Ardent returned the greeting, knowing that the stranger was checking him out as well.

"My name is Dank, and what's yours?"

"Ardent." The calmness in his voice was settling in now that the initial meeting was over and that he got to see what his pairing looked like.

"I guess we have to come up with a pairing name," said Dank, known for his coldness of heart and the lack of fear, not of anything was Dank afraid to face.

"Let me first put my stuff away and wash up," Ardent answered, as he glanced across the small quartering area, aware that Dank was still checking him out.

The quartering area, like the structure, didn't look much bigger than what he had while at Area #26. Right away he noticed that the bedding area was bunked, and since Dank got there first he had already taken the lower bedding. A bold move, he thought.

After emptying his backpack and arranging his things neatly, Ardent went to the wash bowl and filled it with water from the pitcher and started to wash the dust from his face.

Dank sat quietly watching Ardent slowly dip his cupped together hands into the water and as he brought them to his face, carefully trying not to spill any water onto the dirt floor. When he finished drying off his face, he walked over to the table to join Dank.

The table was just as small as his before. At least it had two chairs.

"All right let's think of a good pairing name," Ardent said. A smile was on his face after having thought of how particular he was when washing and of how Dank must have thought the same, having watched him intensely.

"While waiting for you to wash your face I thought of a good name."

"What name?"

"Another word for bravery is bravado. I thought it might make a nice pairing name ... Bravado. What do you think of that for a name?" Dank asked.

"Actually, that sounds good. Ardent Bravado ... Yes that does sound good, doesn't it?"

"Yes and so does Dank Bravado. So, it is Bravado, right?"

"Yes," answered Ardent. "Bravado."

Dank got up from his chair and went over to where Ardent was sitting. After Ardent stood up they both shook hands on it and then they both started laughing. Dank isn't that bad a guy, thought Ardent. I think we will get along just fine. But, I would rather he had left the lower bunk for me.

"When you got here did anyone say what was in store for us tomorrow?" Ardent asked. His shoulders shrugged.

"Yes, that we will get our new identification number put on our arms, and that it may hurt a bit." A sour look came across Dank's face.

When Ardent and Dank Bravado got to the mealing area for the evening meal everyone was quietly adjusting with their pairings, or tired from the long march there. So as soon as Ardent and Dank finished the meal of vegetable stew and corn bread they went straight back to their quartering area.

Ardent lit a couple of candles and threw a log into the stove, and there in the dim light the two sat and chattered for several hours. Outside, the wind was blowing hard onto the structure making a whistling-like sound, and its cold draft caused Ardent to shiver. Then he yawned, his mouth opening wide. It was the latest he had ever stayed awake. It was 11pm before the two finally crawled into their warm beddings.

The intercom's loud morning wake-up call sat Ardent straight up. Forgetting he was in the top bunk he almost hit his head on the ceiling. *I better learn to get used to that intercom for now on, or else*, he thought.

The climb down the ladder steps from the top bunk bedding felt odd to him, very odd. Something he never did before was to sleep in such high bedding. It was so high up from the floor that if he were to fall out he surely would get hurt. He didn't like it.

When his feet hit the cold dirt floor he noticed that Dank was not in his bedding, nor was he in the quartering area. After getting dressed and washed he went outdoors where he found Dank sitting on the ground next to the door with his back against the structure's wall, a sad look printed on his face.

"Is everything all right?" Ardent asked, concerned.

"Oh yes, mate! I couldn't sleep, so I got out of my bedding early and came out here to think." Ardent wondered about what. What made him so sad looking?

"C'mon, let's go, I'm hungry," Ardent said, as he extended his hand to give Dank a lift up from the ground. "What were you thinking of out here in the morning cold?"

"Nothing much, I was wondering if Tome will pick us."

"If we work hard and get on his good side. But I should warn you, Tome is a stern mannered instructor."

"Then we will get on his good side: aye, mate."

"Yes," Ardent laughed out loudly. Even after their long talk just the night before Ardent thought it funny, the accent Dank had.

The morning meal being served by the DIPS was the usual hot cereal with milk and corn bread. There would be no eggs again for quite awhile. The trainees were fed only twice a day, the morning meal at dawn and the evening meal at dust. If you missed one you went without until the next.

Just as Ardent and Dank got up from the mealing table, their stomachs full, they heard, "Hey, over here," and when Ardent looked over his shoulder, he saw Jejune waving his hand, motioning for him to come over.

"This is Dank, my pairing mate," Ardent said when he got there.

"Hello mate," and then Dank extended his hand.

"Hi, and my name is Jejune," and he shook Dank's hand. Then after turning back to face Ardent, "This is Seethe, my pairing mate," a big proud smile on his face.

"I've heard so much about you already," replied Seethe, named so because he was known to have a lot of anger. Then he held out a welcoming hand to Ardent.

"I should warn you about Seethe," Dank said, after Jejune and Seethe left and was far enough away as not to be able to hear him.

"What of?"

"I knew Seethe from the United Communes of Europe, and believe me mate when I say he has a real bad temper."

"Then I will watch out," answered Ardent, now concerned with the mild manner and not very bright Jejune having to train and quarter with a pairing with a bad temper.

⊂⊱⊰ ⊂⊱⊰ ⊂⊱⊰

It was mid-morning when the intercom rang the assembly call awakening Ardent from a rare light nap. There would not be opportunities in the near future for naps.

At the assembly area there were several long lines of trainees waiting to be tattooed with an identification number, a number that would be with them the rest of their lives.

"Does it hurt, you think?" Dank asked Ardent.

"It must, look at the expression on Jejune's face. Seethe has already got his and is waiting for Jejune to finish, and he's got a smile on his face watching Jejune."

"You go first, mate," Dank said, nudging Ardent forward.

"Sit down," and with some hesitation he sat onto the seat, still warm from the trainee before him.

"What's your name?" He was asked by the one that was about to insert pain into his arm, a big grin on his face signaling that he was about to enjoy poking the long needle into Ardent.

"Ardent," he answered, and then being nervous of what would come next he squinted his eyes while turning his head away.

"And your pairing name is?"

"Bravado," Ardent answered, the nervousness showed again in the sound of his voice.

Suddenly Ardent felt the sting of the needle, just as he saw Dank turn his head away from watching. He tried to keep a smile on his face when he looked up at Dank later. It hurt, it really hurt, he thought.

When he was finished being tortured by the needle poking sadist, he looked down onto his left arm nearer the wrist and there in black dye was a marking that would be with him forever. Then Ardent got to smile, as he watched while Dank got his identity markings.

In a second line nearby Ardent noticed that Jewel and Bandy, with their pairing mates, were getting markings also. Soon, he guessed, he would get to meet their mates.

Chapter Three

It was lightly snowing when Tome send Ardent and Dank out on an overnight exercise with nine other pairings. All twenty were armed and with full gear on their backs. Their rifles were lever action repeating rifles with a fixed tubular magazine hand fed end to end, and each held fifteen .44-40 caliber, black powder cartridges.

Their practice mission was to scout the hillsides, as if looking for a zealot's camp site. This was already their forth such mission and they had only been there a month.

"Another mock run he's got us doing," Dank remarked, a tone of sarcasm in his voice. He wanted the real thing, real zealots to shoot at.

"Yes, but soon we will be at the capital doing the real thing," Ardent answered. "This training is important." Dank wasn't really listening. On his mind was the thought of meeting up with zealots to kill.

The snow had just turned to rain, and the water from the rainfall was dripping off Ardent's hat onto his face, already reddened from the bitter cold. A shiver overcame him, followed by a sneeze.

"Maybe we will get lucky and find some apples along the way. That is if they're not frozen," Ardent said to Dank. He was hungry, cold and wet from the rainfall, and tired of eating vegetable stew every evening. "Something in our stomachs should warm us up." On this night all there would be to eat were the raw vegetables they had in their backpacks and the powdered liquid mix they got with every meal.

Soon enough, they did come upon several apple trees grouped close together in the middle of a tall grassed, open field. Most of the apples had fallen from the trees onto the ground and were all brown, mushy and rotten. All but a few of the leaves had fallen to the ground as well. The apples left on the branches looked barren, and with small icicles hanging from underneath, water drops falling from each icicle to the ground.

The hungry trainees each hastily picked a couple of over ripe but eatable apples from the tree.

"It is soft and bitter," Jewel said to her pairing mate Malinger, named so because she always had an excuse for avoiding her duties.

"The bitterness will sour my stomach and make me sick," Malinger answered, but she went ahead and took a big bite out of her apple, chewing it fast. She was hungry.

In a wooded area about a half mile away, right next to a shallow, noisy, babbling brook, the trainees found a good place for a campsite. The dryer ground under the large willow trees nearby provided good shelter from the rainfall.

After building several huts under the willow trees using pine tree branches, the trainees started a small fire for warmth. After the fire got good and hot it stopped raining, so most of the trainees cuddled up close to the heat of the fire to keep warm and to dry off their clothing. Still hungry, three of the pairings decided to go back for more apples.

"Don't forget your rifles!" Ardent yelled out, having noticed they were leaving without them.

"The stupid rookies," Ardent said to Dank, as they watched them come back for their rifles. "Even though this is a mock exercise, if Tome were to check on us and saw them away from the camp without their weapons he would send them right back to Area #56, where they would be cleaning the waste huts instead of the DIPS."

"I hope they get back before the darkness," Dank remarked, and then after a minute's time, "Maybe you're right. Maybe we should not have let them leave the campsite." Dank was the strongest of the two and smart enough to know that Ardent was the smarter one. That formula was what made them a good match.

Except for Ardent, the remaining six pairings and Dank decided to sing poems that they were taught when they were youngsters. Ardent knew his voice would only make the others laugh. Instead, he got under his bedding. He was tired, and an early night's sleep sounded like a better idea, at least to him it did. No one thought to set up a perimeter protecting their campsite. Even Ardent who usually had everything under control and always did as trained.

After about a half dozen poorly sang poems a loud burst of rapid gunfire coming from off in the distance brought them to their feet.

Ardent rushed out of the hut yelling: "Get your rifles and take cover."

"The gunfire is off in the distance!" Jewel yelled out.

"The others, it must be the others," Ardent called out. He was now standing by the fire with his rifle butt shouldered and its barrel pointed ahead. If anyone was to come out from behind the trees he was ready for them.

"Hurry," Dank said. "They're in trouble." Then he started running toward the field where the others had gone for more apples. Quickly Ardent and all the trainees ran after Dank. What would lie ahead they had no idea. They were all rookies, trigger happy, with no battle experience, and they were running wildly to where the gunfire was coming from.

It was dark. The gunfire had stopped and most of the young trainees kept stumbling as they rushed through the woods, stopping only when Ardent held his hand up for them to stop when they reached the woods edge, the apple trees in sight. Next to Ardent and Dank were Jewel and Malinger, both down on one knee breathing heavy, almost out of breath.

"I don't see anyone out there," Ardent whispered. "We must proceed with caution, a trap may lie ahead."

Ardent split up the trainees. Ten were to stay at the wood's edge. From there they would provide cover while he, Dank, Jewel and Malinger checked out the area where the apple trees were.

Moving slowly, their rifles in the ready position, the four nervous trainees approached the trees. Ardent and Dank, in the lead by several steps reached the first of the trees.

"Wait here," Ardent commanded, his hand high up above his shoulder motioning for Jewel and Malinger to stop advancing. "Cover us," he told them.

Ardent and Dank continued advancing, and when they reached the edge of the small group of apple trees Dank separated from Ardent's side, heading off to the left.

When Ardent got under the first of the trees, stretched out along the ground face down by the trunk of the tree was one of the trainees they were looking for. Ardent bent down and turned him over just enough to see his face. It was Restive, a good trainee. But he was always uneasy and impatient with delay. "You won't have to wait again," Ardent whispered, as he lowered Restive's face back to the ground. *There was nothing anyone could do for him now*, he thought.

Dank, from under another of the trees motioned for Ardent to come over to him. When Ardent reached where Dank was standing, he saw the other five trainees lying at Dank's feet, apparently dead. Nowhere in sight were their rifles.

"The zealots must have taken their rifles," Dank whispered.

"They will arm others of their kind with those rifles, zealots that want to kill government troopers, troopers like we soon will be," Ardent whispered back to Dank. The image of Restive's whitened face was still on his mind. "They still might be nearby, so we better leave the bodies here for the night. We can bury them in the morning." Then he noticed that the ten trainees that were supposed to be providing cover from the edge of the woods were standing there with them amongst the apple trees. Upset, he motioned for them to head back to the woods edge where they were supposed to be. Ardent was dismayed that they left their position. He would have to deal with them later for disobeying his orders, he thought.

"What now?" Dank asked. "Do you really think we should leave the bodies here in the freezing cold?"

"Does it matter? They're dead," Ardent answered, still on his mind was the ten trainees that left their position, and it showed in his temperament. "They could of got us all killed. They left our backs uncovered."

"Go easy, they're learning," Dank suggested. There was quietness in the tone of his voice.

"Dank. We've already made one mistake and it cost six trainees their lives, trainees we knew well," and there was no quietness in his tone of voice, just the anger.

"We better get back to the others," Dank suggested. He didn't want to talk about this anymore. He hated to admit it, but Ardent was right. It was their fault the six lay dead.

When they got back to the campsite they put the fire out, for fear it would attract the zealots. Ardent, setting up a secured perimeter, posted shifts of four guards at a time.

"I can't believe we forgot to set up a perimeter," Ardent said, to which Dank shook his shoulders up and down several times.

"I thought you took care of it, or else I would have," Dank remarked.

"That makes two mistakes," Ardent muttered, a look of disgust on his face.

Getting to sleep wasn't easy for Ardent. The worry of being attacked was on his mind throughout the rest of the night, waking him early. The thoughts of what Tome was going to do to him and Dank when they got back didn't help him get much sleep either.

⸻ ⸻ ⸻

Ardent got Dank and the others up before dawn and gathered them together. It had snowed most the night leaving the ground slippery. Under the snow the ground had hardened from the cold. A trail of footprints could be seen leading up from the brook.

The trainees wanted to start a fire. Several already had kindling piled in their arms.

"No fire," Ardent insisted. "The zealots are nearby. They will see the smoke."

"If they come we will kill them all," Bovine said. He was cold and didn't agree with Ardent about the fire.

"Yes, we will kill them all," said Savvy, Bovine's pairing. Savvy was a practical know it all. Ardent didn't like him at all and thought that Bovine and Savvy deserved each other.

"I just got back from scouting the area. About a mile and a half away and by this very same brook is the zealots' campsite. I counted eight stacked rifles and I saw only one zealot guarding the area," Ardent stopped talking and pointed at Bovine. "So put the kindling down. If you really want to kill zealots, then we should go to them. Surprise would be on our side." He watched, as those with the kindling in their arms threw them to the ground and reached for their rifles.

"Well, mates. Let's go get them," Dank said. His eyes lacked all fear. The others all agreed with Dank. They would have followed Dank anywhere. They were all in a rush to get their first kill.

"Ok," answered Ardent. "We'll follow the brook to their campsite. It should hide the sound of us approaching. If we are lucky, all but the guard will still be sleeping. When Dank shoots the guard the rest of us will rush the sleeping zealots," and after putting a half smile on his face: "And make sure you hit him with the first shot." Ardent was looking Dank's way. Dank just laughed back at him. He could shoot. He was the best marksman in the group, and he knew it, so he thought, but Jewel and Ardent thought otherwise.

The brook's water was cold, even through the woolen-lined boots each was wearing. The small rocks beneath the water were slippery and made it difficult to walk at a quick pace. Slowly and carefully they walked, so not to make any noise.

The zealots' campsite was quiet and just a short run up a snow covered embankment. As Ardent had hoped, all but a zealot guarding the perimeter and a zealot, his rifle shouldered, standing by the fire keeping warm were asleep in the tents. Ardent, counted seven rifles now stacked near the fire. He was getting nervous, his hand shaking. He gripped his rifle tighter and the shaking went away. Then he nodded his head at Jewel, pointing to the zealot by the fire.

Dank's shot rang out loud, its echo quickly followed, and then Jewel's shot and its echo. Both shots a clean hit, both in the torsos, and both targets quickly fell to the ground.

Instinctively Ardent started running up the slippery embankment, the others following closely behind him. Bovine slipped, falling to one knee before getting back up with the help of his pairing mate Savvy.

"Don't let them get to their rifles!" Ardent shouted out. His rifle was trained on the stack of unattended zealots' rifles, and as the first out of his tent ran toward the rifles Ardent fired off three quick rounds. The force of his hits, two high up in the chest area, flipped the running zealot over backward, his arms extended he landed on his back.

Ardent turned, aiming his rifle at another zealot running for the stack of rifles, but before he could fire his rifle the zealot spun sideward, blood exiting the side of his head. Then he landed atop the stacked rifles, an arm falling onto the fire.

"I got one! I got one!" Ardent heard Savvy yell out.

"Four left," thought Ardent, when just then he saw another zealot to his left fall to the ground. Then to his right side he saw Bovine down on one knee, his rifle aimed at a fleeing zealot. He heard three shots, and three times Bovine's shoulder was nudged back by the butt stock of his rifle. The fleeing zealot's arms rose upward, and then he fell to his knees, and then face down onto the snow-covered ground. The hot blood that flowed from the zealot's quivering body was melting the snow near, then stillness, all life ended.

Within seconds, that felt like minutes, Ardent's trainees were in the campsite. The zealots never had a chance, including the two that tried to surrender.

"This is for the six you killed," Dank yelled out. His rifle was spitting out the remaining cartridges from his magazine as quick as he could cock the lever, each of the shell casings flying through the air and landing on the snow covered ground, disappearing into the snow. Malinger also emptied her magazine into the surrendering murderers of her fellow trainees.

"Stop," Ardent commanded. A look of anger was on the trainee faces when they turned their heads his way, their rifles pointing at the dead bodies lying at their feet, twisted and riddled with bullet holes, the snow near the bodies soaking up their warm blood, the red markings left — the stains of death.

"Reload. There might be other zealots nearby," Ardent commanded. None hesitated, quickly reloading as ordered.

"We got them! We got them!" with excitement yelled Plaudit, the smallest of the trainees at only five feet tall. Plaudit's hand, Ardent noticed, like his, was shaking almost out of control as he tried to slide more cartridges into the magazine of his rifle.

"They won't kill any more troopers, not now they won't," Dank said, laughing aloud. The laughter was steady, as were his hands. No fear ... No guilt ... In his eyes was a look of satisfaction, the kind that revenge rewards.

"Get their rifles and empty casings," Ardent ordered the others. Lying on the ground next to the stacked rifles were the other troopers' six rifles. Next to the rifles was the zealot Savvy shot, his tunic in flames and the smell of burning flesh lingering in the air nearby.

"Tome will be proud of us now," Dank said to Ardent. "We got our first kills." He finally got excited, and it showed somewhat in his face. A bounce was in his step as he walked closer to Ardent.

"Will he?" Ardent replied back. "Or will he be mad because of the six we lost?"

"Well, I know one thing for sure."

"What, Dank, what do you know for sure?" Ardent sarcastically asked.

"I'll always sleep with my rifle at my side from now on," to which Ardent could not help but crack a smile.

"And that goes for me."

Ardent was right. When they got back, Tome was not pleased. Not when he was told by a nervous Ardent and Dank of the six that were lost.

"It was good that you revenged those lost, but you never should have let the six wander from your campsite." Tome maintained his temper, but his eyes signaled anger. Ardent saw it. "Six dead … an expensive lesson learned," Tome mumbled.

"We won't make that mistake again, sir," Ardent answered. There was no reply from Dank. He thought they should get a medal for their bravery. After all, their pairing name was Bravado, and a medal for bravery would have set their name in stone with the rest of the trainees.

"Now, get out of here before I get really mad!"

"He should have given us a medal for bravery," was all Dank had to say to Ardent when outside.

As soon as Ardent and Dank got to where the other twelve trainees were waiting for them, Ardent called the ten that left their position to his attention.

"For leaving our backs unprotected the ten of you, for the next month, will clean the waste huts every morning instead of the DIPS. Do you understand?" His voice was firm. His order was direct.

"But Ardent ...."

"No but about it," Ardent interrupted Bovine. "You are all dismissed."

"Well, you just made a lot of DIPS happy," Dank remarked, after the others left the area.

⌒⋈⌒ ⌒⋈⌒ ⌒⋈⌒

The 90 day pairing preparedness period was passing quickly, and it was well into the month of December. The full blast of winter had arrived. The snow-covered ground was getting difficult to travel on. For both Ardent and Dank the time couldn't pass quick enough. The two had learned from one another each other's likes and dislikes, blending the best of their talents.

Since each pairing had to work as a team, the Bravado pairing soon became the best trained. Tome took notice, and in spite of thinking them culpable for the incident with the three pairings having been killed during their watch, he promoted both to the rank of Tertiary Pairing. Only Tome and instructor Morose held rank above them.

Morose, another educator/trainer and second in command, was a bit frightening and gloomy looking. He had a scar down his face that started above his nose, crossed his right eye, and stopped under his right ear, somehow missing the eye. The zealot that gave it to him paid the ultimate price of a slow agonizing death. It is said that Morose cut the zealot's heart out after and that he keeps it in a pouch hanging from his tunic's belt as a reminder.

Dank's remark to Ardent after being told of their promotion: "See, I was right. We are being rewarded for our bravery on that day."

Tome and Morose often spent extra time with their Tertiaries explaining the reasons for forming a new elite unit. Of course it was plain to see that both Ardent and Dank were going to be a part of the elite unit. Although Tome had not, yet, told them that they would be.

"A revolutionary group, although small, is causing unrest throughout the country. The primary duties of the new unit will be to capture them, foremost, their leaders, and then send them to the work camps where they will spend the rest of their lives," Tome explained, on one of the occasions alone.

"And just what is it they are revolting against?" Ardent had asked.

"That's not our concern. It's our duty to stop this anarchy before it grows, spreading its propaganda throughout the country. Our job is to enforce the laws of our government, and they are breaking the law." Tome made clear, and when asked when he would make his choices; "In just another three days the training will be completed. Then, and only then, will I make the choices as to who will be selected for the unit, which will be called, 'The Revolutionary Vanguard.'" Then, with a smile on his face, "Can I count on the two of you?"

"Yes, of course," Ardent did answer, and without hesitation.

"And, as for you Dank, is that a yes also?"

"Yes sir," standing up taller as he spoke, a satisfying smile on his face.

⸻ ⸻ ⸻

The remaining three days went by real fast, but on the eve of their last night Ardent had a problem with Jejune and Seethe. It appeared Seethe got into a fight with Jejune.

When word of the fight got to Ardent, he headed straight to Jejune and Seethe's quartering area. When he got there he entered without knocking on the door, in fact, he pretty much knocked the door down having pushed on it so hard.

"Just what the heck is going on with the two of you?" Ardent shouted above the sound of the door slamming against the inner wall. Surprised, both Jejune and Seethe jumped up from the chairs they were sitting on.

"Don't you knock?" Seethe shouted.

Ardent walked up to Seethe, and after putting his face up close to Seethe's face, "As your Tertiary I'll do as I please, and you'll sit yourself right back down on that chair." With that said, Ardent pushed against Seethe's chest sending him backward onto the chair. Then, after looking at Jejune, he noticed the right cheek cut and a bruise under the eye.

"What happened?" Ardent asked Jejune.

"Nothing, he fell down." The wise remark from Seethe didn't rub well with Ardent.

"You just shut up, I asked Jejune."

"It's nothing, really, just a little disagreement between Seethe and me."

"We're shipping out tomorrow and I don't need the two of you fighting. Not right now, and if I have to report this to Instructor Tome the both of you won't be coming with us tomorrow, if you're even selected."

"Everything is all right now, really it is," Jejune said, but Ardent didn't sense that to be true. Just one look over at Seethe, who was still sitting in the chair with a mad look on his face, and Ardent knew Seethe wasn't finished with Jejune, and that more of the same would happen in the future. Seethe was a problem. Dank was right, he had an anger problem and would have to be watched closely in the future, but for now something had to be done.

"I better get back. There is a lot I have to do before morning. I don't want to have to come back here again. Do you both understand?"

"Yes," Jejune answered, but there was no answer from Seethe and that worried Ardent.

"Seethe, come with me. I've got something I need help getting done," Ardent ordered, and without a word Seethe followed Ardent out the door, a suspicious look on his face. He didn't like Ardent at all. He didn't like taking orders from him or Dank either. If it weren't for Jejune, had he been assigned a different pairing mate, they would have been promoted to Tertiary instead, he thought. It was Jejune's fault. He hated Jejune.

"Where are we going?" Seethe finally asked, after a short hike into a wooded area, and just as Seethe got the words out of his mouth Ardent grabbed him firmly by the neck with his right hand. Then after lifting Seethe off the ground by the neck, his feet left dangling above the ground, Ardent yelled:

"You touch Jejune again, I swear, I'll have you in a work camp before you could blink an eye lid. Do you understand me now?"

Seethe wanted to say yes, but the words just couldn't come out of his mouth. Instead, he started gagging. The choke grip Ardent had on his neck was too overpowering.

When Ardent finally released his grip Seethe fell to the ground onto his knees. His hands rushed to his sore neck, as he tried to get his breath back. He kept gagging, again and again.

Without a warning Ardent kicked him as hard as he could right under the ribcage; dropping Seethe the rest of the way to the ground into a curled up position, coughing and gagging even more, almost out of control. He felt like he was going to pass out. He thought he was going to die.

"Remember what I said, because, the next time you lay a hand on Jejune, when I get done with you, you'll never get up." Ardent wasn't smiling, not one bit. He wanted to kick him again, but instead he turned and headed toward his quartering area where Dank was waiting for him.

"I should have kicked him again," he mumbled to himself, just loud enough so that Seethe could hear it. That is if he hadn't passed out already. Ardent didn't bother looking back, he didn't care.

After getting up off the ground Seethe slowly headed back, coughing and holding his side. Once inside and after washing off his face, he walked up to where Jejune was seated and backhanded him across the face, knocking him to the ground. Jejune, shocked and lying on the dirt floor, looked up at Seethe, "Why?" he asked, his hand on his cheek, a look of shock on his face.

"You say one word to Ardent about this and I'll kill you."

Chapter Four

At the mountain's foothills the rain was falling on the Capital Commune, pouring down and splashing hard on the already soaked ground. It was cold, but not cold enough in the lower valley lands for the rain to change to snow.

Stoic, given the surname Taurine because of his bull like strength and largeness … Leviathan, and above succumbing to sensations and pain, struggled pulling a small cart, called a Death Rig in the work camps. It was overloaded with large stones, its wheels deep into the mud.

The death rig was made of wood with a large narrow wheel on each side, cabriolet looking with a deep bin in the rear for hauling cargo. In the work camps it was drawn by a team of slaved workers and not the usual work horses, as it was in the Communes.

"Push it harder!" Stoic yelled. "Harder!" but the death rig wouldn't budge.

The Capital Commune citadel was in sight, but the muddied ground made it impossible to get the death rig there. The other four slaved workers, two on each side by the wheels, were also trying their best. Then the rain started coming down harder, the citadel disappearing in and out of sight.

The whip stung as it snapped into Stoic's back ripping his tunic, already shredded from the whip's previous strikes. This time the whip ripped through his shirt and deep into his back, dropping him to his knees.

"Get up!" yelled Pique, who loved to injure people's pride, and the whip he raised high usually helped. Although smaller than most the guards, he was the one feared most by all the slaved workers. Pique loved using his whip, the whip he named Felicity, the very same whip that made him much larger a man.

The other two guards just stood there. They, too, feared Pique and had no intentions of interfering with the pleasure he was getting out of the beatings.

"We better get out of here, and soon," said one of the guards. "It's going to be a tempest," and a gust of wind's suddenness almost blew him over. "We will all be killed," as he pointed uphill to where the citadel was.

"C'mon, let's go," the other guard said, leaning into the wind, his tunic soaked, the rain falling from his chin.

Stoic got up from his knees and tried to wipe the mud from off his hands onto his pants, also covered with mud. Immediately, from fear of another strike of the whip, he started to pull on the rope again. The death rig moved forward, but only a couple of wheel turns before stopping again.

"Hel—Help!" The yowl got everyone's attention. Lying in the mud with the wheel of the death rig resting on top of his leg, most of the leg buried in the mud, was Bilker. "Help—Help me" his mouth wide open, the raindrops splashing in the puddle around him, his hands on the half buried leg, he continued crying out. "Help me, please!"

Stoic ran straight to Bilker. Then while looking down at him lying there helpless, he saw blood rising up from within the mud, and the blood was thinning out in the puddle of water forming around Bilker's body. From as fast as the blood was gathering, Stoic could see that Bilker was losing the battle for his life.

Bilker, a swindler and cheat, was sent to the work camp after being caught swindling a farming commune out of 100 supply credits. Like Stoic, he arrived to the work camp two years earlier to build the citadel on the high ground overlooking the Capital Commune. It was to be the domicile for the United American Union of Commune's 200 elite troopers that were coming soon. The freedom movement Stoic heard so much about must be bigger than he had thought. Why else would the government be reinforcing its policing forces?

Stoic and the other three work camp slaves started throwing the large rocks out of the death rig to lighten the load. With a lighter load they might be able to lift the death rig and pull Bilker free, thought Stoic. But the wind and rain was making it difficult, the footing bad.

"Hurry!" yelled Stoic, and he kept yelling until finally the death rig was empty and Bilker pulled free from the wheel.

"Now get those stones back into the cart," Pique yelled, the rain still pouring down, falling almost sideward. To make matters much worse, the wind was from off the ocean and felt warmer, a sure sign of a tempest, and if they didn't get under cover soon they would surely die from the storm's fury.

Stoic knelt by Bilker and lifted the ailing Bilker's head resting it on his lap. He knew Bilker was dying and needed someone to comfort him. He was going to have to make a decision and it would be a difficult one to bear. Bilker was going to die anyway, thought Stoic, as he got up from the ground with the thought of leaving him there.

The wind almost knocked his big body back down, as he tried desperately to keep his footing. He stood there braced against the mighty wind, still undecided if he should leave Bilker there to die alone.

"It's a tempest! It's going to kill us all if we don't get to cover right away," Pique yelled out.

"He'll die if we leave him now," Stoic said, having decided he would not leave him to die all alone.

"Just leave him there!" Pique insisted. Bilker's life didn't mean a thing to him. He was just another meaningless work camp slave, a cheat and swindler.

The other two guards are long gone and most likely already in the citadel, thought Pique. Scared for their lives, Pique and the other three slaved workers ran off leaving Stoic standing alone with the dying Bilker.

○>< ○>< ○><

Illuminating chains of lightning were streaking across the now much darker skies, its thunder shaking the ground below Stoic's feet. A willow tree just to the right of him and Bilker was tilting with the wind and looking ready to fall at any moment — For sure a soon to be victim of the wind and soft muddied ground.

Stoic knelt by Bilker again to lift him from the ground, putting one arm around his back, and as he was putting his other arm under Bilker's legs:

"Go, it's too late for me. Save yourself," and just as Bilker finished speaking there was a loud crashing sound, as the willow tree's outreaching branches hit the ground and death rig. The winds furry had finally delivered its mighty blow. The tree was no more, its lifespan ended.

Many of the large and smaller branches had snapped off from the tree and were flying in the wind past Stoic. He suddenly felt a sharp pain in his arm. A large broken limb from the willow tree had lodged itself into Bilker's torso, and its sharp ragged cut end protruding out from Bilker's back, having stopped only after penetrating deep into Stoic's arm. There was nothing he could do for the now dead Bilker, half buried in the muddied ground with the tree's limb protruding out of his back.

Stoic stared down at Bilker's face. The eyes were still open as his face sunk out of sight into the muddied water. The broken limb and Bilker's arm was all that protruded from the muddy gravesite.

Stoic, now afraid for his own life, reached for one of the remaining branches still attached to the trunk of the downed willow tree, and once he steadied himself he glanced ahead through what remained of the tree. He could see, barely, Pique and the other three slaved workers entering the gates of the citadel.

He knew there was no way for him to make it to the citadel, not on his own and not uphill across the open, muddied field. His only chance of survival was too crawl under the large trunk of the fallen willow tree, hold on and hope the tempest's fury would spare him.

Lightning struck another willow tree nearby igniting it, and almost as quickly the rain and wind doused it out. Splinters from the willow tree were everywhere about the ground, many on top of Stoic who was still holding on for his life, barely.

The ground under him started eroding from the down rushing water and mud. Stoic sensed he was not safe where he was so he climbed up on top of the large tree trunk. Then, soon after, it started sliding down the hillside, slow at first. Had he stayed where he was, he thought, he would have been crushed by the moving tree.

Fearing for his life Stoic opened his eyes wide, as the tree trunk picked up speed. The steady flow of water and the strong gusts of wind was sailing it uncontrollably down the steep hill.

⌒⋉ ⌒⋉ ⌒⋉

Stoic almost fell off the tree trunk when it splashed hard into a river's flow. It was the mighty Merrimack River; a wide body of water that flowed past the Capital Commune, where once stood the city of Manchester, New Hampshire.

Knowing that the rapids, then a waterfall that dropped to the ocean's edge were just ahead downriver, he knew he would have to get off the tree trunk soon. But the swift river currents were much too strong to navigate or swim across. Death was waiting for him just ahead, and he would be arriving soon to its arms, he thought.

It was much too dark and stormy to see the Capital Commune, but he sensed he was at its edges. That was when he suddenly realized he was free of the work camp guards, free of Pique, free of Felicity. Now, if only he could get to the shore.

The rain and wind had, as suddenly as it started, stopped. The full moon sky was bright, a bit of pinkish glow showing outside the hazy yellowish glow around the moon. It was calm. It was like being in the eye of a storm, except for the river, which was still as mighty as ever.

The sound from the rapids ahead was deafening, the on-rushing water crashing against the giant rocks, worse yet, the sound a reminder of the waterfall and the certain leap of death into the ocean.

The trunk of the willow tree dropped several feet into the mouth of the rapids, plunging deeply into the water. Stoic was trapped, still riding atop and holding the willows strands like reins, his thighs pressed hard against the tree trunk, its bark scraping deep. He almost fell when the trunk turned backward, and again as it lifted up to the top of the water, then continuing its uncontrollable rush downstream toward a grouping of large rocks, where upon its arrival the trunk smashed very hard up against the rocks almost throwing him off. "Ouch!" he yelled, as his forehead hit up against a branch's limb, and quickly its blood started seeping into his eyes. With one hand he wiped the eyes, and ahead in the tree trunk's path he saw yet another grouping of large rocks.

The crash that soon followed was as hard as the previous was. The trunk of the tree stopped lodged between two of the giant rocks and the rapid's water rushed over it, shaking it up and down. He knew it wasn't going to stay lodged for very long, that the force from the water's flow was too strong.

Cold, wet, and still bleeding from the gash in his arm, he started crawling along the tree trunk. Because most of the willow strands and limbs had been ripped off the sharp points left protruding kept cutting into his already scraped inner thighs, as he rushed to get close to the rocks before the tree trunk broke free.

When he stood up to jump onto one of the rocks, he felt the sharp edge of what was left of a larger limb. It had torn into his left leg, high up on the thigh leaving a large open wound, the blood rushing out and thinning amongst the water. He reached out and grabbed hold of his aching thigh. At that moment the trunk of the tree started breaking loose from the rocks. Letting go of his thigh, he stood up again, reached out with both hands, and leaped to the rock, smashing hard up against it. He started sliding free. Just under him the rushing water flowed, waiting to pull him under and to a drowning death. With one foot already in the cold water, he grabbed onto a ledge protruding out from the rock, stopping his slide.

He then pulled himself up to the very top of the giant rock. Out of breath, his clothing soaked and his body freezing cold, he sat on top of the rock breathing quickly while trying to get his breath back, his heart beating fast, as he watched the tree trunk rushing downstream, smashing aimlessly against rock after rock.

Blood was rushing from the gash in his leg and arm, and his face was scraped and bleeding from smashing up against the rock, but he was alive and free. Right now that was all that mattered. The wounds would heal with time and proper care, he thought. But where would he find the care he needed?

There were three large rocks between him and the freedom awaiting him at the shore of the mighty Merrimack River. He knew he could leap to each of them without any problems, even with the bad leg. He knew he could, because on the shore was his freedom, and for that he could do anything.

When he reached the shore he took off his shirt and ripped one of the sleeves off and wrapped it tightly around his thigh to stop the bleeding. He stood up and put his weight on the wounded leg, testing if he would be able to walk on it. "Ouch!" It hurt, but he continued walking in a small circle.

"I'm free!" he yelled out at the top of his lungs. "I'm free!" He was cold, wet and sore. But he was free for the first time in over eight years. Free of Pique, free of Felicity's sting. "I'm free!" Again, he yelled out at the top of his lungs. Suddenly he didn't feel the pain.

He would not be free very long, he thought, unless he got as far away as possible, and it better be as soon as possible. His afflictions he would have to deal with later. Pique and the other guards would be looking for him now that the tempest had ended. Hopefully, they thought he was dead. That he was taken by the storm's fury; a fool trying to save the life of a cheat and swindler that no one cared about.

Chapter Five

The sun wasn't out yet, so it was cold and dark when the trainees rushed to the parade ground area where Tome, Morose, Dank and Ardent were waiting. It was early, very early. Sleepiness still filled the trainee eyes, watering from the dawn's coldness.

It took at least five minutes for the trainees to get lined up once they arrived, and that didn't please Tome. No, not one bit. He would teach them a lesson, one they wouldn't forget.

"That was a bit sloppy and slow!" he said, as he paced down the front column of the, finally, lined up trainees. "I want you to go back to your quartering areas and when the alarm sounds again; I want you to get out here, and it better be in half the time." He turned his head away, glancing over to where Ardent and Dank were standing. He had a grin on his face. "We are going to keep doing this until you get it right," turning his head back to the trainees, his voice deep sounding, as it always was when he shouted commands or when he was upset. And right now he was upset!

"Dank! Ardent! You both are to take over and don't come to get Morose and me until they all get it right," Tome instructed, but made sure he said it loud enough for all of the trainees to hear.

It took three tries before the trainees got it to Dank's and Ardent's likening. After even then, Tome made them wait an hour in the cold before he came back to the assembled trainees.

"That's much better," Tome started to speak. "I posted a roster of 50 pairings. Listed are those of you that will be assigned to the citadel with me and Morose. Those not coming with us will stay here another week, at which time you will be assigned to a commune elsewhere." Tome stopped speaking for a moment, having noticed the anxiety on his trainees' faces. "New uniforms distinguishing us troopers from the capital COPS will be provided when we arrive." He stopped talking for a moment to think over what he had to say next.

"The departure will be delayed until tomorrow because it looks like a tempest is headed our way. And, as usual the winds will be strong. So you must tie down anything that could blow away." Again he stopped, but this time it was to look up at the sky. He didn't like what he saw off in the distance. A wall of black clouds was heading toward them, and he could feel that the air around him was getting warmer. "Already," he continued. "I can see the sky changing. Hurry! There isn't much time."

The trainees rushed off toward Tome's office area where the names were posted, leaving Tome standing there with Morose. Then, having checked the list of names they went right to their quartering areas to tie down what needed to be kept from blowing away. Time to get to safety was running out fast. Ardent, however, after checking the names on the roster went into Tome's office area and he had a look of dissatisfaction on his face. The wind suddenly slammed the door behind him. "Sorry, sir," Ardent apologized.

Tome was standing alone at his desk, which was a mess with empty backpacks on the floor waiting to be filled with the trainee personnel records. He hadn't looked up when the door slammed shut, as if he expected Ardent. Outside you could hear the winds howl.

"Sir, Lead Trainer Tome, can I speak, sir?"

"Yes, you may speak your mind, but you better hurry."

"Sir, you have the pairing of Jejune and Seethe on the roster."

"Yes I have. Is there a problem with that?"

"Sir, I don't think Jejune is fully capable, sir," he felt like he was letting Jejune down saying what he said, but he knew it to be so. Jejune was not capable or trained good enough.

"Seethe is one of the best trainees in the group, enough so that I think his usefulness outweighs Jejune's inabilities. Don't you think so?" Tome made his point, and didn't think anymore needed to be said.

"Yes sir, I understand now." Ardent stopped short mentioning of the night before, of his thoughts that Seethe was physically abusing Jejune. Maybe because, down deep in his heart, he was glad his friend of so many years was going with him.

"You better get to your quartering area and prepare for the storm, Tertiary Ardent. It's going to be another bad one, and the worst of it will be here soon."

And soon it did come. The tempest, as it had done to Stoic and the work camp detail, threw all its fury onto Area #56.

Ardent and Dank stayed in their bedding while the storm roared outside. Getting to sleep was near impossible. Their quartering structure shook with each mighty gust of wind, and the rains' dirty, muddied water leaked through the roofing. At one instance, Ardent thought it was going to collapse onto them. The creaking, cracking noises were making him nervous.

"Dank, are you awake?" At first there was no reply.

"Yes," it was almost a whisper.

"We've gone through many a tempest before. Don't worry, it will pass. They always do," and then he pulled the bedding up over his head.

When the tempest ended, and it hadn't lasted long, Ardent and Dank went outside to take inventory of the damage.

Two of the structures housing trainee quartering areas were destroyed, flattened to the ground. A few of the trainees received serious wounds. One of which was Genteel, Bandy's pairing mate. When Ardent heard the news of Genteel's injury he felt sorry for Bandy. It meant she would not be going with them. She trained so hard to be chosen, he thought. He would miss her. Maybe they will arrive later with the next 50 pairings, he hoped.

Darkness set in before the area was cleaned up, so the trainees had to work late into the night getting everything back to normal, except for the destroyed structures, the remaining trainees and DIPS would have the responsibility of reconstructing them.

The trainees that were displaced for the night had to sleep out under the stars in the cold. Jejune, his quartering area being one of those destroyed slept on the floor in Ardent and Dank's quartering area. Seethe, however, decided to sleep outside with the others. He didn't want anything to do with Ardent or Dank.

The wakeup call came a little later than usual. Ardent thought that Tome let everyone sleep later. It was the very first time Ardent saw a weak moment in Tome.

Soon after the morning meal of cold cereal, a caravan of supply carts arrived and was waiting just outside the entrance gate. The DIPS were busy loading the supply carts with supplies needed for the march to the citadel. Each trainee's personal stuff would be carried on their backs, packed in backpacks found lying on the ground by each pairing's quartering area door. Each trainee's identification number was stamped in large white numbers across the opening flap for everyone to see. It only took Ardent a few minutes to pack his. He was anxious to get on the way.

Ardent, with Dank right behind him, was the first to arrive at the caravan of supply carts, now fully loaded with the supplies. It wasn't very long before the rest of the trainees got there. Soon after, Tome and Morose arrived.

"It's going to take at least 5 days for us to get to the Capital Commune, what with all these supplies to slow us down. So, if anyone here isn't up to the hard march ahead let them say so now." Tome waited a moment for a reply, and with none coming forward he continued giving instructions.

"From this day forth you will no longer be called trainees; by myself, Morose or anyone else. From now on you are Revolutionary Vanguard Troopers. You will be respected by all those that quarter in the communes where we will be enforcing the law. Also, from this day forth you will call me Commander Tome, and Morose you will call Lieutenant Commander Morose." Tome stopped speaking for a moment. Then, in a loud strong voice command, "Troopers all — Forward march," and he led the trainees down the trailway.

The supply carts were heavy. Each cart's horse struggled getting its cart to start to roll forward. The pots and pans rattled a loud tune against the wooden sides, occasionally one would bounce up against the supply cart's wheel only to be quickly thrown back, hitting hard into the others. Each horse's master pulled hard, leading the horse along. Just behind the row of supply carts were the rookie troopers, their backpacks full and heavy on their backs.

Ardent and Dank positioned themselves at the rear of the column, and just in front of the DIPS that were also reassigned to the citadel. During the march the DIPS would perform their normal

THE LOST CHRIST

duties servicing the troopers. Ardent was also given command of the DIPS, to watch over them closely.

Ardent looked back over his shoulder toward Area #56, and when he did he bumped his nose on the barrow of his rifle, its strap resting on his shoulder. He saw Bandy and the others, those left behind, standing just outside the entrance gate watching the caravan leave. A sad look was on each of their faces, each wishing they were leaving with the caravan. When he looked forward again, he noticed that Dank was smiling. He had seen him bump his nose.

The sun was setting and they had only marched a few miles this first day. A campsite was set up within minutes, and the DIPS were rushing to get the evening meal ready when Ardent entered the mealing area to check on the DIPS progress.

Putting together the vegetable stew was the DIP that all the other trainees thought skillful in the use of his hands and an expert meal preparer. The very same one Ardent had spoken to in the past. At least now he could talk to him without being questioned by anyone.

"That looks good," said Ardent, referring to the cut up pile of vegetables in one of the large meal preparing pots. The DIP stopped cutting some carrots to look up at Ardent, surprised that Ardent spoke to him. A smile was on his face when he answered, after looking to see if anyone was looking their way.

"Yes, they're very fresh."

"I've been put in charge of watching over all of you, so you can feel free to speak to me." Another smile came over the DIP'S face. Then, the DIP opened a large sack filled with a white powder, and from it he scooped out a cup full and added it to the drinking water that was to be served with the vegetable stew.

"What's your name?" Ardent asked.

"Adroit."

"You, Adroit, can call me Tertiary Ardent."

"OK."

"What was that powder you added to our water?"

"We have to add it to every meal we prepare and to the drinking water. They told us it was a natural steroid used to better develop our bodies. We have to put it in our food and water as well. Although, most of the time we eat the same meal we cook for you."

"Thanks, and remember that I'm here if you have a problem with anything." With that being all for the time being that Ardent wanted to say, he headed back to where the other trainees were setting up their bedding areas.

Everyone was setting up their bedding near or under the small two-wheeled supply carts. The work horses were tied up well away from the camp, a sentry posted to watch over them.

Ardent found Dank under a large maple tree. They too survived the holocaust. In fact, they grew like weeds in the lower areas of the hills. Dank had not only set out his bedding wrap, but also set out Ardent's right next to his. Dank knew that the ground was warmest up close to the trunk of a tree, also frost free come morning.

Ardent and Dank sat under the tree chatting awhile about the march. Both were very excited, as most 16-year-old men would be, and men they were. That morning by the brook when they killed the zealots made them men.

⋙ ⋙ ⋙

As Ardent and Dank were getting up to go to the fire pit area for some of the vegetable stew Adroit prepared, Commander Tome approached them with two holstered sidearm weapons.

"Here take these. Everyone with a leader position carries a sidearm along with a rifle. The sidearm is a show of authority."

"Thank you, sir." Ardent replied, and soon came an echo reply from Dank. Commander Tome wasted no time, after handing the weapons to his third in command he left not looking back.

"Look Ardent, they're single action .45 caliber revolvers just like the ones we got to shoot at the weapons firing area."

"Yes, and ready to fire with six cartridges," said Ardent, as he slipped his belt through the holster, and then he put the belt back around his waist buckling it tight, a proud look and smile on his face.

"I can't wait to use it on some zealot," Dank said, drawing the weapon from its holster and waving it in the air. Then while putting it back in its holster, "There'll be plenty of zealots for you to kill also. I'll leave you a couple." But Ardent was already snuggled up in his bedding. He really didn't care about killing zealots, not now. He was too tired to care. It had been a long day, as will be tomorrow, he thought.

It didn't take very long for everyone to get to sleep, all except the first watch detail that Ardent set up around the perimeter of the camp site. He didn't forget this time. Not with Tome there.

The second day of the march went uneventful until late in the day, when on a narrow, icy ledged trailway cut in along the side of a mountain, and with not much space for the supply carts to pass through, one of the work horses spooked and reared up causing the work cart to slide sideward, its right wheel reaching the ledge's edge.

The weight of the supplies in the wagon shifted forcing the work cart off the ledge, dragging the horse and one of the DIPS off with it, and starting a fall of at least 500 feet toward the ravine's bottom. The unfortunate DIP'S echoing screams were in vain as those that were close could only watch his body, the horse and supply cart bounce and tumble down, the cart breaking apart along its way to the ravine's bottom, where one of its wheels kept rolling, wiggling and bouncing until it finally came to a stop crashing into a large rock, the horse continuing its slide went out of sight when it slid off another ledge below.

A sign of relief came upon Ardent's face when he got to the ledge's edge and saw Adroit standing near looking down.

"How sudden death comes," Ardent said, but there was no reply, not from the uncaring and coldhearted Dank. Unlike Dank, Ardent felt emotions and could not help feeling sad for the dead DIP.

Later Ardent learned that that particular supply cart was carrying half of the food supplies including the steroid powder and all the meal preparing and eating utensils. Without them every meal from then on would be half rations of raw vegetables and fresh fruit. Not much for the stomach of marching men and women, but it would have to do until they got to the citadel.

Rain, snow and soft ground the third day delayed the caravan. It would now be a six day march. Everyone was tired, wet, cold and hungry for a hot meal by the fifth night, but again they were given only half a ration of raw vegetables and fruit. Tempers were short.

Even Ardent had a short fuse. That last night Ardent took a turn at perimeter guard duty, the last watch.

When he woke from his sleep for the duty he felt a bit odd. A weird feeling came over him, a sensation of sorts, one he had never had before. He looked over at Dank. He was sound asleep, so Ardent didn't bother waking him. Maybe, he thought, it would be better that he not say anything to him. The feeling was too weird to explain anyway.

After returning from perimeter guard duty Ardent hastily ate his morning meal of half a ration of raw carrots and potato. He was starved. Then Ardent and Dank rushed everyone into position for the last leg of their march, Ardent still chewing the potato.

According to Commander Tome they should reach the citadel by mid afternoon and just in time, thought Ardent. They had run out of food, the last of it served that morning.

The temperature at the lower altitude, being nearer the ocean, was warmer than it was atop the mountain at Area #56. On the ground there wasn't yet snow. *The rest of the march should be easier*, Ardent thought.

On this day both Ardent and Dank decided to march at the front of the caravan. They wanted to be amongst the first to see the citadel, their new domicile. Ardent was getting excited. The pace of the march quickened the closer they got to the Capital Commune and the citadel.

On the mountain's side looking down Ardent could see into the valley and the Capital Commune. It was amazing. *It was so big*, he thought.

"There must be hundreds of villas. The bigger and taller structures — look, some are as tall as three levels. They must be what Tome called workshops, structures in which many citizens work together at their tasks," Ardent said to Dank, who was adjusting his rifle strap and not seeming to care.

When the caravan entered the outskirts of the Capital Commune, immediately hundreds of its citizens came out onto the trailway to greet them. Most of the citizens were cheering them, but at some of the trailway corners they were greeted by angry crowds, their arms raised and their fists closed, booing them.

An older man ran out from an angry crowd and walked alongside the caravan yelling for Ardent and the rest to go back to where they came from. Dank nudged Ardent on the shoulder and pointed ahead.

"Look over there, Capital Commune COPS coming this way."

The two watched as three Capital Commune COPS went up to the old man and started to beat him with their truncheons. Eventually, the old man fell to the trailway and rolled under one of the caravan's supply carts. The cart bounced, as its wheel ran over the poor old timer's legs. The old man was in pain and screaming for help while he was being dragged away by the three COPS and thrown to the side of the trailway where several other citizens came to his aid, the three Capital Commune COPS walking away laughing.

The commune center was crowded with farm vendors showing their previous autumn picked crops. The column of troopers looked on with amazement. The trailway was lined with fire pits for warmth. Near each keeping warm were vendors standing at large baskets, some filled with fruits and some with vegetables, a copious supply set out for all to see.

The baskets of food, however, were of no use to the troopers, as hungry as they were. None of the troopers had supply credits of any sort, and wouldn't until they've been a trooper for a month. Only then would they receive their first monthly credits, which were barely going to be enough to survive, they were told by Morose.

"Look Ardent, over there," Dank said. His finger was pointed down the trailway and to the left of it. In front of a large hastily put up tent was a group of citizens playing instruments, and some were singing poems.

"I wish we could stop and watch awhile," Dank joked, as the column continued on past the revelers. Tome had no intentions of stopping, and Dank knew it.

When the column reached a large park that had many large trees and benches scattered throughout, they saw in its center what Morose, now walking beside them, said was a statue of Regent Querulous; the Supreme Councilor.

The statue stood tall and was out in the open for all to see. A likeness of Regent Querulous was mounted on a horse. His hand was raised high as though he was waving to his subjects. What Morose called bird animals, and the only to have survived the holocaust, were walking on the statue, their droppings scattered all over Querulous's likeness.

"That's funny," Dank said. A big grin was across his face. Ardent just smiled back.

"Shoo, shoo!" Morose yelled, his arms waving. A fluttering sound erupted when the bird animals flew upward and away. It amazed Ardent, not just the sound of their fluttering wings, but also the sight of an animal in flight. He had never seen such a thing before.

"Look Dank, look!" Ardent, excited, yelled out. But Dank didn't seem to care. Not at all, he had other things on his mind. He just wanted to get to work, to face more zealots. He wanted more kills.

Just beyond the statue the column came upon a tree-lined trailway leading to a gated, high walled complex of sorts.

"That's where you were birthed," Morose said, a bit of laughter followed, which was rare coming from Morose.

"Look," Dank said. "There on the walls, more COPS."

"Yes, the Birthing Center is well guarded," Morose said.

The Birthing Center consisted of several structures, all within its walled compound, and all of them were made of stone and mortar. The wall around the center was also made of stone and mortar and stood at least eight tall men in height. The structure with the birthing tubes was the largest structure in the Capital Commune and had its own electric power generating station. The wind source electricity was needed to keep the birthing tubes the proper temperature. The only other two structures in the Capital Commune with electricity were the Government Center and the Government Metal Foundry.

Before Ardent could get a good look they heard horses' hooves. Coming in their direction at a full gallop and in a column of two was a dozen or more horses, and mounted on them were more COPS. In the lead was the vexillum bearer, the bannered troop markings held high. Next to him was the troop's leader.

"They're in a rush, most likely, to raid a hideout of the Pariahs," Morose commented. "You will learn more about the Pariahs later, after we get settled in at the citadel," and right after his comment Morose drifted back into the ranks to check on the others.

"I can't wait to be like him," Ardent remarked, stopping to see if Dank heard him. And once he realized Dank did hear him: "To be leading a troop on a raid," he continued. A look of excitement covered his face. Ardent, with a skip first, hastened his pace to catch up with Dank.

"Yes, and I too," answered Dank, as Ardent got closer, then next to him.

With the Capital Commune now behind them, the column of troopers headed up a steep hill. Along the hillside were many downed trees with their roots half buried in the ground. The evidence left of the damage from the recent tempest that went through the area.

"Look over there," Ardent heard. And when he looked at where many of the others were pointing to, he saw in the almost hardened mud a limb from a tree and the arm and hand of what must have been someone buried there, a victim of the storm. Next to the protruding arm and tree limb were many other broken tree limbs from a willow tree scattered about, and a broken up work cart with a large pile of stones next to it.

"He must have been killed by the tempest, unable to reach the citadel in time," Morose said to Ardent and those standing near. Everyone had gathered to get a good look at the dead man's monument. Some even pushed and shoved their way to the front to get a better look.

"Get back in rank!" Tome yelled out. "You'll see plenty of the dead soon enough." And within seconds the troopers were back to their positions in the column.

Later some of the troopers broke ranks again, but this time to help the DIPS with the supply carts. The work horses pulled hard, as the troopers pushed on the wheels of the supply carts. Without their help the horses never could have pulled the carts up the steep grade.

When the column reached the citadel's entrance gate area Ardent took a long look back at the Capital Commune and the surrounding area. The site was unbelievable, he thought. The Capital Commune stretched out for miles up the opposite hillside, and then all around the bottom of the hill the citadel stood on. Off in the distance he could see a mountain range, its many peaks covered white with snow.

"Look, that's where we came from," Ardent said to Dank, just as the gate to the citadel opened to let the column in.

Tome entered through the gate of the citadel first, his retinue of troopers right behind him. Once everyone was inside he halted the column.

"Amazing isn't it?" Ardent said to Dank. The two just stood there looking up at the walled garrison.

"It's our new domicile Ardent, just look at it. It's so big!"

"Yes," Ardent answered, as he slowly turned around, his eyes wide opened, staring at all that was there, "Amazing!"

The inner confines of the citadel were gigantic. So large was the parade ground area, located right at the entrance that it took at least 5 minutes for the front of the column of troopers to pass through. Along the north and east walls were the quartering structures. A large mealing area structure was located at the west wall, along with the assembly area structure. At the south wall on both sides of the entrance gate were the stable structures for the horses. Horses Ardent could hardly wait to mount. A ride through the Capital Commune leading a column of cohort troopers would be wonderful, he thought. Then he noticed that all of the structures were backed up to the wall and just above the roofs was the security walkway. In each of the corners were high, square, open viewed towers with roofs over them. Within each of the towers were troopers standing, lookouts guarding the citadel's perimeter. Nowhere did Ardent see a tent.

Given the travails of the long march, and now having seen the Capital Commune and its citadel, Ardent thought the sight worth the journey. He couldn't wait to see what his quartering area was like.

Chapter Six

It was damp inside the large, one-area structure. In its center was a fire for warmth. The smoke from the open fire was rising upward to a flute and out into the wooded area above, where it slowly drifted, thinning out amongst the trees with each breeze. Small tables stained with ink filled the confines of the area. Each table had a stool for the copyist whom soon would be arriving.

A large candle on each table was being lit by Salient. The loose fitting sleeve of his long white robe hung down from his wrist, dragging along the desk's top. The robe, a rope-like belt around his waist, his sandals and yarmulke-like cap were the only clothes he would need during his stay there.

Salient, a young man, as were most of the students at the Yeshivan School, was glad he had been chosen to learn of the Lord Jesus Christ's teachings. It was only a year past that he had arrived, and only a month ago was he chosen to work with the copiers. Like the disciple Peter, he had been a fisherman. Although he was only seventeen years of age he had been through a lot the past year since boarding one of the freedom ships to Harbinger.

After almost a year of previously living in Harbinger he departed for the small island of Yeshiva, the domicile of the Yeshivan Pacifists Sect School. There he would spend most the rest of his young life learning of the writings in the Holy Scrolls. Then he would go out into the world to teach others, as the Lord Jesus Christ did.

The copyists filed in, each to his table one behind the other. All twelve were silent. From underneath their tables they each took out two parchments, opening one. Then they began copying the words written on it onto the other blanked parchment. The words they copied were from the Tanakh (Written Torah, 5 sacred books of Judaism) and the New Testament Bible, both, the three educators found in their dig. The three, confused that there were two writings, mixed the two together and added the differences — Thus creating one common belief; one of both the Christian and Jewish writings.

Slowly, they continued copying. Every letter was perfectly scripted, each copy taking months to finish. Then each copier would start all over again. The completed copies eventually to be carried into the United American Union of Communes by the Yeshivan school graduates where, with their retinues, they would spread the word of the Lord to new converts.

Narration One

Four years quickly passed since Ardent and Dank's arrival to the Capital Commune citadel. Four years of which the Revolutionary Vanguard sought out and killed many of the citizens that lived in the Capital Commune and its surrounding farming communes. Citizens with new beliefs of a superior being, a God, or as Ardent and the others were told; a myth. They were given the name Pariahs by the government because of their defiance of the social laws, a name that would stay with them.

The Pariahs that were lucky enough not to be killed were confined in work camps, where they eventually died of starvation or the fever. Those that resisted militarily, the zealots, were hunted down and killed in battles in which they often were outmanned and out gunned by the much better trained Revolutionary Vanguard Troopers. Zealots usually weren't spared the work camps. During the battles, usually all the zealots were slaughtered, even when surrendering. A kill-all order was issued by Regent Querulous. No questions asked.

Stoic, after his unexpected escape found shelter with a small group of peaceful nomad, gypsy-like, Pariah converts that encamped in the dense forest. Although he didn't understand their new ways and beliefs he welcomed their hospitality.

When raiding unarmed Pariahs of a nomad encampment, the same that sheltered Stoic for four years, Ardent, Dank and their troopers killed everyone they found in the encampment including all the women and children. Stoic, along with two of the younger men, were the only ones that managed to escape the brutal onslaught, and only because they were in the deep woods searching for fruit and berries.

In spite of all the setbacks the Pariahs were having in the Capital Commune, their new beliefs were spreading throughout all of the United American Union of Communes ruled lands.

Because it was difficult for the Pariahs to hide amongst the other citizens of the Capital Commune, some decided to venture out to the outer areas joining farming communes. Many others, however, ventured onto the deadly ocean aboard sail ships in search of uninhabited islands that would be difficult for the troopers of any kind to reach. Large seafaring ships called Freedom Ships were used to transport the settlers-to-be. Often they became the victims of a tempest's fierce winds or a free floating iceberg, all lives lost at sea. On the newfound islands discovered they built settlements in which they had the freedom to believe as they pleased.

The first of the island settlements discovered, named Harbinger, was centrally located in amongst the other later settled islands. Although it lacked a deep water harbor, its high cliffs and surrounding mountain range protected it from the violent tempests. A narrow, high cliff valley leading to the ocean provided a gateway to the arriving Freedom Ships, with not only other converts onboard but well needed supplies.

Bandy and her pairing Genteel were never assigned to the Capital Commune as Ardent had hoped. Instead the two were assigned to the Rockport Commune much further away. There in a battle with zealots Genteel was killed. Soon after, Bandy, having found the way of the Lord, deserted and eventually found her way to one of the island settlements.

Chapter Seven

Ardent, while wiping the blood from his hands, watched as the water in the wash bowl turned red. His rifle was by his side leaning against the table. On the table was his knife, the long hardened blade covered with blood.

Lying on the ground face down was Savoir. A stream of blood slowly flowed from under his chest, stretching out from his body. An easy kill, too easy, and it bothered Ardent. Why, he wondered, do most the Pariahs not fight back?

Another glance into the wash bowl, he saw his face. A look of guilt reflected back up at him, reminding him of the many he had killed.

Now, after four years and at least a hundred raids since arriving to the citadel they finally captured one of the Pariah's leaders. It was Savoir, a very informative and all knowing teacher and one of the original three educators that discovered the buried time capsule.

Earlier in the day Ardent and his team stormed the cave that Savoir and his followers were hiding out in, killing all those that resisted or tried to run away. Only three of the thirty or so Pariahs survived the advancing trooper onslaught. The three would be sent to a work camp nearby, a hard labor death camp where only the strongest survive.

Found hidden in the caves were the Pariah's Holy Scroll Writings. On the scroll parchments were the written words of their beliefs. As was ordered by the government council the written propaganda would be burnt and the bodies of the Pariahs' dead loaded onto carts. Then the bodies would be paraded through the streets of the capital, an example for all to see.

The caves were well structured, a community of sorts with stall-like quarters. The area that Ardent was standing in was apparently a meeting area filled with long benches, one right behind the other. An aisle way was in the middle that stretched from the back to the front of the benches. On the wall in front of the benches was a large wooden cross. In front of the large cross were three high back chairs facing the benches, a small table with a bowl and the pitcher of water of which Ardent only just used to wash his hands. Stretched open across the table were more of the propaganda parchments.

Ardent heard someone approaching. When he turned he saw Dank.

"What an odd symbol this society has, a simple cross," Ardent said. Dank had a smile on his face. The killing never seemed to bother him. On his hands and tunic, too, was the blood of Pariahs killed.

"The cave is fully secured. The fools, as usual, they didn't put up much of a fight. Cowards! We had no casualties, just a few wounded," Dank reported. His rifle was shouldered, a sure sign that there was no one else to kill. Ardent knew Dank too well.

"This one," Ardent pointed to Savoir. "A so-called leader he was, just knelt there when I inserted the knife into his chest. Then while dying he said that he forgave me, that I knew not what I was doing." A startled look was on his face while he waited for Dank to respond.

Dank walked over to Ardent, and with a slight nod: "His kind will make him a martyr, even though he died for a useless cause, and so did the other fools in this cave."

Ardent walked away, and with his back to Dank: "Tome and Morose were talking just yesterday of the many Pariahs that have sailed off onto the sea looking for new island lands to settle on." Then, as he dipped his already washed hands, again, into the wash bowl, "Tome said that larger ships were being built by the government to transport its newly trained large force of troopers to those islands." Ardent paused, then lifted his head from over the wash bowl and glanced over at Dank. "Tome was upset," Ardent continued, "Upset because the troopers would not be Revolutionary Vanguard Troopers. Instead the government force was what Tome called a Legion, and the troopers called legionnaires."

Just as Ardent finished telling Dank what he had heard Jejune, Seethe and two other troopers, Tawpie and Yenta, entered the area. Already in chains with them were the three Pariahs that were captured, and there was no sign of resistance from any of them.

"You will pay for this with your soul," said the oldest looking man of the three to Ardent, who was bent down over Savoir wiping dry his twice washed hands using the dead man's tunic. The old man's chains rattled when he lowered his hand to point at Savoir's body. The blood from a bullet wound dripped off his arm onto the ground at his bare feet. His right eye was swollen, a cut just under with its blood running down his cheek. And his lower lip was split open, it too bleeding. All were evidence of a beating, Ardent thought it most likely given by Seethe.

"One day the sky will open and descending from it will be a man, called Jesus. You and your fellow sinners will feel his rapture. For your sins you will be struck down."

Ardent was curious of what he had to say, so he was going to let the old man continue talking of this man he called Jesus. But Seethe struck him in the ribcage with the butt of his rifle to shut him up. From the look on Seethe's face, he was enjoying beating on the defenseless old man.

"Old fool!" Seethe shouted out, hitting the old man again. Only this time in the middle of the old man's back with the butt of his rifle, just as the old man's knees hit the hard dirt ground from the first blow.

Ardent grabbed hold of Seethe's rifle, a firm grip, as Seethe was just about to move the rifle in a downward motion, butt end first, toward the back of the old man's head. Surely, it would have been a deadly blow and another senseless killing.

"Stop!" Ardent yelled, holding Seethe's rifle back. "The old man had enough."

A sign of weakness had emerged, and in front of some of his troopers. This weakness, Ardent knew, was not a good thing for them to see of a leader.

"He's only going to die anyway! He's too old to last very long in a work camp," Seethe shouted back. A look of anger reddened his face.

"Take them out of here. The work camp will shut him up!" Ardent commanded, yelling right back at Seethe. Then he pushed him back away from the old man, a show of force to prove to the others there that he was not weak. Seethe had been getting on his nerves a lot lately. Jejune, the wimp that he was, kept quiet and still.

The other two Pariahs helped the old man back to his feet. And, only because of the help they gave holding him up to keep him from falling down, he staggered out of the cave. Still he kept talking of this man named Jesus that so many others also spoke of, as Jejune and Seethe led them out.

"Do not harm the old man!" Ardent yelled out. He wanted to question him later. He wanted to know why they didn't fight back. Maybe the old man could lead them to the one he called Jesus, he thought. Tome would surely be happy if he and Dank were to capture another of the Pariah leaders. Yes, thought Ardent, I will question him later.

"Imagine, some guy is going to fall through a hole in the sky and kill us all," joked Dank, and a loud laughter started flowing from his mouth waking Ardent from his reverie. Then he, too, began laughing.

"We better get back to the citadel. Tome is waiting for a report. I'm sure he will be glad to hear of our great victory," said Ardent, as he tipped the wash bowl spilling the reddened water onto the ground. Then he released the wash bowl from his hand letting it fall, the wooden bowl shattering into several pieces when it hit the floor. A half smile was spread wide across his face while he watched the pieces scatter along the ground. Then he grabbed Dank by the shoulder to lead him out of the cave.

"C'mon Dank, let's go."

The thought of what the old man said was still on his mind, as the two walked out of the cave's dampness and into the dry cool air of the outdoors.

"What do you think the old man meant?" Ardent asked. A serious look was on his face, which he quickly shook off with laughter.

"He's an old fool, just like Seethe said," answered Dank. "Now let's get back to the citadel and enjoy this victory," when suddenly:

Bang ... Bang ... Bang ... The sound of the three shots startled Ardent and Dank. Each of their heads turned to where it sounded like the shots came from.

"It came from the other side of the rocks. Over there!" Dank shouted out, pointing to a grouping of giant rocks to their left.

Ardent was on the run, leaving Dank standing still, and it was straight for the grouping of rocks that he was heading. He didn't want to think what he was thinking, but he knew the thoughts were probably true. It better not be.

When he got to the other side of the rocks Jejune and the other two troopers, Tawpie, with a mind of a foolish younger person, and Yenta, one of the women selected by Tome, a blabbermouth and often spreading gossip, were standing over the three captives, the three lying dead at their feet, under which three rivers of red flowed to a puddle of blood forming by the outstretched, lifeless bodies. To the side, just a short distance away stood Seethe. The smoking weapon in his hands, and still pointed the captives' way.

Ardent's mind exploded. The thoughts within were running amuck. The fool, the stupid fool; the words kept bouncing off the walls of his brain. Within a wink of an eye-moment, Ardent was upon Seethe, the warm barrel of the smoking weapon in his left hand. Then in one motion he pushed the rifle to the side, his right hand rocketing upward stopped only after having impacted the jaw.

You could hear Seethe's lower jaw collide with his upper. See his face move to the opposite side of the mighty blow, blood exploding out of his mouth and from the tear left across the lip. Following the spray of blood were two teeth tumbling through the air. Then to his knees was the collapse, hitting hard onto the ground. His head tilted upward, a glance at Ardent, but all he saw was a blur of a figure. Then the blackness and the final fall to the ground, his head bouncing hard upon impact ... once, twice and a third time — He never felt the kick that followed, or the next and the next.

"Ardent! Stop! You're killing him," having just got there Dank yelled, his hand on Ardent's right arm he pulled him away before Ardent could finish the kill.

"I told him not to harm them. I should have killed him," Ardent yelled back. His right fist was still closed and the cut across his knuckles had already started to bleed. He turned around, a spinning move, and released Seethe's rifle from his left hand throwing it as far as he could. One step forward put him back standing over Seethe and again, Ardent kicked Seethe in the ribcage. His foot was moving forward for yet another blow when, with a loud crashing noise, the smoking weapon landed against the large rocks nearby.

"Please Ardent, he's my pairing mate, please don't kill him," Jejune begged. A fool he was, for another beating from Seethe.

Ardent stared, a long stare, at Jejune. Then he walked away, slowly, turning once and glancing toward Jejune. A shake of the head followed, letting Jejune know that he was disgusted with him. Ardent was disgusted with everything, the killings — everything!

"Yenta, Tawpie, clean up this mess," Dank ordered. Then he walked away, soon a trot as he tried to catch up to Ardent — His crazy, for at least the moment, mate.

Chapter Eight

It was getting near nightfall and the pinkish-gray, dirty looking sky was beginning to turn its blackened and grayish cloud-like color, as it usually did just as the sun was about to set, its usual ugly sight. The rarely seen, occasionally spaced stars were just emerging. One, always out of the north, shined the brightest, a guiding light there for all to follow.

The inter-perimeter security patrol was entering the gate that led to the center of the settlement, their nearly-emptied backpacks light on their backs. The three days of supplies issued were gone, used up during their required monthly inter-perimeter security detail. All the adults of Harbinger over the age of 16 had to take their turn patrolling the settlement's perimeter.

"I can't wait to get back to the villa to see the mate and kids," said Obtuse. A large smile was on his face in spite of how tired he felt. It had been a long three days, too long to be away from the ones he loved.

Obtuse was only 42 years of age with a poor sense of observation and not very sharp intellectually, yet he was one of the most senior of age living in the settlement. He also was a bit short of height, at only five feet tall. His face was scarred and his neck showed the burn marks he got on the ship twelve years earlier. The ship caught on fire from several lightning strikes during a fierce tempest. Most of the would-be settlers on the ship were burnt alive and taken down to the ocean's floor with the ship when it sank.

Obtuse was one of the few lucky ones. Crewmen and crewwomen from one of the other freedom ships that set sail at the same time managed to take him out of the choppy water, and only because he managed to stay afloat holding onto a piece of debris until they saw him bobbing atop the water.

"And I can't wait to see my mate," said Pristine. Then she took a moment to tug at her rifle, re-adjusting the strap position to better fit her small, thin shoulder. Her tunic, too, needed adjusting. It was much too large for her skinny body.

Pristine was a newcomer to Harbinger, having arrived on the last ship to enter the harbor only three months earlier. Although unspoiled and somewhat primitive, she was a rather pretty girl. Her dark black hair was braided, a long single braid that rested well down her back. And her eyes, also dark black, matched the hair perfectly.

Although she was only 17 years old when she arrived, she immediately had an affinity for the older Onus, her mate, having only recently joined in marriage. She had already blended in with the other citizens of the settlement, all of which respected Onus.

Yet to have children the two were trying almost every night they were together. Pristine feared she was barren and that Onus had suspected the same. Onus loved her very much, and if she couldn't have his children then so it was, he felt.

Onus also survived a difficult voyage and like Obtuse, he was pulled from the ocean. He was the type of person that easily accepted responsibilities. Often other citizens from the settlement came to him for advice. Usually when they had questions about things written in the Holy Scroll Writings, things they didn't understand. Although a tall and thin person, he was very strong both in body and mind. He had a beard that hid most of his well-scarred face and, like most of the men and woman birthed in test tubes, his eyes and hair were brown.

The ship Pristine arrived on was still docked in the harbor, unable to leave until all the damages from the tempest encountered on its voyage were repaired. Not many ships' captains were willing to take the chance making the crossing back. Most came knowing it would be a one way trip. Once here the ship's cargo would get unloaded then the ship itself would get stripped clean. The materials, such as the planking used to build it, would be recycled to build villas for the families.

The aboriginal settlement of Harbinger, a forerunner, was surrounded by a tall square stone wall, garrison style. The wall was put together with a mortar-like substance made of mud from the river's bank and shredded leaves from a strong wiry plant that grew in abundance on the small island.

A wooden walkway was built along the entire wall about one average man's height from the top. The wall was not built for a battle, or to protect its citizens from the troopers, if sent by the government. Instead, it was built to protect the town from the violent winds of the tempests that often and suddenly struck the settlement.

The villas within the walls were also built of the same stone and mortar mix. The roofs were of wood coated with the mortar mix too both firm up the roof protecting it from the winds and to repel the storm's rain water. The villas were built totally without the use of glass, nails or metals. The wood was fastened together with wooden pegs. They were built environmentally safe with small openings left for windows. A wooden shutter that lifted outward and up, with a wooden latch to keep it open, was used both for the sunlight and to protect against the violent winds of a tempest.

There was no fear of wildlife, birdlife or insects entering the opened windows, all having perished during the holocaust two thousand years earlier.

In the back of each villa was a terrace, its two sides a vegetable garden stretching outward beyond the villa. The back of the terrace was where the split wood for the fireplace and stove was stacked. A long table with benches was set in the center and used mostly by the women to do the washing of the clothing, done by hand in a large wooden bucket. Inside the villa was small and furnished with only the basic living needs. The citizens with larger families had lofts built for children's beddings.

Most of the citizens ate all their meals in the commune's mealing area, prepared daily by the women on a rotating basis, just as the DIPS had done in the communes before they left.

The mealing area structure was located next to the meeting area structure. Inside were tables and benches, two large wood stoves for preparing the meals, a wash basin, a large fireplace, a long table to cut and prepare the food and a storage area. Some of Harbinger's families, however, prepared their own meals in their villas. It was becoming a tradition that was spreading quickly throughout the settlement.

Because of the growth of Harbinger, many of the newcomers were building their villas just outside the wall surrounding the commune's center. The villas outside the commune center were built with tree trunks instead of the stone and mortar mix.

The meeting place, a large two-story structure, was built attached to the wall at the very end of the settlement. A steeple with a bell to call its citizens stood high and could be seen from almost anywhere on the island. It was also used as a school for the children, a place to heal the sick, and had a large open area lined with benches and where once a week on a Sunday the three town leaders would take turns reading to its citizens from the hand copied Holy Scroll Writings. They chose Sundays because in the Holy Scroll Writings was written that God created the Earth in six days, and rested on the seventh. Sunday, being the seventh day of the calendar week, was set aside for only rest and prayer. There were no stores, nor any form of currency yet.

The lowlands around the town were cleared for farming. An aqueduct carried water from a spring-fed lake about a mile away to the commune. Those quartering in villas outside the commune had their own wells. Their water was lifted up in a wooden bucket attached to a rope.

Close by each villa was the waste area, a deep hole in the ground. Built around it was a small roofed hut, usually built of stone and mortar to keep it from blowing down in the storms.

The town itself was not well fortressed, it didn't need to be. It was doubtful that the government's troopers would invade their domain. Many troopers would die and vital supplies would be lost to the violent sea if they tried to make the crossing.

The entrance to the valley overlooking the harbor was ravine like and very narrow. Cliffs of at least 500 feet lined both sides. Atop one was erected a giant wooden cross, a beacon signaling the freedom ships of its safe harbor.

Harbinger's citizens built a well-armed small fortress and garrison at the end closest to the town. The men from town manned the garrison on a rotating basis, an un-uniformed, untrained detachment.

Living at the settlement was difficult. Having the freedom to worship, raise a family, and have their minds not controlled by the government, all the lies, made the difficult tasks worth all the risks. There would be no turning back, not now and not after the taste of freedom they were experiencing. No matter what the government thought or would do, would they give their freedoms up. Not now or ever. They would die for their newfound rights, for their families, for their belief in the Lord.

Obtuse, Pristine and the six others had been patrolling the inter-perimeter of the valley — the foothills surrounding the settlement, river and farming areas.

Obtuse's regular duties along with several other men were to care for the cows and horses. Every morning he would make the mile long hike to the caves where they were kept.

The caves were discovered when the settlers first arrived, and were where everyone lived until the settlement center and wall were completed. Inside the caves was well protected from the storms. The citizens, after they moved out and into their own villas, decided to build stalls for the work horses and milking cows. Just outside, next to the caves, were two structures made of stone, one on each side of the caves' entrance against the hillside. One was for the chickens, and the other was for the goats. In amongst the fields, and also made of stone, were several sheepfolds for the many sheep.

Over the years the chickens had reproduced in great numbers, so eggs were of great supply. The feathers of the chickens made good bedding as well. In fact, the chickens were of such supply that the citizens decided to keep their population manageable, so the chickens became edible. For the first time in two millennia man ate meat again. However, the cows, sheep, goats and horses were spared such a fate.

Children were often seen playing games near the meeting area. Usually, skip the rope and one-two-three you're out tag. The children's favorite story from the Holy Scroll Writings was the one of an infant child called Jesus who was born in a stable. And of the three wise men who came bearing gifts.

The names mentioned in the Holy Scroll Writings, so different than theirs, were used by most of the joined mates, given to the children they conceived. Obtuse choose Mary for his daughter and Josef for his son.

Communities like Harbinger were being settled on several of the islands nearby. One such island, Newfoundland, started trading goods with Harbinger. The two islands were only a day's sail apart and being so close usually a safe sail.

The freedom ships weren't coming with new settlers as often as they did in the past. Most of the recent freedom ships that set sail were bringing settlers to newer found islands, so trading with the other islands was welcomed, and so was the news they often brought.

The latest news was that one of the islands nearby now had two settlements. That news troubled Harbinger's leading fathers.

Sordid, Stymie and Cavil had been jointly serving on the council to govern over the citizens since Harbinger was first settled. The meeting area doors were closed as the three met, and the mood wasn't good. Outside, it was getting dark.

"Too much growth too fast would bring the government and its murdering troopers here in spite of the storms. And, if their ships should get through with minimal damage it would mean much bloodshed," Sordid, a tawdry appearing and an undignified type that rarely smiled, spoke up, the concern showed on his face.

"The troopers are too busy fighting the underground resistance within the Capital Commune to be bothered with us. After all, we are a peaceful people. We've never caused them harm," Stymie answered. He was the oldest of the three and usually stood in the way of the other councilors' decisions, blocking progress.

Having finished his comment Stymie stood up, and then paced the ground. The other two kept their eyes upon him, waiting. Then he finally turned about, and while staring at the two onlookers he shook his head as though he was not at all in agreement with Sordid.

"But once the government puts down the capital's zealots they will be coming after us, the murderers. The zealots at the Capital Commune are untrained and unorganized, so it's only a matter of time before they are defeated," Sordid answered right back. The concerned look was still there on his face.

"And if we were to organize, who would lead us? No one among us, that's for sure," Stymie remarked.

"We must at least prepare the things we will need. Stockpile everything in the caves for when the time comes, if it does indeed come," Cavil, a clever man, but he was always finding faults or raising petty objections, got into the discussion.

"But what if they don't come?" Stymie interrupted. "Will all the vegetables and fruit stockpiled spoil? Food our mouths might need, if it be a cold, snowy winter." Then, after he sat back down and with firmness in his voice he spoke again before the others replied: "And what are we to use for weapons? We can't fight the troopers throwing stones at them."

"There is plenty of ore in the hillsides. Besides, we could stockpile the supplies in the mines left from the diggings," Sordid suggested. He thought it a good idea, so he smiled at the others.

"If the both of you agree, than I will have no choice but to stand with you," Stymie said. "But Sordid, remember that it was your idea." He wasn't smiling back at Sordid.

"I suggest that we send couriers out to all the other settlement leaders, asking for a joint gathering in Harbinger or Newfoundland to discuss the forming of a common government. Only if united can we repel the government should they mount a campaign to wipe us out." Sordid motioned.

"I agree," seconded Cavil, his right hand raised.

"I too will agree, but with reservations," Stymie softly spoke, his right hand stayed rested on the table.

"We are probably making a big mistake, for in the Holy Scroll Writings it is written that — Thou should turn the other cheek," Stymie quoted, and then he looked down at the meeting notes he had already taken. Then, looking back up at the other two: "I am agreeing, and only because we must stand together."

Chapter Nine

As Harbinger's council leaders were meeting a small zealot resistance force was attacking the Birthing Center at the Capital Commune. Their goal was to capture as many of the just born FITTs as possible and to destroy all of the birthing tubes.

The Pariahs wanted peace and the right to their newfound beliefs. The zealots, however, believed in militarily getting the right to their newfound beliefs by overthrowing the government.

⌬ ⌬ ⌬

Jingo, a bellicose-like man, a young leader and zealot patriot, was motioning with his hand for his zealots to retreat to the cover of the trees. The troopers on the wall of the Birthing Center had them pinned down, their advancement stopped.

"Brassy!" he yelled, as his head moved side to side looking for her.

"I'm right here behind the tree next to you," she answered, and with her rifle aimed upward at the wall's top she immediately fired off two rounds.

Brassy, who had a bold, outgoing nature, was his best shooter. Kneeling next to Brassy was Ursine, a big woman and strong as a bear. The two were once pairing mates and COPS, but like so many of their fellow zealots they found the way of the Lord.

"Get some of the others and set the work carts afire. Then push them between us and the wall. The smoke should shield us," Jingo's hand extended, a finger pointing behind at the three work carts filled with tree branches just cut, the leaves still green.

"C'mon Ursine, let's go," Brassy said as she stood up, turning to go to the carts. "Let's go … now!" and Ursine fired a quick three rounds, a cover for Brassy, before following her. Then from behind one of the work carts Brassy fired three rounds off as Ursine weaved back and forth her way to the work cart, several bullets landing near at her feet, and one into a tree trunk, the pieces of bark spinning into the air. One of the shots fired by Brassy hit a trooper, his head foolishly exposed. "A lucky shot," Ursine teasingly said with a wide smile on her face. Then she knelt next to Brassy and fired cover shots when Brassy got up to light the torches on fire and then throw one in each cart, as two zealots at each gave them a hard push forward toward the wall.

Ardent and Dank stood alone watching the fires, three in all, from in front of the citadel's forward wall, the sky above covered with a thick, white smoke. Soon, both knew, they would get the command from Tome to mount. They waited with patience, yet were anxious to end this uprising, and once and for all wipe out the band of zealots responsible, and to capture or kill their leader, the one called Jingo.

Ardent thought the armed insurrection was suicidal to have started, that the zealots will all be killed before morning, and right they should be, that there will be some taken alive and questioned, that from them he will learn where their hiding places are, and that soon this will all be over with.

Ardent had questions and even doubts as to why the citizens were rebelling against the government. A government that for so many years; birth, fed and cared for each of its citizens. The same citizens, that when their meeting places were found often just turned the other cheek refusing to fight, only to be slaughtered or the lucky ones sent to the work camps.

"Why do they resist the government only to be slaughtered?" Ardent asked, as he put his hand on Dank's shoulder. "For what are they willing to die?" He knew the other troopers would never doubt the government, so Ardent was careful in what he said, even when alone with Dank. But still he had his doubts, and they worried him.

At first Dank didn't answer. He only smiled back at Ardent. He didn't care, there were no doubts in his mind, none. All that was on his mind was the battle to be with the zealots. Dank, unlike Ardent, still looked forward to the battles and the killings that went with each battle.

"Because they are fools led by more fools," Dank finally did answer, with a worried look on his face. "It's our responsibility to kill as many as we can. So, we will have no more foolish questions."

It was too easy battling the Pariahs, because they did not fight back, thought Ardent, but the zealots were better organized and trained. They fought back using hit and run tactics. Many of his fellow troopers had been killed by the zealots hit and run tactics, and usually in the darkness of the night.

Ardent knew Dank was right. Yes, he was having too many thoughts, but the memory of the educator, Savoir, and what he had said to him as he died haunted him.

"C'mon let's go. Tome is waiting for us at the command center," Dank bellowed out, and while looking straight into Ardent's eyes.

Dank had taken notice of the many questions Ardent was asking the past months, many repeated questions. So much so, that it worried him.

"We've got zealots to kill waiting for us at the Birthing Center."

"Yes, the others too are waiting for us," Ardent answered, he knew the Capital Commune troopers at the West end of the Capital Commune would soon need relief. Together and with one hand around each other's back, the two headed for the stairwell of the tower.

About half the way down the steep, narrow, spiraling, stone stairwell they met Seethe, who was rushing up too them and almost out of breath.

"Tome said to hurry back. The Birthing Center is under siege, and they've asked for reinforcements," Seethe shouted, still out of breath and struggling hard to get it back.

⇂⋊ ⇂⋊ ⇂⋊

When the two got back to the command center Tome was pacing back and forth, upset with what was happening. He had a concerned looked on his face, as he kept pacing.

"There are 60 of your fellow troopers mounted and waiting on the parade ground area. I want you to head straight to the Birthing Center and reinforce those there. You must not let the insurgents take the center. Their goal is to destroy the center and mankind, the fools. I don't care what it costs in troopers. You must hold the center," Tome commanded, and as soon as he got the last of the words out of his mouth, both Ardent and Dank were rushing out of the command center for the parade ground area.

Once the two got outside they quickly mused over the plan. And the plan, it was simple enough. But, would it fool the zealots?

"Yes, it's a good plan," said Dank.

"All right, let's do it," answered Ardent. His reply sounded like a dare, which Dank welcomed.

Once mounted, and without delay Ardent and Dank led their troopers out the main gate and down the hillside into the Capital Commune. Through the streets the troopers' horses galloped, filed two by two in a column. In the lead with 40 of the troopers was Ardent. At his side was the standard bearer. His bugle at his side, he waited for the command to sound the charge.

Dank was right behind Ardent with the remaining 20 troopers. The sound was loud, as the 62 horses' hooves hit the cobblestone, 244 horseshoes. The thunderous storm echoing off the stone villas and alleyways could be heard well before their arrival.

Some of his fellow troopers, Ardent knew, wouldn't make it through the gates of the Birthing Center. Snipers surely would be waiting, each with their finger on the trigger, a trooper in their gun sight and a kill on their mind.

The Birthing Center was surrounded by a large park with picnic tables and lots of trees for the insurgents to hide behind. Ardent plan was to run his column of 40 troopers through the park. Well away from the main trailway leading directly to the gate. With any luck, the zealots would be waiting along the main trailway. Hopefully, the zealots would re-gather to fire at his column. His troopers and he would be most of the way to the gate when Dank, several minutes behind, would come down the main trailway leading to the gate. Hopefully, catching the zealots re-gathering and out in the open.

Returning fire would be difficult for Ardent's troopers. So instead they would run the horses hard and fast, while Dank's column fires at the out in the open zealots. Maybe the loud thunderous noise from the horses' hooves on the hard ground will scare them, thought Ardent, and then he laughed at his foolishness. Once his column is secured inside the center what's left of Dank's column will make their run for the gate.

Ardent thought it was a good plan, at least, one that would get most of his fellow troopers into the center alive. And, as usual, Dank and his column would take most of the heat.

Just ahead Ardent could see the park and the occasional flashes in the dark from the Capital Commune's troopers returning gunfire. And from what he saw of the flashes from the zealots hiding in amongst the trees, it looked like his guess was right.

Ardent turned his column onto the park as planned. Then, while at a full run of the horses, and when they were about 500 yards from the gate, he gave the command to his standard bearer to blow the charge with his bugle. And just as he had thought, when the zealots heard the bugler's charge they regrouped and soon came out into the open to get better aim.

The sound from the bugle also alerted the Capital Commune's troopers inside the center to open the gates. And just in time for Ardent, who was approaching the center at a fast trot.

A volley of gunfire erupted from the insurgents, falling three then a forth trooper in his column. Ardent heard the thud sound of a bullet's hit, and watched, as the blood oozed out of the hole in his horse's neck. Yet, the horse continued well into the center's grounds before coming to a halt, where Ardent quickly dismounted, as he heard the thundering sound of Dank's column storming down the main trailway. The rapid gunfire that must have been coming from Dank's column could be heard, even above the loud sound of the on-rushing column of horses' hooves.

Dank caught them off guard but good, so good that he kept his column out there. He had the zealots well out in the open and on the run. His troopers were chasing many of them down. It was becoming a slaughtering, one that the zealots surely never would forget.

Jewel and Malinger were with Dank's column and the first to dismount, the two horses trotting to the citadel rider-less right behind Ardent's column. Jewel, out in the open, went down on one knee. Malinger stayed standing next to her. The two opened fire on two zealots hiding behind a tree as bullets ricocheted off the trailway near them. Then, from next to them came a sudden noise and dust rising into the air. Fallen to the ground was a horse and its mount. The horse's legs kicked upward, kicking up more dust, before it jumped back up. From the horse, and with a bullet through his chest, rolled one of the troopers atop the trailway stopping beside where Malinger stood. She didn't move, nor look down at him as she reloaded, aimed and fired her rifle, cocked it and fired again.

"Good shot," she said to Jewel as a zealot from behind a tree fell over backward. And then it was the other that fell over backward right after she fired a third shot.

"Good shot," Jewel said, then looking up at Malinger she smiled.

In his rifle sight Jingo had a trooper. She was standing out in the open. He wasted no time pulling the trigger. The shot was true hitting the targeted trooper in the neck. He didn't bother watching her fall. Turning his rifle to the one kneeling near he quickly pulled the trigger again. The bullet hit her rifle, knocking it from her hand. He fired again, but she had moved. The bullet passed its target.

Jewel turned and reached for her fallen mate's rifle, her eyes reddened with hate for the one that shot Malinger. She felt a bullet's breeze pass by her head, a miss. She aimed and fired, and fired again. Misses she thought when she saw the sparks each bullet made when hitting a large rock he was hiding behind. Still the zealot fell to the ground. She aimed again at his body, wounded but still moving, when suddenly Dank's mount trotted across her line of sight. When the dust settled the zealot wasn't there.

"Malinger!" she cried out running to her lying still body, "Malinger!"

The zealots unable to retreat started surrendering, their weapons dropping to the ground and their hands rising high. The Capital Commune's troopers that were manning the wall started target practicing, popping shots into the surrendering zealots.

Jingo was being helped by Brassy and Ursine, each with one of his arms over their shoulder running. He was wounded when a bullet from a trooper's aim hit a large rock he was hiding behind. A chipping from the stone went deep into his left eye. Of the fifty that attacked the center, only the three and a half dozen of their fellow zealots managed to get away.

Ardent watched as Dank trotted his horse into the center's grounds. A big smile was on his face, a victory smile. Then Ardent heard the loud crashing sound coming from behind him. The horse he was riding fell to the ground. It laid there lifting its neck upward, looking over at Ardent who would have to put the mare out of her misery. One shot into its head rang out loud and echoed throughout the compound. Lying still now lay the mare with once her rider standing quiet, his sidearm at his side.

"Tome will be happy now that there are no more zealots attacking the Birthing Center," Dank joked trying to cheer Ardent up, he knew saddened after having to shoot the mare.

"Sir," It was Jewel interrupting. "Jingo and several others got away," and she had a look of sadness and disappointment on her face. She didn't tell him Malinger was dead.

"It would have been nice to have captured a few alive for questioning later," barked Ardent, a bit upset that the Capital Commune's troopers cut down the surrendering, unarmed zealots before he got to question them. "Now Jingo will reorganize his forces with new recruits," he muttered.

It was early in the fall and each day that passed was getting colder, months passed since the attack on the Birthing Center and now, finally, the Revolutionary Vanguard had driven Jingo and his zealots from the Capital Commune.

Defeated, unorganized and his family recently murdered by the troopers Jingo had taken refuse with Brassy, Ursine and about forty fellow zealots in caves on the snowier and much colder, higher elevated regions. Having split up into two unorganized smaller bands, Jingo wasn't ready to call it quits. He had made up his mind that, however long it took, someday he would return to the capital with a larger and trained force. It would be God's will. It would be revenge for his murdered family. In a dream he saw it so.

Knowing that the terrain of the mountains was too difficult for troopers to search out the zealots that hid there, the government was contented with just letting the small bands of zealots barely exist. "The lack of food and the weather elements would kill most of them," was what Tome informed the government council weeks earlier.

On this day and at a meeting with the Capital Commune councilors Tome sat waiting for the council's leader, Regent Querulous, to speak. Given the sir name Querulous because of his constant complaining, since his birthing many would joke. Even now, approaching the last of his years, he still was known for complaining.

"Finally, Commander Tome, you've driven the zealots from the capital and into the mountains. I really don't understand why it took so long," Querulous spilled out the words, a message eagerly sent to Tome of his unhappiness with his performance. Tome, suddenly lost for words, kept quiet.

"Now that the problems here at the capital have finally been solved the council and I have decided to form a legion of soldiers to conquer those dissident Pariahs that have fled to far out westward islands. Ten centuries, one thousand legionnaires have been gathered and trained for this legion. The island settlements will soon feel the sting of our legionnaires." He stopped, and then he looked ahead toward the others there, a smile on his face. The others nodded back, an approval. "Stories that were spread from sailor to sailor and eventually to the work camp guards, whom have informed the Council, tell of separate fortressed communes. We want them destroyed before they unite," and again he paused and again the nodding of the heads.

"The new legion will be given the name '101st Battle Legion of Manchester' and it will be commanded by Austere De guerre," Regent Querulous stopped again, but this time to wait for Tome's remarks, fully aware of the council's decision to pass over Tome for Austere.

Known for his audacious behavior, Austere, years earlier was the head instructor at Area #56 when Tome was young and just starting out as an instructor. The two did not see eye to eye and have not spoken to each other in many years.

The Revolutionary Vanguard defeat of the zealots, Tome thought would put him in good favor with the council. He knew of the forming of a legion month's earlier, however, the news he just received only meant that he was being passed over for Austere, whose methods he disliked. This didn't show well to Tome and the council sensed it when he suggested:

"To put a large force out to sea all at one time could be disastrous. One encounter with a tempest would wipe the entire force out. Instead, a satellite fortress should be established on one of the unoccupied islands nearby. Then, and over several months of sending a ship at a time, we build up a force the size we need. From the satellite fortress the settlements can be engaged and destroyed one at a time." After finishing his suggestion to the council Tome glanced around the table looking at each of the council member's faces. The look on the face of each council member had said it all. None appeared to be listening to what he had said. Quickly his suggestion was tabled when:

"Supreme Commander De Guerre assured us a victory. Your suggestion would take many months longer, time we don't have to waste. The longer we wait the stronger they will be," Plethora, the only female on the council spoke up, the others nodding their heads in agreement. "You can leave now," she continued once the head bobbing had stopped.

Plethora, an excessively heavy woman and a voracious eater who had a lot to say about everything and everyone, was the youngest of all the councilors. She also was very ugly to look at. On her chin was a large wart with hairs growing out of it, and the other councilors often stared at it. Just under her chin was a second and third chin of hanging fat, giving her a turkey-neck-like look.

Tome left the meeting depressed, wondering what Plethora was saying about him now that he left the meeting and of what would happen to his Revolutionary Vanguard. On his way outside, as he opened the door, in came Austere. Not a word was spoken, as each passed by one another. Tome did, however, notice the smirk on Austere's face.

Narration Two

Throughout all of the westward freedom settlements the fall's harvest was a plentiful one. Stockpiled in the mine diggings at Harbinger was the extra corn meal, vegetables, fruit and berries that were donated by all of the settlements.

Made by the women of the settlements and also stockpiled away were enough clothing, tents and bedding for at least 400 of the united settlements volunteer fighters.

With winter coming, however, the training of the settlers would have to wait until springtime. Still the settlers had no one experience to lead them or to train them for that matter. They were well stocked up, but they had no idea what lay ahead.

The building of a foundry in Harbinger that would be used to forge the knives and what was needed to build the firearms, was just completed. Since the planting was done until springtime the farmers of the settlement were being used for the assembly of the weapons.

In the Capital Commune things were getting out of hand. The new believers had split into separate groups and each with different beliefs. The largest of those groups still remained the Pariahs, the believers of the Lord Jesus Christ.

Of the other groups some worshiped the sun, some animal idols, and some even believed in sacrifices. However, all practiced marriage, childbirth and wanted to be free of the government's rule. The spin-off groups would often turn on the Pariahs for the supply credits offered as a reward.

The desire for a safer place to hide and to practice their new beliefs, the Pariahs began moving away from the capital to the farming communes located in the outer areas. Those with enough supply credits to buy their way boarded freedom ships leaving for the settlements.

Mike Difeo

Jewel had a hard time getting over the death of Malinger. The killings of past had been many, and it began bothering her. She had many doubts, and with her grieving she found the Lord Jesus Christ. Soon after she joined the underground movement and upon a freedom ship she sailed to the new settlements in search for a new life.

Chapter Ten

Springtime came early at the Capital Commune and the newly trained 101st Legion of Manchester was out to sea heading southwest toward where they thought the new settlements were, their ships bouncing hard into the oscillating ocean's waves.

Commander Austere stood tall, his hand a hold of the railing top deck, a firm grip. The waves were high, the strong winds of a tempest only beginning.

The Mt. Pocono's sails were still full. The crew struggled with the wind trying to lower the sails, and the wind was winning the battle.

Austere ducked down when he heard the main mast sail tear. Then he glanced upward when he heard the snapping noise being made as the wind tossed the tattered sail about. He had sailed before into a tempest. Many a good man he knew was lost that day. He feared the fury of a tempest, scared for his life. But he knew there was nothing he could do. His life was in the hands of the crew.

Austere stool tall again. A show of strength, he thought. Then the Pocono's starboard side was hit by a towering high wave's might. Austere felt the coldness of the water as it crashed down upon him. He had no control of his motion. The wave's wake and the broaching portside of the ship threw him onto the decking, and then into the sternpost head first just as the Pocono headed down the backside of the wave. With a broken neck Austere lay still. His fear of the tempest was no more.

The force upon the Pocono as it shifted, broaching starboard again, snapped the sternpost midway down, its sails still full of wind as they crashed to the decking and atop the already dead Austere.

Aboard one of the other ships, the Springfield, were 50 of Tome's Revolutionary Vanguard troopers that were under the command of Morose. Tome, as usual, stayed behind at the citadel with the remaining 150 troopers. The troopers' mission once they reached the settlements was to stand guard over the captured Pariahs. There would be no women or children survivors. Only the strongest of the men would be spared and only to be sent to the work camps. Austere had given his legionnaires a "kill-all order."

Below with Morose and the others were Jejune and Seethe. On deck with the crew, helping with the lowering of the sails, were Ardent and Dank. But it was too late. The storms winds had already torn most the sails.

"Dank!" Ardent yelled out, the wind stealing his words before they could reach Dank's ears.

"Dank!" again he yelled, only much louder.

"Yes mate," he finally heard Dank yell back, barely. From what he could see, in spite of the sharply stinging salt smashing against his face, Dank was half bent forward into the wind trying to make his way to him.

The streaks of lightning were lighting up the sky even more than before. Its thunder was now instant. The full fury of the tempest was right over the convoy of ships.

Below deck, most of Ardent's fellow troopers were motion sick, overcrowded and wet from the water seeping in from the separating seams. From bow to stern — the panic amongst them was evident — the look of death's nearness was on all their faces — the creaking of the planking's deafening — and the calls for help cried out through the darkness — But all alone they were! All alone … all alone and at death's final moment — without forgiveness?

☙ ☙ ☙

Just ahead starboard Ardent could see the command ship, The Mt. Pocono, with Austere and 100 legionnaires aboard. Ardent watched, as a giant wave crashed onto the bow of the Mt. Pocono driving it deep into the water. White breakwater rushed to the stern, taking anything not tied down with it. The ropes, chains and tackle of what remained of the sternpost were swinging free and out of control.

Ardent watched as the crew on deck were being dragged overboard, splashing into the water. One sailor, his head smashed into by a heavy boom that swept across the deck of the Mt. Pocono, plunged into the blackness of the ocean, smashing first through the railing.

Unmanned and out of control the Mt. Pocono was met by the next wave. Then rising slowly to the wave's peak it turned starboard

THE LOST CHRIST

half out of the water, and came rushing down to the bottom of the rear side of the wave. The next wave's crest crashed into the ship, swamping it. Its keel faced the darkened sky, as the next wave, the next, and another smashed hard against the bobbing upside-down death trap; until it finally ripped apart and sank out of sight. Floating debris and lifeless bodies of some of the brave aboard were all that was left in its place, rising upward to the breaking whitecap of the next wave's anger.

⌒⊲ ⌒⊲ ⌒⊲

Ardent, even over the sound of the wind and thunder, could hear the flapping of the torn sails above him.

The Springfield's stem post, hit by lightning, had snapped and was lying across the deck. Ardent, after struggling with the wind to get to the downed stem post, reached around it and held on for his life. Not far away, near the ship's railing aft, was Dank holding onto one of the rigging ropes. Right next to him was one of the crew-women. A large splinter from a downed mast was lodged into her neck. Her lifeless body was sliding back and forth along the deck flooring.

"We're never going to make it through this storm," Ardent yelled out to Dank, while still holding onto the stem post, afraid to let go of it.

Looking over toward Dank, Ardent could see his mouth moving, but he couldn't hear what he was saying. Just behind Dank, Ardent saw the bow of another ship heading right at them and it, too, was out of control. The stem post and sternpost snapped off clean and the stem post hung over the side dragging in the water.

"It's going to hit us," Ardent shouted, but he knew Dank couldn't hear him.

The sound of the two ships colliding was vociferous, and upon impact the force snapped off the Springfield's sternpost. Ardent could feel the ship rolling starboard. Then he heard the crashing sound, as the separated section of the sternpost landed on Dank crushing him to the decking, he never saw it coming.

"No, oh please no," Ardent screamed out. The taste of the water's salt was in his mouth — the splinters from the decking and planking flew past him with the wind — the crushed bodies of some of the troopers from below pushed upward by the bow of the oncoming ship, and then thrown upon the Springfield's decking — crushed against the wall of the captain's quartering area with a splintered planking through the torso, was what was left of Morose.

The Springfield kept broaching to the starboard side from the force of the crash. Then it came to a rest on its side, and only for a moment, throwing both Ardent and the stem post he was holding onto out into the cold sea — just as the tempest winds came to a stop — and as if it were meant for Ardent to be spared the others untimely, wasted deaths.

⋈ ⋈ ⋈

The water felt frigid, its salt stinging his scrapes and cuts. He grabbed onto a rigging rope still attached to the stem post and then climbed up onto it tying himself to it. Off in the darken distance he could see the two joined ships sink out of sight. Alone, cold and bleeding from a small gash on his arm, Ardent wept for Dank, Jejune, Morose and all the others that must have perished. Then he wept for himself. He knew he couldn't last long in such cold waters. Already his legs felt numb.

A half hour passed and Ardent didn't know how much longer he would last. At least the sky was cleared of the storm clouds and the ocean had calmed down, he thought.

Afloat in the ocean's river-like current and still tied down to the stem post, Ardent fell off to sleep. Just off in the distance, unknown to him, was the silhouette of a landmass and a lone ship anchored in its harbor.

⋈ ⋈ ⋈

Ardent slowly opened his eyes and saw that he was in a strange place and bedding. He felt weak, sweaty, and his whole body hurt. His arm, he noticed, was bandaged and taped to his waist. His other arm was free, so he used it to lift himself up in a sitting position. Then he sat still for a moment, his head hurting, his eyes blurred.

The surroundings, he thought, were very modest. Then he noticed that he was in a small separate area and a door was left open. He could hear the snapping sounds of a well fired-up wood stove coming from the other area, and he could feel the draft of its radiant, distant heat. From the other area he also heard sounds of women talking and laughing. *Where could he be?* he wondered.

Ardent turned and lowered his feet to the floor, and after removing the bedding covers he stood up. His legs buckled and he immediately fell to the floor knocking over the chair that was next to the bedding.

Ardent felt the soft, warm hands that grabbed his arm. When he looked up, helping him back onto the bedding were two women.

"Where am I?" he asked, the words coming quietly from his mouth, which felt dry. There was no reply from either of the women.

"Did anyone else from the ships survive?" Again, there was no reply from the women.

After the two women got Ardent comfortable, back under his covers and some water; which one of the women helped lift the container to his mouth, the two headed back to the other area. One of the women, the one that kept laughing, stopped at the door and turned back toward him, "My name is Pristine, and what is yours?"

"Ardent," ouch, his lips were sore, his voice hoarse. "Ardent Bravado."

"Soon my husband, Onus, will be back from his work detail. He will answer any questions you have and, I'm sure, ask many of you."

"Husband — What is that word?" Ardent said to himself. And right after he shut his eyes and soon fell back to sleep.

⸻ ⸻ ⸻

"Wake up Ardent, wake up you fool. It's me — Bandy." The sound echoed in his ears, and for the moment he thought he was dreaming. When he opened his eyes he saw Bandy standing there next to his bedding. While wiping the sleep from his eyes he sat up. A look of disbelief was on his face when he realized that standing there next to his bedding really was Bandy.

"Bandy — Is it really you?"

"Yes, you big fool, it is me."

"But what are you doing here? And where am I?"

"I came here from the settlement of Newfoundland on one of the trading ships. After I arrived I heard that someone shipwrecked was sheltered here and that he was found wearing the uniform of a Revolutionary Vanguard Trooper. When I heard the name Ardent

Bravado, I rushed over hoping that the Ardent they spoke of would truly be you, and it was."

Ardent just stared at Bandy, lost for words to say to his dear friend, so he let her do most the talking, until others, some he did not know, entered interrupting. All of them with smiles on their faces, and each appeared happy to see him sitting up on his own.

"Dank and Jejune are dead," he blurted out the words, suddenly.

"Let's not think about that right now. Instead, tell me how you feel. Is there any pain?" Bandy asked, but the sadness from the news of Jejune did show on her face.

"No. I just feel weak in the legs."

"You are in the settlement of Harbinger. The citizens living here in Harbinger are good people and they will take good care of you. I told them that I knew you from the COPS training school and that you were indeed a Revolutionary Vanguard Trooper, but that didn't seem to matter. God, they said, will show you the way."

"You mean a Pariah settlement!"

"I, too, am a Pariah, a believer of the Lord Jesus Christ," Bandy snapped back.

Ardent was surprised to hear her say that she had become a Pariah, and it showed on his face. He always thought Bandy was strong minded. He would never have thought she would believe their propaganda. And she was a trooper like I was, the thought rushed through his mind.

"And what of your pairing mate Genteel?"

"She was killed by zealots."

"Tell me, who is this man you Pariahs call Jesus?" Ardent asked. He had sensed her sadness of Genteel's death and changed the subject.

"Later, my friend," Bandy said, and she started to laugh, "I will talk to you again tomorrow," and right after she finished speaking, smiling, see turned and left. The others, all except Pristine, left with her.

"You have been sleeping for three days since you woke before. My husband Onus was worried that you would never wake again. We both prayed each night for you to recover and God answered our prayers."

"This man named Jesus, will he be coming by?"

Pristine started to laugh at him. The laughter made him angry, because, now two women had laughed at him, a Tertiary.

"I have chicken meat with vegetables and broth on the stove. It will make you strong again," said Pristine, and then she left, still laughing.

⊂✕ ⊂✕ ⊂✕

Ardent spent a long time lying in the bedding wondering how he was going to get back to the Capital Commune and Tome, or if any of the ships got through the storm undamaged.

"Is everything all right? You look confused," Pristine said, as she entered to bring him his bowl of broth with chicken and vegetables.

"Everything is fine."

"But you look confused."

"I said everything is fine."

"Here, eat this." Pristine wasn't happy with Ardent for having snapped at her. "It will make you strong. It's the meat of chicken with vegetables and broth. Before you know it you will be up and walking again," insisted Pristine, a steaming bowl in one hand and a spoon in the other. She placed both on the table next to the bedding and sat in a chair that was next to the table. Then she spooned out the hot mixture and held it out to feed him.

"I can feed myself," again Ardent snapped at Pristine. It stood her straight up from the chair.

"All right, go ahead and feed yourself," She snapped right back then put the spoon back into the bowl and left him alone.

The mixture from the bowl was hot and tasted very good. He hastily drank every bit of the broth, wishing there were more. Still hungry he even ate what must have been the meat of the chicken Pristine spoke of, which he had never tasted before. These people even eat the meat of animals, he thought, how strange, but he admitted to himself that the meat of the chicken did taste good.

Chapter Eleven

The months passed slowly for Stoic, long and cold winter months. Since his escape when the gypsy-like nomad encampment was raided, he wandered around from one farming commune to another, working in the fields for his food and bedding to survive.

Eventually, Stoic found himself in the seaport commune of Rockport where he labored for his shelter and bedding on the cargo ship Halcyon, then anchored in Potomac Bay at the foothills of the mountains of what once was the state of Maryland. And now it had just anchored in Manchester Harbor, the Capital Commune's seaport. A place he didn't want to be.

Because of his vast size the ship's captain assigned him to cargo duty. Any duty would have been fine with Stoic. All he wanted was to get as far away from the capital and those that might still be searching for him. The memory of Pique and his whip, Felicity, was deeply embedded in his mind. Now here he was right back near the capital, and until the ship leaves it was best he not go ashore. He feared a guard from the slave camp might see and recognize him.

It was known throughout the Capital Commune's underground that the Halcyon was setting out to sea as a freedom ship. Its arrival port was to be Harbinger. A hard sail through, what the crew told Stoic were the roughest waters to sail, waters with free-floating icebergs, high seas, strong river-like currents and sudden tempests that could strike at anytime.

Once all the cargo was loaded into the holding area, and under the darkness of the night, the ship would set sail with only the crew aboard. When the Halcyon got out of sight of Manchester, along its coastline and about a mile out to sea, it would drop its anchor. There, the Halcyon would wait for the passengers that eventually would arrive aboard smaller shore boats.

In the bilge over the keel were barrows loaded with black gunpowder to make bullets and the much needed supplies the Harbinger citizens would need to make it through the coming cold months of winter.

The captain, Abstruse, was of middle age, overweight and difficult to comprehend. He, like those he would soon be taking to Harbinger, was a believer of the teachings of the Lord Jesus Christ. This voyage would be his last. He, too, would be settling down in Harbinger.

Aboard one of the small shore boats to come was Prudent, his wife-to-be. Although she had good sense in dealing with practical matters, she was having some difficulties dealing with the fact that she was only half his age. But she loved him very much and wanted to have his child. To her that was more important than what other citizens had to say.

Prudent had long black hair, and unlike most the FITT women her eyes were of a green color. Before leaving for the settlements she worked in the Birthing Center as an assistant to one of the electrical engineers.

The Halcyon finally set sail under the darkness of the night. Then, when it got to deeper water and well away from the seaport commune each of the crew was given firearms. There was no turning back now. If a government ship came about they would have to make a run for it.

"Stoic," yelled Abstruse. "Did you feed and tie down the livestock?"

"Yes, sir," yelled Stoic.

"Good, now come forward. I want you up here at my side." A monster of a man at his side would be a good show of strength to the rest of the crew, was Abstruse's thought.

"What should I do now?" Stoic asked when he got to his captain's side. A surprise look was on his face, surprise that the captain knew who he was. His rifle was shouldered, although he had no idea how to use it.

"Just stand right here near me and look as mean as a mad cow," which Stoic did. First by snapping his feet together, then by putting his shoulders straight back, and then came the mean-looking frown on his face.

"Good, that's real good," Abstruse said, followed by a chuckle or two. His big belly bounced when he laughed and the space where there once was a tooth showed. Stoic wanted to laugh, but instead he kept the frown on his face.

The crew was nervous with the Halcyon anchored and its sails down. If a government's ship saw them now they would be caught dead in the water. The fact that the waves were hitting hard up against the ship's side, rocking it back and forth, didn't help matters either. It would make it difficult for the passengers to board, most of all the youngest of the children.

Quietness swept over the ship making the squeaking of the plankings and riggings that echoed through the night fog sound ear splitting, when suddenly:

"Over there!" Stoic yelled out, pointing to the sound of oars hitting the water, and soon after he saw the bows of the shore boats protrude through the fogs edge. "I see four, no, five shore boats."

The crew rushed to help board the passengers, as each of the shore boats reached the starboard side. The waves smashed the crafts hard against the ship making it difficult for the passengers to board as thought. As each of the shore boats emptied the oarsmen headed back to shore, fearful of being caught with a cargo of Pariahs.

When the last of the shore boats was unloaded the captain quickly brought the anchor up and set the Halcyon's sails for Harbinger, to the relief of the crew. It would be at least a month long sail.

"Many that came aboard are women and children, so it will be a most difficult journey," Abstruse told Stoic, a concerned and worried look upon his face, because he knew some would not survive the journey.

"Yes, a long journey indeed," answered Stoic. He had no idea, this was his first long sail having recently boarded. He was still learning his way about the ship. He felt more comfortable when below with the livestock. But, most of all, he was proud that the captain choose him to be at his side.

"Check the lower deck after the passengers get settled in and make sure there is enough space for all of them. Then tell them that they will not be able to get to any of their belongings that we've loaded until we reach Harbinger."

"Yes sir," Stoic answered. A smile appeared on his face. He knew how anxious his captain was to see his lovely Prudent who was waiting for him in his quartering area.

Chapter Twelve

Ardent was enjoying his daily walk with Bandy along the outer perimeter of the settlement. Since he felt stronger they started taking longer walks. The daytime sky, he noticed, was its usual gray, dark-pinkish color, but the sun felt warmer than normal. Warm enough that he removed his hat and gloves and put them into the pocket of his tunic. After brushing his hair back with his fingertips he stopped walking and sat down onto a large rock next to the pathway. Bandy stood next to him for a moment and looked down at him, a smile on her face.

"Are you tired?" Bandy asked when she sat down onto the ground right next to the large rock Ardent was sitting on, and then rested her back against the rock and her shoulder against Ardent's left leg. She was playing with a dead twig from a nearby tree, twisting it around and around in her hand, every now and then writing Ardent's name into the sand by her feet.

"It's such a beautiful day."

"Yes, and you're lucky to be alive enjoying this day."

"I can't stop thinking about Dank, Jejune and the others," a now sadder Ardent spoke. He missed Dank, his smile, his accent. Jejune too, the sadness changed to a smile thinking of Jejune, and some of the fun times they had. Then he told Bandy of that morning when Jejune fell with his hands still in his pockets as he hit the ground. A smile broke out on Bandy's face, and soon after Ardent started to laugh, remembering he and Jewel promise never to tell anyone.

"I think of that day often," Ardent quietly said, as he watched Bandy throw the twig into the sky, and then she rested her right arm on his lap and her hand on his knee.

Ardent was getting nervous. He could feel an odd feeling in his stomach.

"What's wrong?" Ardent heard Bandy say, a look of concern showed on her face when he pulled away from her.

"Nothing," he answered back. But there was something wrong, and why this feeling had come upon him, he had no answer. He just knew he enjoyed being close to her, but he did not understand why.

Bandy was always honest with him and to the point. Because of the talks he was learning of these strange citizens. He wanted to learn more. He was in no hurry to get back to the Capital Commune or Tome.

"A few days ago I saw Onus press his lips against Pristine's lips, and afterwards Onus said the words; I love you. What is this word love? I've heard it before." He was facing Bandy as he spoke. The odd feeling he had in his stomach went away.

"There are a lot of things you must learn, and soon you will. Onus, Pristine and I will soon take you to a meeting. There you will learn much."

Bandy was now standing next to Ardent. She put her hand on his shoulder, a smile decorated her face. "Love must come from your heart, from deep inside. Pristine and Onus have that love for each other, and they express it by being close to each other, always," and then she removed her hand from his shoulder and placed both of her hands in his hands, lifting both and placing them over his heart. "You someday will love a woman and the two of you will become a pairing."

"Me paired with a woman!" laughed Ardent, interrupting Bandy.

"Yes, a woman," Bandy said, after stepping back and removing her hands away from his heart. "God made us all equal and in his image."

"God, you mean this man that will drop out of a hole in the sky?"

"No Ardent, he will send his son Jesus."

Ardent started walking up the pathway. He had heard enough. Suddenly Bandy ran past him and gave him a push as she passed, almost knocking him down. Mad, he ran after her, eventually catching up to her in a field on a hillside overlooking Harbinger. She fell to the ground rolling over and over and laughed uncontrollably. Ardent knelt next to where she finally stopped rolling and then laid next to her. He was smiling as they stared upward into the gray-dark pinkish sky, which was now filled with puffs of darker blackened clouds. An all-blackened sky usually meant that a tempest was brewing.

"Can you feel that?" Ardent asked, suddenly sitting up.

"What?" Bandy asked, as she stood up. "You're scaring me."

"The ground, it's shaking," Ardent answered, as he laid softly back down and put his ear to the ground.

"Yes, I feel it now!" shouted Bandy, a real nervous look on her face. Then the ground began to shake harder, eventually hard enough to make her fall to the ground. Scared, the two laid still on their backs, each holding the other's hand tightly, still staring upward into the sky.

The earth's tremors soon stopped and the blackened clouds began to move quicker, and then very fast, a spinning-like motion. Every two of the closest clouds merged together, and then every two of the merged clouds merged, etc, etc; until there was only one cloud left, a merging of every cloud that once was there.

The one cloud left started moving across the sky like a river's quick current's flow, finally disappearing off in the distance leaving the sky its usual gray-dark pinkish color. But, as it had never been before the sky was left cloudless.

"Look," Ardent said, pointing to the far distant sun. A black circle started slowly moving across the sun, eventually covering it entirely. It was suddenly like night, as complete darkness fell across the land, a cold darkness.

"What's happening?" shaking and scared, Bandy asked as she moved closer to Ardent, lowering her head and resting it onto his shoulder.

The blackness soon began moving slowly away from the sun. Until finally the sun took its usual shape, but brighter and more yellow became its glow and its heat stronger upon the land.

"Look! The sky, it's a beautiful color blue," shouted Ardent.

"And look! The clouds, they are white," Bandy, pointing to the puffs of white, shouted out with excitement in the sound of her voice.

"The sky has turned a beautiful blue and the clouds white," Ardent, a nervous, excited tone in his voice, said as he quickly got up off the ground and stood on his feet.

"It's God's doing," Bandy cried out, as she got up onto her knees and started praying. The words from her mouth Ardent thought were strangely spoken. Many of the words he had never heard of, nor knew what they meant.

Amazed and puzzled at what he had just seen and of her speaking in prayer words, Ardent just stared at Bandy, as she continued on with her prayer to the one she and all the others called God. These people he now was amongst were very strange, his thoughts continued, as he again looked up into the new looking sky in wonderment.

"Hurry Ardent. We must go and be with the others," shouted Bandy, after she got up off her knees. Then grabbing his hand she led the way, running down the hillside to Harbinger. The both of them would occasionally look up into the new looking sky in complete amazement.

The main trailway through Harbinger was full of its citizens, many on their knees praying. Others just stood gazing upward at the new looking blue sky, crying out "Jesus is coming! Jesus is coming!"

"It's a sign from God," yelled an older man, as Ardent and Bandy walked down the trailway and past him. His arms were outstretched and his head tilted back looking up into the sky, the unusual looking sky, its brightness.

"The Lord Jesus Christ is coming!" yelled the same old man who had just fallen to both his knees. With his hands embraced he started to pray aloud. Bandy knelt next to the old man and she, too, started to pray. More strange words Ardent was hearing. His mind was confused, too much was happening too fast. He felt out of place just standing over the two. The thoughts were rushing through his head, and doubts. Ardent was uncertain, especially, as to whether the old man spoke of the truth, but he did see the sky change. Was it the work of the one they all called God? Was the one they called Jesus really coming? he wondered.

It was getting very warm, in fact, quite hot. Many of the townspeople had removed their outer clothing. Hats, gloves and tunics were scattered about everywhere along the trailway.

"Ardent, this is a wonderful day. A day for us all to rejoice," Bandy said after getting up off her knees. She saw the doubt in his face. "You, someday, will understand and believe as we do — That the Lord Jesus Christ is coming again, the Lost Christ. I too had doubts at first. The old ways, those taught us by the government were well planted in my head, as they are in yours."

"I saw, with my own eyes, what has happened. I do not understand," remarked Ardent, still lost for the right words to say he felt out of place, all alone. He missed Dank. He missed Jejune.

"Later, many will meet at the meeting area to rejoice. You must come with us. It is there that you will begin to learn."

⌒>< ⌒>< ⌒><

When Ardent got to Onus and Pristine's villa after leaving Bandy, it was hot inside and the air was very still, warmth he never felt before. Like all the others had done earlier, he removed his tunic to get comfortable.

After rolling up his sleeves he poured water from the pitcher that was on the bedding side table into the washbowl. Slowly, and with his hands cupped he brought the water to his face. When the water in the bowl became still again he glanced down at the image of his face. Who am I, and why was I spared the death of my fellow troopers? Why was I brought here amongst these people?

Upset, he grabbed the bowl and threw it against the wall. The water splashed everywhere, and the bowl made of wood bounced off the wall onto the floor, rolling back and stopping at his feet.

"What is wrong?" Ardent heard, and when he looked up Onus was standing by the doorway. A look of surprise was on his face, as he walked up to where Ardent was standing. He had taken a liking to Ardent and understood the doubts Ardent had. He, too, once had many doubts. Jesus showed him the way, his beliefs strengthened by those around him. Ardent needed someone to show him the way of the Lord, his thought.

"I don't understand why I am here, here amongst you that are rebelling against our government. The very government I swore to defend."

"Sit, there on the bedding, and I will try to explain. I will tell you things you will doubt but they must be said," Onus paused for a moment, putting his hand to his chin, then to his head, and then with his fingers he scratched at his hair.

After Ardent sat down on the bedding's edge, Onus reached for a chair and pulled it up close next to Ardent.

"Many, many years ago, before the holocaust changed the world, man and woman lived together mating in pairs of one man and one woman. Each paring was bonded together by a thing called *Love*."

"What is this word you call love?" Ardent interrupted, maybe he thought, Onus would explain it better than Bandy had.

"It comes from deep within your heart and comes in many forms. There's the love of God, the love for your fellow man, the love of your child, and the love that a man and a woman have for one another." Onus paused for a moment to put his hand on Ardent's shoulder. Then, while staring into his eyes: "A child is born out of the love a man and a woman have for one another. Not from out of a test tube as your government made you think."

"Not out of a test tube? A child, what word is that?" Again, Ardent interrupted. Onus saw the confused look that was on Ardent's face. He smiled trying to comfort him.

"When you were first birthed from out of a test tube and very young you were what we Pariahs call a child. Mankind was not meant to be birthed from a test tube. We were meant to be born of love, birthed from a woman's womb.

"A womb, what is that?"

Onus started laughing, and after removing his hand from Ardent's shoulder. "That, my friend, you will discover for yourself." Onus continued laughing until he realized Ardent was getting mad at him.

"The feeling you have right now, the feeling of wanting to hit me, that mad at me feeling. Well, love is just the opposite feeling. It's a feeling of wanting to comfort me, help me. It's a feeling of wanting to be with me. In the case of the love of a woman, it's a feeling that you want to be with that one person the rest of your life. The pairing of a man and woman that have much love for one another is called a *marriage*. Together, the pairing's love will birth a child. The three become a *family*." Finished talking for the moment, Onus got up from the chair, reached down and picked up the washbowl, and then he put it back on the bedside table.

"The Carbonaceous Holocaust changed the world," Onus continued, sitting back onto the chair. "You do know about the Carbonaceous Holocaust?"

"Yes."

"But the government didn't teach you much of how things were before the Carbonaceous Holocaust, two millennia ago and before."

"No, just that mankind abused the land."

"Yes they did abuse the land, and as a result there became too little land with too many mouths to feed. The government's solution was the controlled birthing and pairings of men with men and women with women ...." before Onus could finish Ardent interrupted.

"Yes I know all that."

"But what they never told you was that to control mankind's natural desires of reproducing themselves they put a powder in the food and drinking water."

"What?" Ardent blurted out, remembering that day when Adroit put the white powder in the drinking water. "They said it was a steroid mixture for strengthening our bodies."

"That's what they want you to believe," Onus laughed after he spoke, and quickly stopped laughing because he realized that he would only get Ardent upset.

"Then, that feeling I get when with Bandy ...."

"That feeling, my friend, was meant to be," Onus interrupted. "It was given to mankind by God, so that mankind, in His image, could reproduce. And, if you were to take more of that reproducing stopping powder — You would be committing a sin in the eyes of God."

"And this belief in the God you talk of, what place did that come from?"

"Recently three educators discovered what was called a time capsule, and inside that capsule were writings and pictures describing that period of time and before. The different parts from two of the writings has been copied many, many times and distributed throughout the land. A copy is kept at the meeting hall for all to read or review. Ardent, my friend, you will have to read it to understand much of what I've told you, and to understand the way of the Lord Jesus Christ."

Ardent stayed very quiet. Savoir, whom he had slain in a cave, was an educator and one of the leaders of the revolution. Could he have been one of the three that found this capsule Onus talked of? He wondered.

"Are you all right?" Onus asked, after the long silence.

"Yes I would like to read from this scroll you talk of," Ardent responded, and for the time being he felt it best he did not mention Savior.

"You know I am a Revolutionary Vanguard Trooper and swore my allegiance to the government. So why are you telling me all this?"

"We are a peaceful people. We just want to be free, free of the government, free to worship our Lord Jesus Christ, free to raise our families and free to love one another."

"Many citizens have armed themselves. Zealots have attacked government areas inside the Capital Commune killing COPS and troopers. Some were my friends."

"That's all being done by fractions that refuse to leave their communes for new settlements like Harbinger. Their beliefs are very much like ours. However, their methods are very different," Onus answered, pacing back and forth.

"It'll soon be mealtime. Ardent, will you be joining us at the table?" Pristine asked, standing at the open doorway waiting for an answer from Ardent.

"I would be honored to join you both," answered Ardent, as Onus sat himself down again in the chair, nodding his head toward Pristine who immediately left upon his clue.

"What do you think about what has happened today?" Onus asked.

"An older man told Bandy and I that it meant the coming of the one you call the Lord Jesus Christ."

"Ardent, according to the Holy Scrolls Writings the sky used to be blue, the clouds white, the sun shined bright and you could see many stars in the sky at night. The Carbonaceous Holocaust changed all that. So yes, it must mean the re-coming of the Lord Jesus Christ."

Ardent sat again on the edge of the bedding next to Onus and put a hand on each of Onus's shoulders resting his head against his chest. And, in the company of his new found friend, and with the feeling of emptiness overcoming him he began to weep. He wept for Dank, for Jejune, Morose and even for Seethe.

"So many good men died on the voyage here, a thousand legionnaires sent to kill you all," Ardent said, still weeping, struggling to get the words out of his mouth.

"Some of us are armed, poorly trained I may say but armed. We would have fought to the last one of us to protect the ones we love, and our right to worship the Lord Jesus Christ freely. The Lord Jesus Christ protected us, preventing your onslaught. The Lord Jesus Christ works in mysterious ways."

"It was the tempest that prevented our onslaught, which would have been mighty. This Jesus I hear so many speak of, who is this man?"

"In the Holy Scroll Writings; a male birthing is called a *son*, and a female birthing called a *daughter*. Jesus, whom once walked this earth preaching love and peace, was the son of God. He gave his life for mankind's sins."

"Sins, what is this word?" Ardent asked, the tears now gone, yet still the sadness showed on his face.

"Any act or thought that is against the way the Lord Jesus Christ wants us to act or think," answered Onus, who was interrupted by his wife Pristine.

"The meal is on the table," Pristine yelled out from the other area.

"We must go and eat now. Pristine worked hard preparing vegetables and cornmeal. We will continue this talk at another time. After you read some of the scriptures from the Holy Scroll Writings you will have many more questions. Do not be stiff-necked, read and study with an open mind."

"Yes," Ardent answered, after finally removing his hands from Onus's shoulders.

"These are good people, kind, forgiving and caring. I must read the scrolls they talk of," the passionate side of Ardent, in his thoughts, told him. Also in his thoughts was the devoted side of him, his devotion to the government and Tome.

"Yes I must read the scrolls," Ardent said to himself, as he walked to the table to join Onus and Pristine to meal.

Chapter Thirteen

A month passed since the miracle of the changes in the sky. Even the sea was calmer. Nor was there a tempest since the miracle. Plant life was changing and the crops were ahead of schedule. These changes brought much concern to Harbinger's forefathers. If the seas stayed calm it would not be long before the government sailed again with its legion of troopers, they thought, and without a tempest to destroy them they would get through at full strength.

Sordid, Stymie and Cavil were at the meeting hall. A gathering of Harbinger's citizens were before them, including Ardent who was sitting next to Bandy.

"We are gathered here today to discuss the changes that have taken place over this past month," Stymie brought the subject up.

"The government's legionnaires tried to get here once before, but were stopped by a mighty tempest. Now that the seas are much calmer they again will try," Sordid interrupted.

Quietness overcame the crowded meeting area and it was getting hot inside, even with the doors opened wide.

"We've met with the leaders of the other settlements and they each have the same concerns as we," Stymie said.

"We talked of forming an army of our own, but some of the settlement leaders didn't agree with our proposals. They said that the Lord Jesus Christ will come to our aid and destroy the government's legionnaires just as before," Cavil paused, as a cheer came from the crowd.

"God didn't strike back when the Romans nailed Jesus to the cross, so what makes anyone think that God would now?" a loud shout from within the gathering got everyone's attention.

"We must put our trust in the hands of the Lord Jesus Christ," another yell from an old man standing at the rear, as those there became restless, the whispers and chatter getting out of hand.

"All but a few of the settlements have decided to stand together with us should we decide to fight back defending our freedoms.

Those that didn't agree will follow when one of their settlements feels the government's wrath," Stymie, almost yelling continued, but was quickly interrupted.

"May I speak, I have good news," the shout coming from the rear of the meeting area quieted everyone. Not a whisper was heard as the young man quickly walked down the aisle to the front.

"My name is Michael, and I only arrived here today on a trading ship from Newfoundland."

The lad Michael was very young looking, at most 14 or 15 years old and surely not a FITT, not with the name of Michael.

"Before I departed Newfoundland, he continued, a new arrival, a freedom ship from the Capital Commune docked. I talked to one of the crewmen of that ship and he told me of a birth of a child, and at the same time of his birth the sky over his birthplace opened up and angels descended to earth down a beam of light from a star and sang praises at the child's side. Another crewman told me he witnessed it himself, a non-believer until then, he said he was."

"And where is that child now?" a woman nearby interrupted.

"A couple days later, the crewman said, after word spread throughout the commune of the miracle birth, the Revolutionary Vanguard searched for the child. Every newborn they found they slaughtered. Many of them right out of the arms of their mothers, and all this was done at the order of Supreme Councilor Querulous."

"Murderer," shouted a woman nearby with a look of sadness on her face. "Murderer," again she shouted and her shouts were followed by others from within those gathered. It was getting noisy, out of hand.

"We must have order! We must have order!" Sordid yelled, getting everyone's attention.

"What else did the crewman have to say?" Stymie asked.

"Only that the child was never found. Also, as word spread of the birth, many of the capital's citizens converted to the way of our Lord Jesus Christ. Many are calling the child the Savior, the Christ Child — The Lost Christ."

"Christ has died, Christ has risen, Christ is not forgotten, Christ has come again," a praise that was yelled out from within the gathering and quickly followed by its continued chant; "Christ has died, Christ has risen, Christ is not forgotten, Christ has come again."

Bandy wrapped her arms around Ardent, and in her joy started jumping up and down.

"Bandy, please be careful."

Ardent still had much doubt even after all he read and learned from the Holy Scroll Writings. The boy, Michael, he also doubted, although he knew that it was not unusual for the government to order the slaughter of the non-FITTs, and most likely the citizens found with them as well. It was common for Querulous to give kill-all orders. If he and Dank had been there, for sure, Tome would have sent them instead. He had before, to a nomad encampment.

"Oh Ardent, relax. Don't you understand that God has, again, sent His only begotten Son," and with her arms still around his neck she put her cheek against his and whispered into his ear. "I love you, Ardent, I love you."

Ardent took a step back. He didn't know what to say to her. His face was turning reddish, blushing, as he turned and started walking toward the exit. Bandy followed him, saddened and disappointed because he didn't respond.

"C'mon, let's go. There is too much confusion and rejoicing to continue. We will continue at another time, alone." Cavil told the other two councilors.

Chapter Fourteen

It's been five years since Salient's arrival at the school and still he was cleaning and preparing the copier's work area. Worse yet, now he was behind with his studying of the Holy Scroll Writings and the teach master was upset with him. The rest of the students knew of his troubles so they kept away from him. That was all except Pathos, also not in good standings with the teach master.

The news of the Christ Child's rebirth and witnessing the changing of the sky brought much excitement to the school's population. But even the good news of Christ's rebirth hadn't motivated Salient. He loved the Lord Jesus Christ, yet still the learning was too difficult for him.

"Where are you going?" Pathos asked, named so because of his emotions of sympathetic pity.

"I'm going for a walk on the pathway to the ocean."

"So you are going to your favorite tree where under it you most likely will fall to sleep?"

"Yes, as usual."

Salient continued his walk along the hillside. The pathway was well worn from the daily walks many of the students took. There wasn't anything for the students to do at the school for pleasure except take walks. Their days were very long and filled only with work duties and their studies. The nights were for praying, and there were many prayers.

The view was always beautiful, thought Salient, as he sat down under his favorite willow tree. He was looking down the hill and out onto the bay, which was spotted with small uninhabitable islands, each with large boulder size rocks at the bottom of the high cliffs that encompassed the islands. He was always amazed at how the white-capped waves rolled hard against the rocks and then crashing into the cliff's bottoms, the occasional small rainbow in amongst the misty spray of water left.

He leaned back against the trunk of the willow tree, daydreaming, wishing he was somewhere else. Then he went to sleep, sinking deep into his dreams.

‹›‹ ‹›‹ ‹›‹

"Wake up Salient, wake up," the sound was faint and got louder as he opened his eyes. Standing at his side was Pathos. "If we don't hurry we are going to be late for the evening meal," Pathos shouted, his hand reaching out for Salient's. "I knew you would fall asleep. I just knew it."

"What's the hurry? All they ever feed us is that awful vegetable stew and corn bread," Salient complaint, as he stood up with Pathos's helping hand. Then he rubbed his tired eyes with his other hand, trying his best to wake up.

Pathos was facing him with his back to the bay, their hands still clasped together. Then, when he removed his hand from his watery eyes, from over Pathos's shoulder he saw the sight. A fearful sight it was. His eyes widened.

"Look!" Salient shouted. His hand, its finger extended, pointed out onto the bay. "Over there." A look of shock fell upon his face. His chin dropped leaving his mouth wide open, as he stared out onto the bay.

"It's the government troopers," Pathos shouted. "We must hurry back and warn the others."

The two ran back toward the school ground area as fast as they could, each stumbling along the way. Salient's knee started to bleed from his fall.

"Revolutionary Vanguard Troopers!" yelled Salient when he approached the school ground area where everyone had gathered readying for the evening meal.

"In the bay there is a ship with government banners," Pathos yelled.

From the school ground area you could not see the bay, so the teach master asked if they were sure.

"Yes," Salient shouted. He was bent down from the waist with his hands on his knees breathing heavy.

"Hurry!" shouted the teach master. "We must hide the Holy Scroll Writings in the caves as practiced."

There were hundreds of rolled-up parchments to hide, each just a portion of the Holy Scroll Writings, and each in canisters made of leather. If found they would be destroyed, and years of hard work and time lost.

Everyone knew what to do. So, as soon as the teach master yelled out for them to hurry the students scattered. Salient headed straight for the copier area and gathered up as many of the parchments as he could, his arms stacked full to his chin. Also filling their arms with the parchments were the others.

When Salient got to the first of the caves, a mile's run from the school ground area Pathos was already on his way out of the small cave, the parchments he gathered safely inside. Salient gave him a nod, as they passed by one another.

Inside the small cave there were holes dug into the walls for the parchments. After Salient inserted all his parchments he rushed out of the cave and ran as fast as he could, passing by others going to the caves. Again, he fell to the ground and landed on the same knee with the cut, and it started to bleed again.

When he got back to the copier area the parchments kept there were all gone, so he headed for one of the student learning areas. Maybe there were still some parchments left there, he thought. And he was right. There were enough still there to fill his arms, again to his chin.

When he got back to the cave site both its caves were full, and so was the second site's caves. Finally at the third site and only after crawling deep into the narrow cave using his elbows to pull him along, he found holes for the parchments he had in his arms.

Outside waiting with his arms full to enter the cave was Pathos, so he waited for his friend. Then when Pathos wiggled out of the cave's opening he told Salient that there were no holes left for more parchments.

"We better stay and cover the opening," Salient said. "We can use the rocks piled up over there," his finger pointing to the rocks.

When they finished stacking the rocks against the cave's opening, with their hands they dug and threw dirt against the rocks until they were covered and hidden well from the troopers.

The run back was difficult for Salient, now limping and exhausted. When about halfway back he stopped running and rested against a tree, trying to catch his breath. Pathos, noticing Salient had stopped, stopped as well. Then, just as they were about to start running again, they heard gunfire coming from the direction of the school.

"None of us are armed, so why is there gunfire?" Pathos asked, but there was only silence from Salient. Looks of shock and anger were on both their faces.

It was nightfall by the time Pathos and Salient approached the school ground area, where hidden amongst the trees and bushes they knelt still, staring out onto the school ground area. What they saw were that all the structures were burning, the flames lighting up the school ground area. The loud cracking sounds from the glowing sparks could be heard, as they rose upward with the smoke and into the darkened sky. Scattered along the ground were the dead, much of the ground soaked with their blood. The two shivering, scared students continued watching, as the troopers tied up the remaining students, separating the teachers.

"Take these fools to the ship," one of the troopers commanded, pointing to the tied up students. "They are young. They will be good hard workers for the work camps," and then the trooper nodded his head at the troopers that guarded the teachers and walked away.

The troopers guarding the teachers waited until everyone else had left, and then they raised their rifles and fired upon the defenseless teachers, and quickly three of them fell to their knees, blood spraying out from their bodies before they clumsily dropped face first to the ground; and then two more fell, and another three, two more — Until there were no more teachers left standing, but just a tangle maze of bodies.

Two of the troopers, with smiles on their faces, drew their pistols and walked amongst the lying dead and wounded, and as they did they fired a shot at each. The innocent teachers' bodies bounced upward, an arm or leg shaking, upon the impact of the death proven shot.

The sight before them shocked Pathos. He started to stand up, as if he were going to rush out to help. He stopped when Salient grabbed him by the shoulder pulling him back to his knees.

"No," Salient whispered, the tears blurring his eyesight. "You'll only get killed."

"Look!" one of the troopers yelled. "This one is still alive."

On the ground at the trooper's feet was Genial, a kindly teacher with a pleasant disposition and loved by all the students. "Let's teach the teacher what real pain feels like," as loud laughter bellowed out from the mouth of the trooper, making Salient and Pathos shiver. Again, Pathos started to get up only to be pulled down by Salient again.

The trooper took his knife out from his accessory belt, and then he held it up for Genial to see its blade, as it reflected the nearby fire's glow. Then, with his fist firmly around its handle he moved it side to side through the air, as the other troopers gathered closer.

Pathos would never forget the sound that followed … The screams from Genial as the trooper, after ripping Genial's tunic and shirt off, carved deeply into his chest a large cross. The bleeding from the opened wound was bad, worst as Genial's chest expanded from each anxious breath. Then while Genial begged for mercy, *"Please kill me, please. Dear God, please!"* the trooper ran the blade across the begging Genial's throat. The blood quickly filling Genial's mouth, bubbling as he gargled his last breath; a mouth from which once came the teachings of the Lord Jesus Christ, silenced for good, forever. It was an abject suffering that no man should ever have to bear.

Pathos' eyes were the camera's lens, his brain the negative. Forever a photo of what he had just seen would be in his dreams. Why did God let this happen? Why to his children was there such suffering and so cruel death? he wondered.

"Please! Dear God guide me. Show me the way to forgive." Pathos cried in prayer to himself. There no longer were tears in his eyes. There was just the pain that he should live, spared such a fate.

After the slaughtering of the innocent and the unarmed, the remaining troopers left. Salient and Pathos waited a long while, not speaking. Once they thought it safe they walked out onto the burning school ground area amongst the dead. The heat from the fires was intense. Ashes, some still hot, were falling from the sky onto Salient and Pathos.

"What will we do now?" Pathos asked. He paused to brush the ashes from his shoulders. The smell, the charred bodies, life's bloodstains left on the soil.... All of which engulfed him. "They murdered them all," and then to his knees he fell upon the ground at Salient's feet and wrapped both his arms around Salient's legs. Then with his head buried deep against Salient's legs he cried, the tears falling from his eyes. Next to him lying on his back was the teach master, his body charred from the fire, his eyes opened and staring up at the stars.

"We should look for anyone that might be wounded. Then we should go to the hillside overlooking the bay to watch for the ship to leave. In the morning, if the ship has left, we will bury the dead and say prayers for their souls," Salient suggested, to which Pathos nodded in agreement. Then Salient knelt next to Pathos and together they prayed for those dead; the teachers all, in God's Kingdom.

Their search for wounded was of no avail. They were alone and worse yet, there would be no food. All the food that was harvested for the coming cold season was stored in one of the burning structures, as were the beddings and anything else they would need to survive. Their only chance to leave this dreadful place alive now was if a supply ship was to come, if so — It better come soon.

Chapter Fifteen

The Halcyon had been out to sea a week when the miracle of the changes in the sky happened. The passengers and the crew, confused because of what happened, started spreading rumors throughout the ship. The crew couldn't understand what they witnessed. The passengers, however, believed it to be the work of the Lord. But worse things had come upon them. The Halcyon's sails since the miracle hung flat from lack of a good wind, a week's sailing lost and a week's rations used up as the Halcyon sat still on the water.

The heat below where the passengers were quartered was warmer than Abstruse had ever experienced before, resulting in much more drinking water being used. This worried Abstruse, so much so, he gathered those of the crew he could trust, including Stoic, and told them that they would have to take turns guarding over the passengers. He was worried of what his crew might do, that if this lack of good headwinds continued the crew would turn on the passengers to survive. Because of his fears he commanded the passengers to stay below, allowing them to come above deck once a day and only for an hour.

Stoic stayed right at the captain's side, even sleeping top deck next to his quarters. On this particular morning Abstruse asked Stoic to come inside his quartering area. It was the first time Stoic had been asked in, so it worried him.

Abstruse's quartering area was in a mess. The charts were scattered everywhere making it difficult to move about. On his desk was a sidearm and next to it a partially un-rolled parchment from the Holy Scroll Writings. Other rolled up parchments filled the shelf behind his desk. In the corner neatly stacked on top of a chest were Prudent's things.

"Stoic, I am worried. Soon, I will have to ration the food and water. It will bring much trouble. Tell me, what do you hear from the crew?"

"The crew is restless. I, too, fear much trouble. There are many rumors. One, many say, is that the miracle was a sign that the Lord

Jesus Christ is coming." Stoic stopped for a moment to wait for a reply from his captain, but there was none. "Another rumor is; that if there were to be no more tempests to stop the government ships, then the settlements would soon be attacked. Some below are even talking of returning to the Capital Commune, that it might be safer there now."

"All the more reason to get the black gunpowder we bring to the settlements. They will need it." Abstruse replied.

"Yes, that is true," and Stoic moved closer to the desk.

"Stoic, do you believe that the Lord Jesus Christ is returning after all the many millennia that have passed since Jesus last came?"

"I only know that the sky has changed and that the sun is much clearer and warmer. It must be a sign of something to come."

"It may be a sign of our death, if we don't feel the wind soon," the captain said, and from the look he had on his face he was concerned for the safety of everyone onboard.

"Tell the crew that their daily rum ration will be rationed every other day for the time being."

"That will stir up much talk," Stoic answered.

"Yes, but it has to be. If we run out of rum there will be much more talk, and then trouble for sure."

"It will be as you command," answered Stoic. He, too, would miss the rum rationing.

"If there be no headwinds tomorrow we will have to lower the shore boats. The crew and strongest of the passengers will have to tow the Halcyon. However, do not tell them until tomorrow. Today they may have their rum ration."

"Is that all, sir?"

"Yes, you may go."

When Stoic got out onto the deck he first looked up into the sky. To his surprise there were many white clouds, some a light gray color. One large darkened cloud partially covered the sun. A cool dampness had suddenly engulfed the Halcyon, sending the crew to adorn their tunics and hats for the first time since the miracle. *Maybe it was a good sign*, he thought.

Stoic, now with a sense of some relief yelled over to Osmo to come forward. Osmo was once the captain's mate until Stoic arrived. He was demoted because of his bestial treatment of the crew, but a trustworthy sort and not a nemesis, thought Stoic, and like him, Osmo knew the hardships of the work camps and he knew the touch of Pique's whip "Felicity." The long scar down his cheek and onto his neck was evidence of their meeting.

"Get up into the lookout nest, for if there should come a tempest we shall need the early warning," Stoic commanded, but in a tone of voice that one would speak to his equal. Without a word, Osmo heeded the command and started climbing up the center mast to the lookout nest, a dreaded place to be if a tempest should suddenly strike.

When Osmo was about half the way, suddenly, and followed by loud banging sounds; the sails became full of strong wind. The Halcyon was finally, again — *Running before the wind.*

⊂⊱⊃ ⊂⊱⊃ ⊂⊱⊃

While delighted that the Halcyon was on its way, Stoic was unsure that it would gain back the time already lost. They weren't out of trouble yet, and he had no idea what lie ahead. That was the captain's problem, he thought. Right now he would have to start his usual morning check of the passengers, and on this morning there were many questions asked of him.

A young neophyte approached him as soon as he got below. At his side was an older woman.

"My wife just gave birth, a son," he said, but a look of concern lingered on his face. "Will we be to Harbinger soon?"

"You knew it was a month long sail, so why should you ask?"

"Because many are getting sick with the fever and want to return to Manchester," said the youngster, and after pausing for a moment: "I shall name my son Halcyon, after the ship we sail."

It stayed quiet for a short moment, quiet enough that you could hear the squeaking of the keel's plankings.

"Last night I cared for a frail older man," the older woman started to speak, breaking the silence. The lack of sleep was evident and a ring of black showed around her eyes. Then suddenly, from the rocking motion of the Halcyon, she stumbled forward into the arms of Stoic. Without hesitation and while still being held up by Stoic, she continued: "He is very sick and soon will be with the Lord Jesus Christ. What then are we to do with our dead?" Anger was in her upward glance. Her eyes were staring straight into Stoic's eyes.

THE LOST CHRIST

"The dead, if any, will be buried at sea. A sailor's farewell," answered Stoic, after letting go of the frail old woman. But he knew that the "if any" might be many.

Suddenly, interrupting his rounds and while others started shouting out their demands, Stoic heard Osmo ringing the alarm bell from the lookout nest.

Stoic rushed back onto the deck at the first sound of the alarm. Atop deck he took a quick look forward out over the bow and up into the sky over the distant sea. About a mile or two away, what looked to be a tempest was approaching the Halcyon?

On deck some from the crew were rushing about reefing the slackened sails, a procedure that is done to help prevent the heavy booms from breaking in the wind. Others from the crew were securing the folded canvas with the small ropes.

Stoic was standing at the ship's center deck next to the captain's quarters and watching as the crew finished getting the Halcyon ready for a tempest.

A half hour passed and the winds were mildly blowing and the waves but a few feet. It was unusual for a tempest to move in so slow. Usually it would hit quick and without much warning, but at least the Halcyon was ready, Stoic thought.

The Halcyon was drifting atop an ocean's current with its bow facing the wall of black clouds ahead. Flashes of light sparkled, here and there, within the oncoming dark destructive-looking force. Bobbing up and down the white-capped swells in an upwind direction with its sails reefed, the Halcyon would be helpless against the winds' mighty fury and in the Lord Jesus Christ's hands, thought Stoic.

Some from the crew went below and readied themselves to repair any of the plankings that may separate and leak. Stoic sent the others from the crew, including Prudent, into the hole to ready and aid the passengers, whom were already on their knees in prayer when the crew and Prudent arrived. Many of the passengers, their faces white as ghosts, had buckets at their sides. Most of the buckets had already been used.

Stoic wrapped a ship's rope around his wrist and held on. The Halcyon was already engulfed by the tempest, as the sideway wind threw the rain's downpour hard against his face. Nearby, the captain's quartering area door flung open wide, smashing against the wall. Standing there in its opening was Abstruse, a lantern's candle light blowing quickly out behind him. His tunic opened like a sail, driving him inward as he leaned forward to shout:

"Stoic … You fool! Come on inside! You'll only get crushed by a falling mast," and right after he yelled out the Halcyon's bow crashed into a wave slamming shut the door.

The Halcyon's sudden rise upward knocked Stoic to the decking. The rush of white water flowing over the bow encompassed him. The impact threw him uncontrollably against the captain's quartering area, his head smashing hard up against its wall knocking him unconscious, and then to the decking he was drawn back, and there against the main mast he lay still, as the wave's wake receded. The rope was still around his wrist when yet another breaking wave's wake from over the bow engulfed him, sending him again on a ride to the wall — Just as the Halcyon bottomed out.

⌒⌒⌒ ⌒⌒⌒ ⌒⌒⌒

Stoic woke up with an awful taste of salt in his mouth. Then he coughed, gagged and finally the sea water bubbled out from his lungs. Standing over him was Abstruse, and Prudent with a blood soaked cloth in her hand. His head ached with pain when he lifted it to get up from the floor.

"Ouch!" He quickly put his hand to his forehead. He was getting dizzy.

"Lay still you fool. The storm is over. A tempest it wasn't, and if it was none of us would be alive," Abstruse insisted, his voice commandingly loud. He was glad to see that Stoic was alive. He smiled.

"If not a tempest than what was it?" A look of confusion was on Stoic's face. Then he held his hand. It was very sore and a large blackened spot was where he must have bruised it.

"It was just a torrential rain and wind storm, and it was the calmest I've ever encountered. When the storm broke there were good strong winds again. We are at full sails and running before the wind." Abstruse bellowed out his joy.

"The passengers and crew, is everyone ok?"

"For now yes, and all are glad to feel the wind upon their faces," answered Abstruse, a comforting smile still lingered on his face. "If these winds continue we will make up much lost time."

Prudent bent down next to Stoic, her long hair brushed across his chin. She wiped the blood from his forehead, just above a swollen right eye.

"You must get some rest," a soft whisper, the sounds from the wind and waves almost drowned out her voice. She rested his head on her lap.

"Many of the passengers have fever and the water supply is low. With this unusual heat we are having, more drinking water is needed," and then Abstruse paused for a moment, kneeling next to his Prudent. "Some of the passengers and crew will not see land again if we don't find water soon," he continued, the smile was suddenly gone.

"We must make the sick as comfortable as is possible," Stoic suggested.

"Right now you must get some rest, just as Prudent said. Others are seeing to the passengers," Abstruse commanded.

"No! I must see to them now," Stoic insisted, but when he lifted his head from Prudent's lap the pain streaked through his head. As stubborn a man as he was he stood the rest of the way up, when suddenly the dizziness overcame him. Abstruse stood up quickly, reached out and grabbed a hold of him, steadying the big man.

"Lay on my bedding. Prudent is staying below tonight to help with the sick. You needn't worry. Tomorrow you can tend to the passengers, and that's an order," Abstruse commanded, and the firmness in the captain's voice convinced Stoic to walk over to the bedding and lay his head down. They were right, he thought, he didn't feel strong enough yet.

Prudent, again, wiped clean the blood from the side of his head and eye. A small cut showed just over his eye amid the egg-sized welt. Abstruse already had a bandage prepared for her to wrap around his head and handed it to her. And when she finished wrapping the wound a portion of the bandage covered part of his right eye.

"Now you look like a sailor," Abstruse gravely laughed, making Stoic laugh as well. But Stoic was really laughing because of the way

Abstruse's stomach bounced when he laughed so gravely. He fell right off to sleep, Abstruse's stomach still bouncing.

"I have a feeling about this monster size of a man. He shows great interest in the Writings. I believe God sent him to us for a reason."

"Then you must teach him the way of our Lord."

"Yes, Prudent my dear one, yes I must."

Chapter Sixteen

The dark of night had fallen over the settlement of Harbinger, and on this night the moonless sky was filled with bright stars, countless sparkling spots of light against a black sky, almost as if you could reach out and grab any one. A site that had never been seen before the miracle of the changes in the sky, it was a beautiful sight to behold.

Downward from one of those stars, the brightest, shined an illuminating beam of light that reached to the ground. From each side of the star and upward from the top of the star were shorter beams of the light, each outward beam wider at the tips. The four beams formed a large cross that shined over the land.

Overlooking the peaceful settlement from in the sky, on each side of the downward illuminating beam of light, were the gathering of Seraphim Angels singing praises:

"Holy, holy, holy is the Lord of hosts. All the earth is filled with His Glory."

Over and over the singing continued. The praises sung were heard all over the hillsides and into the valley, where Harbinger's citizens were running out from their villas, drawn by the praises being delivered by God's messengers. Their wings, all white and glowing, were spread open wide against the darken sky.

Ardent, Onus and Pristine were just finishing the evening meal when they heard the praises and quickly ran outside, the praises ringing in their ears. The trailway through the center of the settlement, they saw, was beginning to fill with inquiring citizens.

"There, on the hillside," shouted Pristine, pointing to the illuminating cross in the sky and the glow of the angels.

Harbinger's citizens were running past the three, while others stood still staring upward in awe, some with tears in their eyes.

"It's Jesus, he's come back," a shout from amongst those running.

Ardent became confused. First, about having witnessed what the Pariahs called the miracle of the changes in the sky, then what he had learned from his readings of the Holy Scroll Writings, and also of the long talks with Onus and Bandy, of their beliefs — And now this. Could there really be a God? he wondered.

He hastened his steps when he saw Bandy across the way standing alone in the dark with a lit candle in her hand. He would go to her, he thought.

"Over here, Ardent, over here," Bandy yelled out as she stepped toward him, and then ran right up to him throwing her arms around him, the candle falling to the ground, the flame gone. His arms quickly encircled her small waist, and then he lifted her up off the ground spinning her around.

"We must hurry," Bandy said, after Ardent let her down.

"Yes," his heart racing with excitement when he answered, an excitement transferred from her to him.

⊂⊃⋊ ⊂⊃⋊ ⊂⊃⋊

When Ardent and Bandy reached the hillside they approached the crowd having stopped half of the way up. Those that gathered were just standing there with their eyes staring upward at the Angels singing their praises.

Bandy had Ardent's hand tightly in hers and she was dragging him along, as she moved through the crowd zigzagging her way to the front. The glow from the illuminating beam of light was reflecting off her eyes, and just below upon her cheeks, tears had gathered.

Ardent couldn't stop staring at her. She looked different when excited and happy. This new life she had as a Pariah was making her appear different, he thought, and he was happy for her.

⊂⊃⋊ ⊂⊃⋊ ⊂⊃⋊

Hours had gone by and not one citizen from on the crowded hillside left for the comfort of their villas. Everyone stayed, listening to the Angels continuing the praises over and over: *"Holy, holy, holy is the Lord of hosts. All the earth is filled with His Glory."*

Onus and Pristine joined Ardent and Bandy after having searched a long time for them. The four overcome with tiredness and anxiety, sat down on the hard ground.

Pristine rested her head on Onus's shoulder with her arm around his neck. They too were different, thought Ardent, as he watched her press her lips softly upon his cheeks.

Awakening him from his thoughts was the sound of everyone rising to their feet. When he looked over at the beam of light, as did everyone else — he saw emerging from the sides of the beam of light; one atop the other from the Angels to the ground were many Cherubim — the servants of God. Some of them had the faces of children and some the faces of animals and all had two pairs of wings.

After the appearance of the Cherubim, and slowly moving downward within the beam of light, an Archangel descended. His wings were extended open and as white as fresh snow. A golden halo glowed bright over his head, and in his right hand was a long sword that sparkled from the beams' bright, illuminating glow, and in its left hand, a shield.

The Archangel emerged from the beam of light, its arms extended. And there before the many gathered it stood, quiet and supreme looking.

The sighting of the Archangel was overwhelming, leaving many with tears in their eyes, as they fell to their knees, praying to the Heavenly Father.

After the Archangel stepped forward closer to the gathering of the faithful, and after the Seraphim Angels stopped singing their praises, the voice of the Archangel was heard throughout the valley:

"The second coming of Christ is upon you. For a Child was born, born the Son of God. Thus, the Anti-Christ's control over this land and of human affairs will soon end."

The gathering stood still and in awe when suddenly the Archangel pointed his sword up into the sky, the stars sparkling bright above him, blinking, as if at his command.

A streak of lightning from the heavens descended down upon the sword's tip, sending the gathering a step backward in fear. Then with one mighty arched motion downward, the Archangel plunged the sword's point and the lightning bolt's golden glow at its tip into the earth at his feet. Then the earth trembled as he withdrew the sword, raising it high above his head, his arm fully extended, back to the heavens.

A large, expanding hole appeared where the sword was, and from it a golden firefly-like fluttering light glowed upward. From out of the light's glow flew the birds of every kind — pheasants, sparrows, robins, turkeys, seagulls and others — a continuous flow of the birdlife not seen since the Carbonaceous Holocaust came forth onto the land.

The Archangel lowered his arms again, and with his elbows at his waist he slightly raised his hands in the direction of the crowd. From behind him and out from the beam of light from the star came the animals. All sorts and sizes and all, too, never before seen by the gathering. All the animals, just like the birdlife, having perished during the Carbonaceous Holocaust; the deer, the rabbits, the dogs, the cats, the bears — all God's animal creatures.

Above the Archangel were the birds in flight both large and small, and at his feet the animals. All were sent from God's Kingdom. God was replenishing the earth with its once-lost wildlife, a gift to mankind in celebration of the rebirth of his Son, Jesus Christ.

Suddenly the Seraphim Angels began the singing of their praises as the Archangel, his message brought, ascended to heaven to return to God. The Cherubim, beam of light, and lastly the Seraphim Angels departed. In their place, again, was the darkness of the night and those gathered left standing quiet.

Slowly, and far behind the many others that had gathered there at the hillside to witness a miracle, Ardent, Bandy, Onus and Pristine walked back toward the settlement.

"In the Holy Scroll Writings it is written that Jesus, many thousands of years ago walked the land preaching of love. Do you suppose he will again?" Pristine asked, but the others didn't reply for they too wondered if it would be.

"Ardent, will you stay with me tonight? I'm afraid to be alone after what we've seen. And all those strange animals, what do you suppose it means?" Bandy asked, staring into Ardent's eyes she squeezed his hand tightly.

"Yes, Ardent, you should stay with her," Onus said, and Ardent noticed a look of concern on his face.

Ardent never answered Bandy, but when they got to her villa on the edge of the settlement he followed her in.

Ardent found it to be very comfortable inside Bandy's small, one-quartering area villa. Except for the small wood burning stove used to heat the villa there were no furnishings. Bandy's bedding was spread out over straw atop the dirt floor. A cut tree stump was used as a table for the wash bowl and water pitcher. Two candles atop another tree stump placed in the center were all that lit the area. A mirror was leaning up against the wall next to the stump with the water pitcher and wash bowl. Bandy used the settlement waste area and ate all her meals in the settlement mealing area, sharing the meal preparing and cleaning duties.

Bandy put Ardent's hand in hers, and then she took him over to her bedding. She knelt there next to the bedding and with a tug she pulled him down with her.

When morning came Bandy was wrapped under the bedding still asleep with her warm body cuddled up close to Ardent, who had just awakened. He stared into her face, as he thought of what had happened and of how wonderful and relaxed he felt being with her. He didn't want the feeling to ever go away.

It felt warm when he got up from the bedding, having first removed Bandy's arm from around his shoulder. Then after putting his tunic on he walked over to the door and opened it to let the cooler fresh air in.

"Ardent," he heard Bandy say.

"Yes."

"Please come back to my arms." And Ardent did. Then, wrapped in each other's arms, they talked, deciding it best that he move in and quarter with her.

Chapter Seventeen

Every day that he could Ardent spent several hours at the meeting area reading the Holy Scroll Writings, and often at night Onus and Pristine would go to Bandy's and his villa and the four, crowded together, would discuss that which was written in the Holy Scroll Writings.

One night Ardent asked: "The Holy Scroll Writings warn of false Christs, and of deceivers who would appear claiming falsely to be the returned Christ — So, why would I believe that what we saw on the hillside was a sign of the real Christ's coming?"

"There will be many doubters and disbelievers," Onus started telling Ardent. "Some of God's children will deny the Lord Jesus Christ's rebirth. Even some among those that witness the Archangels message with us will deny what they saw and heard. Ardent, the Holy Scroll Writings teach us that the Kingdom of God is in your heart and soul, and that what you learn of Jesus will be with you forever …."

"When the children of the land once called Canaan, lead by Moses, came out of slavery did they not make golden idols of false Gods? And after Jesus died on a cross for mankind's sins did not his disciples deny knowing him?" Pristine spoke of the examples, interrupting Onus.

"If the government forces were to come we will find new lands. Like those that followed Moses we will wander, even if it takes a thousand years," Onus spoke, a serious look on his face.

"What we? There will be no we, if the government legionnaires were to come and you turn your other cheek, as the Holy Scroll Writings teach you to do." Ardent started to laugh, which only made Onus upset.

"Next week will start the Pesach and the Pascha festivals. It's a time of celebration for when the Israelites were liberated from Pharaoh's slavery and allowed to become followers of God instead, and a time when Jesus rose from the dead on the third day after his crucifixion. As mentioned in the Holy Scroll Writings — the account of the exodus from Egypt and of the last supper. — It's a day of abstention from work, special readings of the Holy Scroll Writings and a holiday feast of lamb," Onus told Ardent. "You must go. You will learn more of Jesus our Lord then."

"Lamb, you mean you eat the meat of the lamb also, as you do the chicken?"

"Yes Ardent, it's when we thin out the lamb population by sacrificing the old and weak, so that there is enough grass for the others to graze upon," Onus answered, and he was getting frustrated with the remarks Ardent was making. Bandy sensed it.

"I have cornbread and milk, so for now let's rest our minds and have meal," Bandy said, thinking it was time to interrupt before things got out of hand. "Tomorrow is an important day for us. We should thank the Lord with a prayer before mealing."

And when tomorrow came, and after a long walk through the woods and up a steep hillside with many caves, Ardent and Bandy, with Onus and Pristine at their sides, removed their sandals before entering the domicile of the cave-dweller named Josef, said to be a Seer.

"It's cold and so damp," Pristine remarked, once they were inside the cave. She spoke softly, a whisper. It was dark. Ahead could be seen the dim light of candles.

"Why would anyone live as a recluse in such a place? Live a life of only prayer and meditation?" Ardent spoke, but there was no answer, as they continued walking deeper into the cave.

Inside the cave was cold and damp, just as Pristine said. The sand beneath their bare feet was wet, sponge-like. On a large rock at the cave's far end were the many lit candles they saw. Next to the rock was yet another cave's opening and from within it came Josef.

A plain, white mantel covered his body, with only a belt made of rope tied around his waist and the ends of the rope hung down along his side. Josef, too, was barefooted. In his hand was a small vase filled with ointment. The cave smelled of mildew, its fungi matter hung from the walls of the cave.

Josef stopped in front of the large rock and placed the vase of ointment down on it next to one of the lit candles. After turning to face the four visitors he raised both his arms, leaving his elbows at his side he opened both of the hands stretching his fingers outward with the palms facing upward.

Ardent and Bandy both stepped forward close to the Seer. Right behind them followed Onus and Pristine. Bandy looked happy. Her hair was let down straight, lying onto her back to just below her shoulders. A red flower stuck out through the side, its stem in behind her ear. In her hand was a bouquet of mixed wild flowers, a rainbow of blue, yellow, red and white.

The Seer, Josef, stared into Ardent's eyes for a long time before continuing. Finally, and with a tear forming in one eye for what he had seen, Josef turned reaching for the vase of ointment.

"Before the eyes of the Lord Jesus Christ I will join you both, and then may He guide you through lives many burdens," said Josef, as he removed ointment from the vase and sprinkled it onto the heads of both being joined together. "God sent Jesus to die to take the punishment for the sins of all mankind. I see before me a child coming to you both. A blessed child, an Archangel that God send to free mankind," the Seer Josef, again stopped. There were more tears forming in his eyes as he reached for Bandy's left hand and placed it out in front of her. "This is LOVE, the first step to Heaven's Gate," still with tears in his eyes he reached for Ardent's right hand and placed it over Bandy's outreached hand. "This is PEACE, the second step to Heaven's Gate," then, slowly he reached for Bandy's right hand placing it over Ardent's right hand. "This is FORGIVENESS, the third step to Heaven's Gate," and after placing Ardent's left hand over Bandy's right hand. "This is SACRIFICE, the forth step to Heaven's Gate."

Then from the vase he poured the remaining ointment out onto both Bandy and Ardent's stacked atop one another's hands. Ardent watched as the ointment flowed off the top of his left hand, stepping downward finger to finger and then off their hands onto the ground.

"This, the blood of Jesus was given for mankind's sins," and then the Seer Josef stepped back. His legs appeared weak, as he reached out to the rock to hold himself up.

"You are joined in marriage," he continued. "So now go. For what I have seen in your eyes — I must pray," the Seer said, while looking right at Ardent.

THE LOST CHRIST

When the four returned to the villa they sat at the table in the new food preparing area that Ardent and Onus only recently finished building. In the fired-up oven were two chickens, a gift from the settlement's citizens in honor of their vows.

Bandy got up and put the pot of vegetables she had prepared earlier on the top of the stove, and then she added some more water. Ardent watched her move about in her new area, as crowded as it was with the four squeezed in. He was glad he had built it, he was glad for her. She looked beautiful today; the long hair she'd grown out, the flowers, the smile she had when they took the vows. She didn't have the looks of any one of the men anymore. She was a woman. She was his woman, and he loved her very much. Love, a new word he learned, one he, now, knew the true meaning of.

The week passed quickly. It was the day of the Pesach and Pascha festival, and while Ardent and Bandy were rushing to get to the meeting area where the festival was being held it started to snow, a dusting, a late spring snow.

"It's snowing," Bandy said, stopping to look up into the sky where she saw the snow falling ever so lightly, a flake or two resting upon her eyes. She blinked, having felt the cold of the snow melting in her eyes. She turned her head to Ardent, then with her hands outstretched she spun around, and around again. "I am so happy. We're married and joined together as one, bonded by our belief in the Lord. Would you have believed this to be true a year ago?" and she took his hand, putting it to her heart she told him how much she loved him. He smiled. "I love you, I love you!" she began to shout aloud, and releasing his hand she spun around again.

"Be careful," he pleaded.

"What's all the noise about?" And when the two turned they saw Onus and Pristine approaching them.

"It's Bandy. She's gone crazy."

"C'mon, we will walk together," Pristine said, grabbing Bandy by the hand. "Let the men talk."

The meeting ground area was filled with citizens. In its center Ardent saw several large fires, and over each was a slaughtered lamb, its body with a picket of wood through it. Standing at one of the picket's end was Obtuse turning the lamb around and around. From the lamb's fat, drippings were falling into the flames igniting a burst of fire that rose up to the skinned body of the lamb. The aroma made Ardent hungry for the taste of a meat he never ate before.

"Look, over there," Bandy said, nodding her head toward where some of the citizens were getting ready to dance. No sooner did she speak, the musicians started to play their instruments and the citizens began dancing.

"Dance with me," Pristine asked Onus.

Ardent watched as the two danced along with the other citizens. They were all holding hands and moving in a line column-like, he thought.

"Dance with me, Ardent. Dance with me," Bandy followed Pristine's clue.

"I don't know how," was his reply, his face getting red.

"Nor do I," and Bandy laughed aloud. "Let's just follow whatever they're doing." And she grabbed his hand. "C'mon Ardent, c'mon," and she pulled hard his arm.

Ardent ate all the lamb that Bandy put on his plate, and seconds. The dancing made him hungry. The dancing, it was fun, he thought. But he didn't want to do it again. He was too tired, and his stomach too full. He was ready to go back to the villa. Life here is so peaceful, he thought. He didn't ever want to go back; to go back to the Capital Commune; to go back to the way things were; to go back to all the killings.

Chapter Eighteen

Since the storm ended the days went by quickly for Stoic, days that turned into weeks. Each of the days brought good strong winds and the Halcyon made up much ground. His eye had healed well, the bandage long removed. Eleven of the passengers had died of the fever, many of them women and children. The newborn child that Stoic watched coming from his mother's womb, named Halcyon, was among the first to die.

On deck, and again at the crack of dawn, Stoic stood starboard watching out onto the sea. The ocean moved quickly under the Halcyon's swift advance, its water's wake spreading outward from the hull. The loud slapping sound of the sails and the creaking of the plankings pierced the quietness.

Stoic stood tall, watching the sunrise's red and golden glow light up the horizon. Never before had the ocean and sky looked as beautiful as it did on this day. The blue sky and the sun rising on the horizon had a look of calmness. God-like were the streaks of gold that shined downward from the clouds. A look he still wasn't used to. If the captain was right, and he usually was, they should soon sight land, he thought.

⊂╳ ⊂╳ ⊂╳

It was midday, and while the passengers and Prudent were on deck getting their one hour of fresh air allotted them daily, a shout came from the lookout nest: "In the sky, starboard side approaching us."

When Stoic looked starboard he saw many animals, all with wings, moving about. Another sight he had never seen before. The flying animals were a white color, some with black markings. Swiftly they flowed through the air; occasionally one would dive downward skimming atop the water, and then would rise back up with a small fish in its mouth.

"Strange isn't it?" The sound of Abstruse's voice was coming from right behind Stoic. "It has to be the work of the Lord Jesus Christ."

"I didn't hear you approach, sir."

"It's a sight I've never seen, but passed on from sailor to sailor over the millennia were tales of giant fish and of animals with wings. All such God's creatures had perished during the Carbonaceous Holocaust. Those you see, I believe, were called seagulls. They are a good sign, because where there are seagulls in the sky there must be land nearby, so thought sailors of past."

"Seagulls ...."

"Yes, before the Carbonaceous Holocaust wiped all of them out there were many such animals with wings. They flew with the wind, high up in the sky. They were called birds."

"Birds," a still confused Stoic said.

"Yes, Stoic, animals that fly are called birds."

Stoic knew Abstruse was well educated and that he also read the Holy Scroll Writings many times over. Some nights the two and Prudent read together, and Abstruse would explain in detail that which he didn't understand.

"In the Holy Scroll Writings is also mention of the birds," Abstruse told Stoic: "Tonight we will read of the doves — The birds of peace and love."

"Doves," a much confused Stoic said. The many different names made it difficult for him to understand.

"Yes Stoic, doves," and Abstruse smiled. "It is time to get the passengers below deck."

On this day Stoic had a difficult time getting all the passengers below. Many were still with fever, thirsty and hungry. The crew, too, were becoming difficult. The rumors that were being spread throughout the ship were causing most the difficulties. Having run out of rum rations several days earlier only made things worse.

Soon after Stoic got everyone settled down, some of their questions answered and the sick separated from the healthy, Abstruse came below, a rare visit.

"Stoic, I need for you to stay below this day and until we reach land," Abstruse whispered. "Here take this sidearm."

"I've never used one before," Stoic whispered.

"Well then use it to hit anyone who should try to harm the passengers."

"Ok," Stoic answered, as Abstruse handed him the weapon wrapped in a cloth, which Stoic put in the pocket of his tunic.

After the captain left a young male passenger that Stoic knew only by the name Sully approached him. A sad look was on his face and tears flowed under his reddened eyes down onto his cheeks.

"My wife is very sick and needs more water," pleaded the younger man.

"Bring me to her."

The young woman, who he soon found out was named Jewel, was very sick just as her husband said. Her face was white and a hot feverish shiver overcame her just as Stoic spoke:

"We will soon be approaching land, so you must hang on longer."

"She needs more water because she is sick. Look, this cloth I use to wipe her down is dry and the heat down here is unbearable."

"Many need the water, so she'll have to wait for her daily ration, I'm sorry."

Stoic knew that if she didn't get plenty of water to drink soon she would die. Although he didn't show it, he cared. With each that died, he felt like a little of him also died.

"Ardent, Jejune, wait for me," she suddenly yelled out in a fever pitch, with her eyes wide open. "Over here, Bandy, over here," she continued before finally closing her eyes.

"She was a Revolutionary Vanguard Trooper before finding the Lord Jesus Christ," Sully told Stoic. "We thought things would be nicer if we could get away to one of the settlements. She hated being a trooper."

Stoic looked down at the young woman. It was hard for him to believe that anyone that small could have been a trooper.

"Land ahead," yelled Osmo down into the hole to Stoic. "Land ahead," the shout was heard by all. Excitement overcame the passengers, as they rushed past Stoic almost trampling over the poor dying woman.

The Halcyon soon anchored well off shore in a coved harbor, Stoic and Osmo, with a small detachment, went ashore to find water.

Abstruse told them that they must have sailed off course, and that the land he was about to explore was not the settlement of Harbinger. But right now finding fresh water was the only thing on Stoic's mind, for without water many more that he cared for would die.

Once on shore Stoic left two from the crew to stand guard over the shore boat. He and the remaining eight, with empty water bags in each hand, went into the wooded area leading to a high hill. From atop the hill he hoped to see a river or lake.

In the woods were many strange sounds, and birds of all sizes. Small furry animals with long bushy tails were climbing the trunks of some of the trees, rushing to hide from the oncoming detail.

Just before reaching the top of the hill, and in an open field were many apple trees with the fruit ready for picking.

"On the way back we will fill our tunics with as many as we can carry," Stoic said to the others, each of whom picked a couple for themselves as they passed through the unattended orchard, none of the apples lasted very long in the hands of the hungry, including Stoic's apples.

"These are good," Osmo said, the juice from the apple in his hand running down his chin.

"Yes," answered Stoic, his mouth stuffed.

"Don't eat too fast. You'll get a sour stomach."

"I don't care. I'm hungry."

"Well then don't cry to me if you get sick," Osmo chuckled.

"The top of the hill is just ahead," Stoic said, as he threw the core of the apple away, after which he burped. It brought a laugh from Osmo.

"There, at the bottom ... Look, it's a lake," and Stoic smiled. Then the thought of finding water for the passengers almost brought a tear.

"Look, over there," and as Osmo spoke he pointed to a clearing and what were left of burnt structures.

"Tomorrow morning we will take a look there, but first and most important we've got to get to the lake and fill the water bags."

"Yes, tomorrow," Osmo answered.

After returning to the Halcyon with the fresh lake water and apples Stoic and Osmo went back ashore with the detail. When enough water bags were again filled and more apples gathered Stoic sent the detail back to the ship. He and Osmo stayed ashore to look for other fruit or berries and to check out the burnt structures. The detail would return in the morning for more water and to meet up with them.

It was getting dark quickly, so once they reached the top of the hill again, Stoic decided to make camp before it got too dark. From atop the hill they could see the lantern's candle light from the Halcyon anchored in the harbor. He was sure that the others on the ship could see their campfire, a sign to them that all was well with him and Osmo.

Before he got into his bedding he knelt and said a recovery prayer for the young woman Jewel and the others that were ill.

"Dear Lord Jesus; watch over the young woman and the others. I ask that you spare any more suffering and death, and make the young woman Jewel well again."

⊂⤫ ⊂⤫ ⊂⤫

"Wake up," whispered Osmo, his hand shaking Stoic's shoulder. "There is smoke coming from the burnt area below, a campfire, I think?"

Stoic jumped up quickly, immediately looking over toward the burnt out site.

"Do you know how to use this?" Stoic asked Osmo after removing the revolver Abstruse gave him from his pocket.

"Yes, of course I know how."

"Good, then take it. I've never fired one before."

Osmo smiled, as he took the weapon from Stoic's hand. And then, after eating a couple apples each Stoic and Osmo headed for the burnt-out site and the rising smoke.

"Look, over there," Osmo whispered, his hand pointed down the hillside to a tall tree standing alone in a field of tall grass. "What is that?"

Under the tree was a strange looking animal eating grass. It was standing on four legs, its coat a golden brown, and what looked like leafless branches were sticking out the top of its head.

"That is strange looking," Osmo said, when suddenly the strange animal looked their way with its head held high, and as suddenly it started to run quickly down the hillside.

"Look Osmo, you've scared it away."

"Look how fast it runs," shouted Osmo and the two soon broke out in paroxysms of laughter as they watched it quickly change directions, a giant bounce-like leap in its stride.

"If only we could run like that," Osmo said, and then he ran on ahead of Stoic, changing directions and hopping as did the strange animal until finally he fell to the ground tripping over his own feet. Stoic, again, broke out in paroxysms of laughter, as he watched Osmo roll over on the ground and on down the hillside, finally coming to rest against a large bush.

When Osmo got back up to the top of the hill where Stoic was waiting for him, he saw, standing about half the way down the hill, two young men.

"There," Osmo pointed, and then he took the revolver out from his tunic's pocket and held it low at his side, hiding it.

"No, put it back. They might be friendly."

Slowly, and with great caution, the two walked down toward the strangers.

"Who goes there?" Stoic shouted, after stopping about twenty yards in front of the strangers.

"Salient and Pathos, students from the Yeshiva school," with scared looks on their faces they took a step back, afraid of what might happen next. Before them they saw a giant of a man with as many stitched wounds as a rag doll. The longest of the stitches stretched down his thigh.

"Then this is Yeshiva Island," Stoic asked, remembering that Abstruse had said that he thought they might have anchored there. If so, Abstruse said they would only be a day's sail to Harbinger, a good sign, thought Stoic.

Stoic knew of the school and its teachings. Abstruse talked often of the place during their readings of the Holy Scroll Writings. After assuring Salient and Pathos that they came in peace the four went on into the burnt-out school ground area. Once there Stoic could see the freshly dug soil he knew could only have been the burial place of those that died there.

After gathering what few belongings Salient and Pathos had, the four headed back toward the bay. Stoic noticed how thin looking the two were, and he noticed that Pathos was in poor health. Pathos kept weeping, as he often spoke of the troopers' raid on the school and of the mass killings. It saddened Stoic.

"We thought we too were going to die," Pathos wept, the words stuttering out of his mouth. Neither Salient nor Pathos spoke of hiding the written copies of the Holy Scroll Writings.

When the detail arrived back to the Halcyon with Salient and Pathos the captain took the news of the raid on the school poorly.

"We must pray for all those that died while serving our Lord Jesus Christ," Abstruse said, and then he went straight to his cabin with tears in his eyes, a strong man of the sea, but human enough to cry.

Chapter Nineteen

It was a beautiful morning. The fields were copious with wild flowers, many of which had not been seen before now by any of the settlers. Flowers, Ardent thought, that must have perished during the holocaust.

Ardent had just finished most of the vegetable plantings in their garden and was leaning against a hoe in his hand and enjoying the beautiful sight. Then he glanced over his shoulder and saw Bandy approaching him. She looked tired. Her hair hung straight down, moving side to side as she walked. In her hand was a small basket of clothing to be washed.

"Want me to carry that to the stream for you?" Ardent asked.

"No, finish the garden."

"It's done. The seeds are all in the ground."

"Then walk with me."

Ardent rested the hoe on the ground and reached for the basket, carrying it anyway. Then the two headed toward the stream, about a half mile away.

"Ardent," and he looked her way, waiting for her to continue. She kept walking, her eyes staring down.

"Yes," he answered, still waiting for her to continue.

"I would like another area added onto the villa, a small area."

"But we have enough area," he stopped walking, shifting the basket to his other side. She only smiled at him, not saying another word the rest of the walk.

⌒⌒⌒

The stream was flowing swiftly, still cold from the winter's melt. He placed the basket upon the ground, and then watched her kneel and take the soap from the top of the clothing, and then as she soaked and started scrubbing a pair of his pants. His old pair, he only had two.

Ardent sat down on the ground and glanced up into the sky, waiting to carry the basket back when Bandy was finished with the washing. The sun was shining bright, hurting his eyes. The sky looked a beautiful blue, he thought. He squinted. Then put his hand out shielding the sun from his eyes.

The clouds seem to just float, all different shapes and sizes, a modicum of bright white against the vast amount of blue. They looked like the vast floating icebergs of the northern ocean, he thought.

"Look at the clouds, Bandy. They are so beautiful, so majestic."

"So God-like," Bandy remarked, just as Ardent got up from the ground and walked closer to the stream. Again his eyes were wandering, only this time at the swiftness of the streams flow. Below the water's surface he saw a fish animal swimming upstream, wiggling hard fighting the current's flow.

"You could have Onus help you build the new area," she broke the long silence, trying to get his attention away from the stream. A smile was on her face when she looked up his way. "Help you cut the trees."

"Look!" Ardent pointed to the water, at a pool next to a large flattened rock. "Another fish, no, there's two of them." He had an excited look on his face, a look of a child.

"They're God's gift given us for the rebirth of his son, Jesus Christ," she said, pausing, while he pointed to yet another pool.

"Look, there's more," and then he ran off toward the nearby wooded area.

When he came back, he had a long stick in his hand and a big smile on his face, from ear to ear.

"I will catch us this evening's meal," he boasted, as he removed his knife from his belt. Bandy watched him while he cut a sharp point on the end of the stick. She started to smile.

He climbed onto the flattened rock. Then with both his hands on the end of the spear-like stick, he pointed it at one of the fish. When it stopped its circle-like swim he plunged the spear into the water. It missed and the fish swiftly swam off. He looked disappointed. He knew he could do better.

"This might take all day," Bandy joked, laughing.

Ardent was determined now. He wasn't going to leave without one. Down he drove the spear again, and another miss … and another miss.

Bandy got up with the basket in her hand.

"Should I prepare the vegetable stew for tonight?" and she laughed as she walked away.

"I'll show her," Ardent said aloud to himself. "I'll show her!"

⸻

When Ardent got back to the villa, hanging on a line he put up from the corner of the villa to a tree nearby were the clothes Bandy had washed. He rushed to the door of the villa, opened it and then stood there. A big "I did it" smile was on his face.

"About time" Bandy remarked, when she saw him standing with the spear in his left hand, its point flattened. In his right hand was a twine-like twig and hanging from it were three of God's gifts, very small fish about the length of a man's hand. So small she couldn't stop laughing. It angered Ardent.

"Here, clean them," he said, a frown on his face.

⸻

The very next morning after hitching a work horse to one of the settlement's two-wheeled work carts, Ardent was going to head westward toward the other end of the island to cut trees for the small addition. Onus was on his monthly three day perimeter guard detail and this was the only day that a settlement work cart and work horse was available to him. Ardent would have no one to help him.

After putting a prepared snack of fruit and raw vegetables under the seat of the work cart, Ardent headed westward as planned. He was in a rush, so he loosened then snapped on the reins signaling for the horse to trot, and so it did. He leaned back, and then he started to sing a poem. He was happy with his new life. However, his singing was not good; it got the horse's attention.

Once he arrived, and after unhitching the work horse, he tied the reins to a nearby tree where the work horse could graze on grass. Then, with his saw and prepared snack in hand, he headed into the woods.

When he finished cutting down and trimming half a dozen trees, he decided it was a good time to relax and enjoy his snack.

Before finishing his snack he heard a noise coming from the woods to his left. Being the curious person that he was, he headed in the direction of the noise. Each time he got close to the noise it stopped, and soon after it started again, but from further away.

Deep into the woods he had ventured, and just as he was about to quit chasing the sound he came upon a small shallow babbling brook. On the other side were several berry bushes, so he crossed over to pick some to eat and bring back to Bandy.

After eating a couple handfuls of the berries he sat awhile, with his back resting against the trunk of a large tree. The sound he had heard was gone so he was enjoying the quietness, as he sat there staring upward at the small blue openings at the trees tops, the rays of sunlight shining downward. *How beautiful it was there*, he thought.

Riding one of the sunlight's rays upward was a beautiful, large and colorful butterfly. Its wings, very large and black with bright yellow spots, were fluttering back and forth, as if waving down to Ardent. Behind the butterfly and much closer to the ground, were three small plain white butterflies following one another slowly upward in a circle-like motion.

The rays' ends shined down on a lonely flowering plant, unlike any Ardent had ever seen. The plant, centered at the foot of a large rock, had dark green lance-shaped leaves and on top of a long stem from its center was a single, large, white cup shape flower.

Suddenly, a large fire-like glow emerged from the earth at the ray's end, encompassing the flowering plant. Above the glow, with their hands together as in prayer, were three Seraphim Angels with their wings opened wide. A golden halo circled each Angel's head.

Ardent rubbed his eyes. Could he be dreaming, he thought? But then a voice coming from the glowing, flowering plant spoke to him.

"I am the way, the truth, and the light. God's children need your guidance."

Then, after getting down onto his knees, there came the praises from the Angels, as he had heard before on the hillside with Bandy and the others:

"Holy, holy, holy is the Lord of hosts. All the earth is filled with His Glory. Holy, holy, holy is the Lord of hosts. All the earth is filled with His Glory."

When the Angels stopped their praises, Ardent heard the voice again:

"Go forth and lead God's children against the influences of the Antichrist."

The glow from the flowering plant began to get dimmer and the Angels ascended into the sky, quickly disappearing.

"Show me a sign, Lord please. Show me a sign," the words came from his mind, his mouth never moved.

It remained quiet, and there was no answer. No longer was the flowering plant all aglow. Confused, Ardent got up from his knees to leave when suddenly the voice spoke again:

"You will be told soon that you shall have child, a son, and he shall be blessed."

Then, as when he first sat under the tree, there were only the usual sounds of the woods and the wind. The butterflies, too, were gone. The sun had disappeared behind the clouds, its rays gone, darkening the woods.

Ardent, an all-alone feeling lingering over him, headed back to load onto the work cart the few trees he had already cut and trimmed. Not much to show for the long time he had spent there.

⊂✕ ⊂✕ ⊂✕

When Ardent arrived back to where the work cart was, lying next to one of the work carts wheels was a strange looking animal. An animal he had never seen before. It had four legs, a thick fur covering its body, a long tail, and it made an odd sounding noise when it tried to talk; a woof-woof-like barking sound. Also, its tail swayed back and forth, as if the animal was excited. It made Ardent nervous, very nervous.

The strange animal seemed harmless, as it approached him still wagging its tail. Then it pressed its nose against Ardent's boots, sniffing as if it smelled something.

Suddenly the animal lifted itself up onto its hind legs and put its front two legs onto Ardent's chest. Its long tongue then started licking Ardent's face. Nervous and a bit startled Ardent stood still and let the animal have its pleasure. At least until he noticed the long, sharp teeth in its mouth, at which time he grabbed the animal by its front legs and rested them back onto the ground with its hind legs. The strange animal stared up at him, its tail still wagging back and forth. It was then that Ardent knew it was harmless and just wanted a friend.

The animal stayed at Ardent's side while he loaded the tree trunks onto the work cart. Ardent found himself talking to the thing.

Occasionally he got an answer back, the barking-like sound and the tail wagging.

When Ardent got back onto the work cart to leave, the strange acting animal jumped up onto the seat and sat itself down next to him.

"Go!" Ardent shouted, but to no avail. It just sat there with a sad look on its face, its head tilted to one side, its tongue hanging out.

Ardent stared back, feeling sorry: "If we are going to be friends than I must give you a name," and after thinking it over: "Since you are wryly amusing, strikingly odd and funny, I shall name you … Droll."

The work horse moved slowly along the narrow trailway. Ardent just sat still and sloped downward, Droll still sitting at his side.

"Was I asleep, a dream, or was it the berries that I ate?" he spoke, as if talking to a friend that might have been sitting next to him. "No one would believe me. I will be called a fool. Me, a deserter trooper, to have been chosen to lead the Pariahs against the Antichrist? Murderer of many just like those I now find myself among. Savoir, one of the original revolutionaries was martyred by my own hand in a damp dingy cave, and for what?" Ardent looked over at Droll, but of course there was no answer back.

Upset at himself, Ardent grabbed the whip from under the seat, and with a quick snap of his wrist the whip's end cracked loudly just above the work horse. After a brief lift of its front two legs, it went into a fast trot. Droll stuck its tongue out and lifted its head high. Apparently it was enjoying the wind blowing against its face, as the work cart raced down the trailway.

When Ardent got back Bandy was waiting outside of the villa for him, and Pristine was there with her.

"What is that thing?" Bandy asked, pointing toward Droll. A look of surprise was on her face, as was also on Pristine's face.

"My new friend," Ardent answered. "I named it Droll."

"I sent him for tree trunks to build me a new area, and instead he comes back with but a few tree trunks and a strange animal," Bandy said to Pristine, now a smile on her face. The two women started to laugh at Ardent who had just driven the work cart away to unload the tree trunks.

After Ardent was finished with unloading the few trees he had cut and trimmed from the wagon, Bandy walked up to him and reached for his hand. Behind her was Pristine, a smile on her face. Running in circles around the work horse and making its barking noise was Droll.

"I have news," Bandy said.

"Yes," answered Ardent.

"I am with child," she wasted no time getting right to the point.

Before she could say another word Ardent fell to the ground onto his knees and started to pray. The very first prayer of his life emerged from his inner self.

"Ardent, many have had child. There is no need for prayers now, save them for when I am in pain giving birth."

"We are going to have a son, Bandy — a son!"

"What if it is a girl?" Bandy asked. "After all, there's a good chance that it could be a girl."

"It will be a boy. I just know it to be so," and then jumping up and down Ardent ran over to Droll, lifted its front legs up high and started dancing in a circle, Droll's rear legs clumsily moving about.

"Look Droll, my love Bandy and I are going to have a child. This is the happiest day of my life!" he yelled it out loud as he released the hold he had on Droll. "We are going to have a child," its echo rang out over the entire valley.

Chapter Twenty

The Halcyon sat still in the harbor, its anchor well secured on the water's floor. The valley leading to the settlement of Harbinger was in plain sight. Already, a dozen of the passengers were in a shore boat and on their way to the docks. Because Harbinger's harbor was not a deep water harbor shore boats had to be used to ferry the passengers and their belongings.

A second shore boat was being loaded when Stoic, with the young woman Jewel in his arms, approached it. Her husband Sully was already in the shore boat waiting for Stoic to hand her to him. The fever still had its grip on Jewel. Now, only prayer, the proper care and the medicines they had at Harbinger could save her.

Most of the crew kept busy carrying the passengers' belongings up to the top deck to be loaded onto the shore boats, and then brought to the shore's dock after the passengers had embarked. Osmo, after waiting for Stoic to finish putting Jewel into the boat, gave him back his revolver.

Salient and Pathos would have to wait for the first of the shore boats to return before boarding for shore. It would take the rest of the day and most likely into the night to unload all the passengers and their cargo. Last to be unloaded would be half of the much-needed weapons and black gunpowder stored in the bilge.

The Halcyon would then sail for Newfoundland, its last journey. There the remaining black gunpowder and weapons would be unloaded, and the ship stripped of all its plankings, decking and furnishings. The captain, his lovely Prudent and the crew had decided to settle there instead of Harbinger. Stoic and Osmo, now the best of friends, decided that they would return to Harbinger on a merchant ship to live there amongst the passengers they were familiar and friendly with. They had enough of the sea life, and were looking forward to what might lie ahead.

Many of Harbinger's citizens were waiting at the docks for each of the shore boats to unload, and many of them were offering the comfort of their villas until the new settlers built their own. Bandy and Pristine were at the docks when the shore boat carrying Jewel and her husband Sully arrived.

"Someone please help me. My wife has the fever," Bandy heard a young man in a shore boat yell out. The citizens at the dock stepped back. A look of fear was on their faces, the fear of catching her fever illness.

Bandy stepped closer to the boat where she saw, all wrapped up tightly in a blanket, what must have been the young man's wife.

"I'll help. My name is Bandy and you and your wife can stay at my villa until she recovers. It's a small villa, but we will make space for the both of you."

"Thank you and may God bless you," the young man answered. "My name is Sully," his hand extended to help Bandy into the boat. On the dock kneeling was Pristine. She too was willing to help.

Bandy, once inside the boat knelt down to remove the blanket from the woman's face.

"Water, she will need water," and as soon as she asked Sully handed her his pouch of water.

"Oh! My God it's Jewel!" and she dropped the pouch as she shouted, its water spilling onto the decking. Sully, confused, looked up at Bandy while picking up the pouch from the boat's decking.

"Pristine, hurry and get Ardent. He and Onus are west of the settlement cutting more trees down for the addition to the villa. Tell him it's Jewel, and that she has a fever. Tell him to hurry."

Pristine remembered the many stories Bandy had told of her friend Jewel. The same Jewel, she assumed, that was with fever. So, she got up from her knees quickly and started to run, as fast as she could, in search of Ardent and Onus.

⸻

When Pristine approached where Onus and Ardent were gathering the tree trunks Droll started barking, a warning that someone was near. It got their attention. They had just lifted a trimmed tree trunk. Each had an end, but quickly dropped it to the ground and ran to meet her. Droll ran past both Ardent and Onus and when he reached Pristine he jumped up putting his front two legs on her chest, happy to see her and wanting her to play. Pristine was out of breath, breathing heavily. She almost fell over backward when Droll jumped up.

"Down Droll, down," Ardent yelled. He could see from the look on Pristine's face that something was wrong.

"What's wrong," Onus asked. "Are you ok?"

"Ardent," she turned her head his way. "You must hurry to the villa," a catch of breath, and: "Bandy is there with Jewel who just arrived aboard a freedom ship. Jewel is sick with fever."

"Jewel … She is sick with the fever?"

"Yes hurry, they need you," shouted Pristine, still out of breath and barely getting the words out. Then she bent over resting her hands on her knees, gasping for air while Onus rubbed her back, and then a pat or two with his hand. He was worried.

"Are you all right?" Onus asked. A greater look of concern overcame him. He started breathing heavy, anxious.

"I'll be fine. Ardent you must hurry," the words stuttered out.

"Go Ardent, Pristine and I will finish here. Go!"

⌒⋊ ⌒⋊ ⌒⋊

When Ardent and Droll arrived at the villa, inside were Bandy and a young man who got nervous when he saw Droll. In Bandy's bedding was Jewel, her face and arms exposed and as white as the clouds in the sky got after the miracle changes.

"Is she all right?" Ardent asked Bandy, as he knelt next to Jewel.

"She needs to eat. Ardent, go to the mealing area and see if they have any soup broth. Meanwhile, I will keep washing her body down with water."

"My name is Sully," the young man introduced himself to Ardent. "Jewel is my wife."

"Your wife, is she really?" Ardent, first surprised to see Jewel, and now to find out that she is married. That could only have meant that she must no longer be a trooper, he thought. She must be a neophyte, having found the way of the Lord Jesus Christ.

"Yes," Sully proudly smiled, as Ardent shook his hand and welcomed him to their villa. Droll, nudging Ardent aside, jumped up putting its front legs on Sully's chest, scaring him. So much so, he stepped back.

Don't worry, he's harmless," Ardent grinned, hoping to settle Sully down a bit. But the size of Droll and his large sharp looking teeth still made Sully nervous. "Droll, get down, now!"

Jewel woke up not knowing where she was, the surroundings unfamiliar. Her fever had broken leaving her lips dry and cracked open, a hardening of blood upon them. A worried Sully was at her side as he had been all night.

"Where are we?" her mouth dry, she barely got the words out.

"With Bandy and Ardent, they have extended their quarters to us."

"Bandy and Ardent; are you sure or am I dreaming?" Again the words came out slow.

"Yes … I mean, no, you're not dreaming, and yes with Bandy and Ardent. Now let me get you more water," and Sully rushed to get the water.

When he got back with the water Bandy was at his side, excited knowing Jewel was awake. She had much to tell Jewel and questions to ask.

"My God, it is you," Jewel said, a wryly smile on her face. "Are we at Harbinger?" It hurt her to smile or speak.

"Yes, but be still for now. I will bring you some broth to drink," then Bandy, with some water on a cloth pressed it against Jewel's lips to moisten them.

"We have a lot to talk about, but first get some more rest," Bandy said, before leaving Jewel alone with her Sully.

Jewel was soon on her feet, and very soon after she was working in the settlement mealing area. The town council, having known she was trained to be a trooper, asked her to help with training Harbinger's citizens to fire the weapons, which she gladly did. Bandy and Ardent, what with a child coming had declined to help. Instead, Bandy agreed to sail to Newfoundland on the Halcyon's last voyage. There she, along with Jewel, would represent the women of Harbinger in the writing of the Articles of Independence and with the forming of a theocracy government, but one also of the people. Traveling with them representing Harbinger were its councilors; Cavil, Stymie and Sordid.

Before leaving, Ardent and Onus helped Sully build a small villa for him and Jewel to live in with the tree trunks Ardent finally finished cutting for the addition Bandy wanted. Later the three would cut more tree trunks for the addition Bandy wanted, the child's bedding area.

Chapter Twenty-One

Tome was lying in his bedding, rankled with the coldness of his thoughts, thoughts that Morose, Dank, and Ardent were dead, and of all the others that perished. It sickened him, the news that Jejune and Seethe brought, themselves picked out of the ocean. It was discouraging.

Of the ten ships that departed, only three had returned. The ship with his troopers on board rested now at the ocean's floor. Only Jejune, Seethe and three others survived, spared the other troopers useless ending. Truly not the ending a warrior would have expected.

At least 800 of the government's newly-formed legion, and the months lost before the survivors returned and when he learned of their great lost, all uselessly spent, he thought, and now it would be months more before he would get trained reinforcements and months, if not years more, before the government's ships were rebuilt and their crews trained. Until then he would have to get by with the 150 troopers he had left and most of them newly trained and fresh from Area #56. Also a replacement for Morose would be difficult to find. Most likely he would have to pick a replacement from the instructors at Area #56, none of whom could possibly replace Morose.

First thing come dawn he would promote Jejune and Seethe to Tertiary Pairing, replacing Dank and Ardent. After all, except for Bovine and his pairing Thespian, they now were his most experienced, his continued thought.

It was late into the night when Tome blew out the candle by his bedding, near its wick's end. The wax having overflowed hardened around the base of what was left of the candle.

It was late before he could fall asleep. He couldn't get the death of Ardent off his mind. His thoughts kept wandering, thoughts of all the years he spent training Ardent, a special student he knew upon their first meeting. Ardent, he always thought, would have replaced him someday as Commander of the Revolutionary Vanguard.

Chapter Twenty-Two

It was raining when Ardent, Bandy, Sully and Jewel boarded the Halcyon with caution, aware of the dangers boarding with the high seas the rain storm brought. The Halcyon was not steady, nor was the shore boat.

"Careful," Ardent said. He wouldn't let go of Bandy's hand when a giant of a man, he thought, grabbed his left hand. Quickly he was lifted up onto the deck, and then Ardent quickly pulled Bandy up with his right hand still a hold of hers. The monster of a man then helped Sully and Jewel up next.

"What's your name?" Ardent asked, his neck bent back looking up at Stoic. The hard rain that already soaked his tunic was falling onto his face. The wind was blowing Bandy's long hair back away from her face exposing her cold, wind-reddened cheeks. She pulled the hood of her tunic up over her head, holding it tightly just under her chin. A shiver oscillated up through her shoulders and head. She was cold.

"Stoic," he answered.

"Where's your captain?"

"In his quarters, he's readying for the voyage," then Stoic brushed the palm of his hand down his face to wipe the rain water off. "Let me bring the four of you to your bedding areas below."

His hand still holding Bandy's, Ardent followed behind Stoic. He was worried. Worried that Bandy might catch a fever. He was worried for the child inside her.

It was cold and damp below, but dry of water. It would have to do, Ardent thought.

"Here, cover yourself." Ardent insisted. In his hand was a woolen from the bedding. Then he handed another to Jewel.

Sully helped Jewel wrap the woolen over her shoulder. He wasn't happy about leaving Harbinger, or their new villa. He was not happy that Jewel was getting so involved. Not at all, and it showed on his face when he thought about it.

"I will tell the captain that you are here and quartered," Stoic said, as he turned to leave them alone. When Cavil, Stymie and Sordid arrive the seven of them would be the only passengers on this, what was to be the Halcyon's last voyage.

Tied down and taking up most of the space in the area were the trade goods loaded earlier. At the far end were the beddings for the crew, and the mealing area. Ardent could smell the stew being prepared. It reminded him that he was hungry.

"Hello mates. I'm Captain Abstruse," and when Ardent turned, behind the captain he noticed Cavil, Sordid and Stymie also approaching them. All three of the councilors were also soaking wet. Following well behind were Stoic and Osmo, each with their arms full with the seven guests backpacks.

"Put them there," the captain ordered, pointing to what appeared to be the only freed-up space left below.

"The evening meal will be served at six o'clock sharp, after the crew meals. Prudent will be joining us," a smile crossed his face when he glanced at the women. The both of them bundled up in the woolens, a polite smile it was. "We have much to talk of."

"He seems quite the jolly type," Sully remarked, right after the captain left, again following him were Stoic and Osmo.

"Yes, so I heard," Ardent answered back.

"The stew was good. Thank you," Bandy said. It got a smile from the captain who, while he ate never looked up from his eating utensil. Neither had Ardent or Sully, both were starving and ate like they were.

"You are going to Newfoundland to draw up the Independence Articles, we were told," Prudent remarked, breaking the long silence that proceeded.

"Yes," Cavil answered her inquiry. "There will be representatives from eleven of the settlements."

"Will you be there very long?"

"No," Ardent rushed to answer. "It is most important that we return to Harbinger before that. Bandy is with child."

"You mean, more important than our freedom from the existing government's rule, freedom to worship as we please?" Abstruse asked. There was no smile on his face.

"Ardent is new to our faith. He's just beginning to learn our ways," Bandy interrupted.

"We should arrive midday tomorrow. Is there anything else I can help you with?" Abstruse spoke as he stood up. He was ready to leave for his quarters. Enough had already been said, he thought.

"Yes" Sordid spoke up.

"What, may I ask?"

"We are also forming a defense force to defend ourselves should the government forces invade our settlements. A ship like yours is much needed. We would like …."

"The captain isn't interested. We will marry soon and settle down in Newfoundland. The ships plankings are to be used to build our villa," Prudent interrupted. She did not want to hear anymore about it from Sordid.

"We are tired, so please excuse us," Abstruse explained. He did not appear happy that Prudent spoke for him. He was birthed with sea salt in his test tube. It would be difficult for him to settle down on dry land, for sure.

"C'mon Prudent, we must go."

Ardent awoke before the others and went topside. His feet ached. A good walk would do them well. Topside by the rail was the captain. His stare was outward toward the horizon.

"Morning," Ardent said.

"Morning, mate." His stare stayed on the horizon, apparently deep in thought. "There," he pointed ahead to a grouping of giant-sized fish, some almost as large as the Halcyon. "Whales," he said.

"Whales, can they harm us?" Ardent couldn't imagine anything so big not being dangerous.

"No, not as long as we leave them alone, they're harmless enough, I think. This is the first time I've ever seen one."

"Then how do you know if they are harmless?"

"I don't," Abstruse smiled. "I just know that the world is changing, I suppose."

"Look!" Ardent shouted. Some from the crew were starting to gather along the railing to view the sighting. "They're on their backs, water is spouting upward!" It got everyone's attention.

"Yes, they're amazing," Abstruse said. Then suddenly and close to the Halcyon one came up from under the water. A gusher of water spouted up from a hole on its back and just as suddenly it dove back under the water, its giant tail lifting then smashing downward atop the water making a big splash before it disappeared leaving a wake. The Halcyon soon started rocking side to side as the wake rushed against it. Ardent grabbed the railing and held on tightly.

"If Bandy were to see this she would have said that they were God's gift to mankind for the rebirth of His son Jesus."

"They were."

◦≺ ◦≺ ◦≺

The meeting area was full, and Bandy was excited with everything that was happening, unlike Ardent who wanted to leave to get some fresh air outside. The walk, he thought, would do him some good. All the talk of forming a United Republic and an army to protect the settlements was boring to him anyway. When he left the convocation was arguing over which of the settlements would be the nascent republic capital.

Ardent no sooner got to the center of the settlement when he saw Yenta walking toward him alone.

"Yenta, what in the New World are you doing here?" His hand already extended grabbed hers. The handshake was firm.

"Ardent," she bellowed out. "Ardent."

"You've deserted too?" Ardent asked.

"Yes," she lost the smile. "I've found the way of the Lord."

"I thought you were dead," she continued. "We all thought you were."

"Dank's dead."

"Your pairing, I'm sorry."

"Bandy and I are joined. She's with child." He felt proud telling her. He was delighted that he saw Yenta.

"Tawpie is dead. Shot by a zealot during a raid. It was right after that I found the way of the Lord. I see you have also. I always thought you might, what with all the questions you often asked, but then we heard you were dead."

"I'm still searching for the Lord, still with many questions," Ardent confessed. "My wife Bandy has found the Lord and is helping show me the way."

"I've yet to marry … But soon, very soon, and it will be to a good man," she smiled, "But I haven't met him yet," and she laughed. Ardent started laughing also. That was funny, he thought.

Ardent enjoyed the long chat with Yenta. He found out that she was helping train the volunteers at Newfoundland in the use of the rifles. She was surprised when he told her he and Bandy had declined to.

Ardent wondered if they would ever meet again. One thing he knew for sure, everyone Yenta knew would soon learn that he was alive.

⊂⋊ ⊂⋊ ⊂⋊

Another twenty days would pass before the Articles of Independence reached an accord, and another two days to write and for all involved to put their signature upon the nebulous doctrines. Bandy and Jewel, along with the other women there, fought hard to include as an article that all citizens would be equals. It became the first article written on the covenant's parchment.

To Ardent, the Articles of Independence was just an understanding. To the others it was a holy covenant. However, he was glad to hear that Harbinger was chosen as the nascent republic capital. Now all he wanted was to get back to the comforts of the villa and to see his friend Droll.

⊂⋊ ⊂⋊ ⊂⋊

At the dock, while waiting to board the merchant ship that would take them back to Harbinger, two much older men approached Bandy and Ardent.

"Bandy, it was nice to meet you, and I'm sure we will meet again someday," one of the men said.

"Ardent, they are the educators that discovered the time capsule. The ones that are responsible for where we are today, responsible for our freedom."

"Hi, I'm Hubris."

"And I'm Placid."

"There was a third but he was killed," Bandy remarked. Ardent's face dropped.

"Yes, Savoir was killed by troopers and then his body paraded through the streets of the capital," Hubris said. "We miss him and all the others that died that day."

Ardent was lost for words. Did they know it was he who put the knife to Savoir? Facing the two before him bothered him, the guilt, so he swore to himself that he would never kill a citizen again. Like Savoir, he would not fight back.

"It's time to board," Ardent reminded Bandy.

"Have a safe voyage and, May the Lord always be with you," Placid said, as Ardent reached for Bandy's hand to help her onto the ship.

"And also with you," Bandy answered. Ardent couldn't speak up. His head still hung low. He wanted to cry out that he killed Savoir. He wanted their forgiveness. He couldn't ask.

Chapter Twenty-Three

At the Capital Commune the United American Union of Communes government council was meeting regarding an appointment of a commander for their new legion yet to be formed, of which would be sent to the settlements to end the mass exodus that was taking place, to wipe out the Pariahs and end, once and for all time, this foolish thought of a God.

Caution was the tempo during the meeting. The councilors were afraid of moving too fast as was done before, which led to the demise of most of the legionnaires and ships that were sent before.

Finally, and only after a long debate was a choice to command the legion made. Surfeit Serpentine, in spite of the objections of some, was their choice and only after many compromises. Those that objected did so because of the reputation Serpentine had of being violent and abusive with his captives in the past, and with his own men.

It was common knowledge that after raiding a farming commune north of the capital some of the citizens were found to be Pariahs. Commander Serpentine had his troopers gather a dozen and line them up facing the others.

It is said, Serpentine walked along the line of Pariahs, each with their hands tied behind their backs. Then, after shouting out a warning to those forced to watch he removed his knife from its sheath, and while walking from one to the next, he slit the throats of each and every one of them. The blood of the innocent, it is said, soaked his arm, tunic and face. As the last in the line fell to the ground he licked the blood from his knife and the clutched hand that held it.

"I hope we've done the right thing having chosen Commander Serpentine. After all, he is the most nefarious beast of a man we've ever known," Councilor Plethora said, as she fixed her hair getting ready to leave.

"He'll get the task done and that's all that matters," answered Querulous, a bit upset with Plethora's remark. "It would be nice if you did your tasks as well as he's done his in the past."

"Yeah, but at what cost in human life?" Plethora's response, although said quietly to herself.

✧ ✧ ✧

As the councilors met, and months after the defeat at sea as Tome thought, a hundred newly-trained replacement troopers arrived. With the reinforcements came Avarice, their instructor. He was no Morose, but he would have to do, Tome thought when deciding to choose him.

Avarice, a big man, extremely greedy and a seasoned instructor had been given the same rank as Tome by the government council. A move, Tome thought could only have meant that he was being pushed aside.

The government council didn't like having him around as a reminder of their mistake sending their legion after the Pariahs all at once. And now they were doing it again, forming another legion, and this time it would be even larger a force.

Things were changing fast, he thought. For one thing, there were the three newly-built, giant foundry structures from which large, round smoke stacks stood high above. From the smoke stack tops black smoke rose upward into the sky, and falling from the black smoke were the white ashes that covered the nearby hillside.

Inside the structures big guns unlike any ever seen before were being assembled, guns that were called cannons. Two of each would be mounted on the new ships, one forward and one aft. This was in violation of the treaty signed millennia earlier by all seven of the governments. Tome knew it so, but to say anything would surely mean his removal or death.

A goal set by Querulous, was to build a new ship every two months. Already completed and its two cannons mounted was the first of such ships, the Merrimack; named after the river that flowed past the Capital Commune.

At the mouth of the river a waterfall emptied into the deep water harbor just a mile away beyond the rapids. There by the waterfall was anchored the Merrimack. For its trial voyage the crew was assigned to the Revolutionary Vanguard under Tome's command and would be used to check out the Yeshiva Island School to make sure it wasn't being reconstructed. That did not sit well with Serpentine, he thought it a waste.

Chapter Twenty-Four

The citizens at Harbinger's docks were busy loading the shore boats with trade goods to be brought to the ship anchored in the harbor, its cargo heading soon for one of the new settlements nearby.

"Ship Ahoy," was the yell from one of the citizens on the dock.

Entering the harbor was another ship. Its sails full, a string of colorful, long banners waved with the wind. A large, bold red cross was painted on the center of its stem sail. It was the Halcyon, tilted starboard and running before the wind, two months after its supposed last journey.

Anchored and the sails fully reefed, a shore boat was lowered into the water. Aboard was Captain Abstruse and eight from his crew. On the docks waiting was an anxious crowd.

Abstruse, as big and clumsy as he was, stumbled, almost falling into the water when he climbed up onto the dock. The first to greet him was Stoic, and the excitement on his face showed. The grin on his face was from ear to ear.

"Captain, I thought by now the Halcyon would be made into your domicile."

"Stoic, you big slob, it's good to see you again, old friend."

"So you've come back, maybe to settle here instead of Newfoundland."

"No," Abstruse laughed. "Sea salt is in this old timer's blood, and apparently not in Prudent's. We have parted."

Stoic's smile turned to a frown, surprised to hear of Abstruse's news, as were the others, suddenly quiet.

"I heard that the settlements are uniting, so I thought you may need the Halcyon and its good crew. We want to be among the first to sign up for duty. My crew and I are ready to do whatever you ask."

"Yes, we could use the Halcyon and its crew. You, however, an old fool we could do without," Cavil joked, and that broke the quietness, as everyone started laughing, including Abstruse.

"Aboard my Halcyon and a bit seasick are 24 good souls. All of them recruited from Newfoundland. They, too, want to sign up."

"Good, we could use them to help build the garrison wall. I hope they are good and strong," joked Stoic, put in charge of the garrison wall construction.

"When they feel better and get their legs back they will be coming ashore."

"Captain, captain, it's me, Salient," the shout came from the other end of the dock. Salient's happy feet rushed toward Abstruse. Right behind him was Pathos.

"Salient, Pathos, what are the two of you still doing here? I thought you would be back at the school by now, fixing it up."

"Soon, after the plantings they will be going with the new United Settlement Army to reconstruct the school. It'll be part of their training and strengthening," Cavil interrupted. "That is if we can find someone to take command."

"Well, than I came along just in time. We'll use the Halcyon to ferry your army and any supplies you may need."

"Now we can get a head start making the furniture and accessories," suggested Cavil. Nodding in agreement was Sordid and Stymie.

―――――――――

Ardent was alone at the villa stacking split wood next to the stove when Bandy got back from visiting Pristine. Walking in behind her were Sordid, Cavil and Stymie. Droll was off in the woods chasing after smaller animals, as he often did.

"Ardent, they want to talk with you," and then Bandy walked into the bedding area, leaving the men alone.

"Captain Abstruse told us that not only were you and Bandy troopers, but that you were ranked a Tertiary," Cavil spoke for the three.

"Yes, my pairing Dank and I."

"As third in command of such an elite force, you must have been battle hardened."

"Yes, a part of my life I now wish never happened."

"The United Settlements Army needs someone to be its commander in chief. Someone that can not only train our freedom fighters, but also lead them in battle." Cavil, of course, was asking Ardent in a round-about way.

"If you're asking me, my wife is with child and I must be here for her."

"You must think longer of this. The United Settlements Army needs you. We will ask again another day soon," Stymie spoke up.

Ardent, being polite, led them to the door. Then he waited awhile after the three left before joining Bandy in the bedding area.

⌒⊂⋊ ⌒⊂⋊ ⌒⊂⋊

"Are you going to take the position?" Bandy asked, as Ardent crawled under the beddings.

"No." His answer was simple.

"Good," her reply, as she snuggled up to him.

"Bandy, there is something I never told you, something that happened to me."

"What happened?" and she stared into his eyes, where she saw a serious look.

Slowly, Ardent explained his experience by the rock in the woods on the day he was cutting trees for the new area she had asked for, and when he mentioned the three angels and the glowing, white flower that looked like a horn, Bandy sat right up. "Then what happened?"

Ardent continued, first telling her of what the voice said, and then of having asked for a sign, and of how the sign came true.

"What's wrong, Bandy?" Ardent asked when Bandy started to cry.

"That was God, Ardent, and he has plans for you. You have been chosen to lead his children, chosen, as Moses was chosen to lead the children of Israel out of slavery. God wants you to lead his children away from the influences of the Antichrist and to the path of freedom, love and peace, as our Lord Jesus Christ taught."

"How Bandy, how?"

"Cavil, Stymie and Sordid were sent here tonight by God to guide you in the direction He wants," Bandy answered, a river of tears flowing from her eyes.

"I can't leave you, or the son you bear inside you."

"You must, Ardent, you must. It is the will of God that you do," words she hated speaking, but it being the will of God she had to help show Ardent the way. "I will be strong, you needn't worry," and to herself she prayed for God's guidance, for Ardent's safety.

Ardent agreed to command the United Settlement's Army's "Solders of Christ" as they soon became called. The soldiers-to-be first assignment, however, was to help Stoic construct the garrison wall and the training grounds; to be located at the foothills of the narrow valley gateway, between Harbinger's Bay and the settlement, and stretching cliff to cliff across the gateway.

The garrison wall was built with thick, round tree trunks two deep and stacked lying down twenty feet high. Five feet from the top of the garrison wall was a walkway with stairs at each end. At the very top of the garrison wall were sandbags for the riflemen to shield themselves and rest their rifles on when firing them at would be invaders.

Inside the garrison wall and extending outward from it were the bedding quarters for the defenders, also made from thick, round tree trunks. The quartering areas were modest, each shared by a team of thirteen Soldiers of Christ.

Into the cliffs overlooking the valley's gateway were dug out caves for riflemen, sandbags stretched across the openings. Inside were stockpiled water and food supplies for the defenders, six in each cave and enough to last a month.

In a large field between the garrison wall and the settlement was where the training exercises were practiced. Ardent set up teams of twelve soldiers each and a team leader. Among the team leaders were Onus, Stoic, Sully, Osmo, and Jewel. Each of the team leaders was trained by Ardent, and then each leader trained their team.

After just a month's training Ardent felt that his Army of Christ's Soldiers were almost ready.

Now all that was left was to wait for the government legion to arrive, which Ardent felt was only a matter of time.

The Halcyon, while the garrison wall was being constructed, made one journey to the Capital Commune. The cargo it brought

THE LOST CHRIST

back was of more converts and supplies. Much needed were the kegs of black powder stored in its bilge.

The news Abstruse brought Ardent was discouraging.

"There are many new ships anchored in Manchester harbor, ships that will soon bring the government legion upon you."

"We will be ready, that is if those trained will fight back and not turn the other cheek."

"Yes, to learn how is one thing, but to face the enemy and kill them is yet another," agreed Abstruse.

"Have you heard who will command their legion?"

"Yes, Surfeit Serpentine was picked."

"A butcher," replied Ardent, and a look of concern came upon him. "I have worse news."

"What could be worse than Surfeit Serpentine?"

"Upon each new ship are mounted two very big guns. Guns that fire large metal balls filled with black powder, and explode after hitting in amongst those they fire upon. With the explosion is left the dead and a large hole in the ground."

"We will be fighting on land, not the sea. Their big guns will be useless."

"The guns are called cannons. They can reach a long way."

"Will they reach the garrison wall from the middle of the harbor?"

"No, I think not, but surely the docks and villas nearby," a questionable look was on his face. "I have yet more to tell you," he was smiling as he spoke.

"What?"

"Cavil, Sordid and Stymie asked me to send you to them when we finished. They await you," and the smile turned to a jolly laugh.

"Go, you brought me enough bad news," and Ardent smiled as he extended his hand out to Abstruse. It was a friendly, firm handshake.

The meeting area was a bit dark. The only candle lit was that which was on the table near Cavil, Sordid and Stymie. After adjusting his eyes to the dimness Ardent spoke first:

"You wanted to see me?" he asked, while still standing.

"Yes, but first sit down," Cavil spoke up, while still looking down at the papers in front of him. "We are writing a message to the

Newfoundland council asking that they send us 65 men to be trained as you've trained the others, five teams of thirteen." Cavil continued, after finally lifting his head to stare at Ardent.

"The soldiers we've already trained plus the armed citizens should be enough to hold back the government forces if we pin them down at the gateway," Ardent questioned the council's decision, because it only meant more mouths to feed.

"We have a detail for you and 65 of your soldiers. It's away from Harbinger, and the men we are asking Newfoundland for will be reinforcements until you get back. Then they will go back to Newfoundland," Cavil, glancing over at the others said.

"When the reinforcements get here you are to take your five teams, supplies and Salient and Pathos to Yeshiva Island to reconstruct the school and copying center. Abstruse will take you there in the Halcyon. In two weeks time he will return with more supplies for the school, which will be made here. The teachers and new students will also arrive with the Halcyon," Sordid finished speaking for Cavil, as the others looked on.

"It is important that the Holy Scrolls Salient and the other students hid in caves are protected, at all cost," Cavil continued.

"In the name of the Lord Jesus Christ, we must continue getting the words He spoke to the people," Stymie, with a serious look, interrupted.

"If that is what the Lord Jesus Christ wants of me, than I shall obey his command," Ardent said, and then he got up from the chair and excused himself. The three watched with concern as he left. They knew Bandy would soon give birth; a child born that Ardent might never see.

Droll was outside waiting for Ardent. His tail was wagging to and fro.

"How will I tell Bandy?" Ardent said, his hand rubbing deep into the fur around Droll's neck. "C'mon, let's go."

Bandy was saddened when she heard from Ardent that he would be leaving on a mission for God, and for many a night after, and while Ardent slept, she sat all alone in the new bedding area Ardent built for their child, a son Ardent insisted, and she would cry.

Her life had been blessed since finding the Lord Jesus Christ, she thought on those nights while crying all alone in the darkness. Christ had brought Ardent to her, and now Ardent's seed was planted inside her. "God" she would pray, "Please watch over the love of my life. Protect him, he who goes forth in His honor to bring freedom, peace and love to the children of Thy kingdom."

The Halcyon arrived with the reinforcements, the first of its shore boats were approaching the dock area.

Ardent was at the docks waiting. He wanted to supervise the unloading of the gunpowder that the Halcyon was bringing. The first of the shore boats had only reinforcements. Ardent had hoped they would unload the black gunpowder first.

With the first of the reinforcements disembarking Ardent saw Adroit, his DIP friend. Ardent was thrilled. A large smile crossed his face.

"Adroit!" yelled Ardent, and immediately after getting his attention Ardent walked up to his side. "It's so good to see you."

"Ardent," Adroit answered, with a surprised look on his face, quickly followed by a smile, as he reached his hand out to Ardent. "I heard that you and Dank were killed at sea with the others."

A real happy look was on Adroit's face, as Ardent's hand embraced his; happy to suddenly see that Ardent was indeed alive.

"When did you escape?" Ardent asked, after throwing his arms around him in greeting. The hand shake wasn't good enough for an old friend.

"Many of us tried, but only a few of us made it. The others are dead. Killed by the troopers, all of them unarmed and shot in the back trying to escape. I was lucky."

"They're with the Lord Jesus Christ now," Ardent replied.

"Amen," replied Adroit.

After the gunpowder arrived and loaded onto the supply carts, Ardent walked to the garrison wall with Adroit, who filled him in with all the news of the Capital Commune, most of which confirmed what Abstruse already told him.

"Where will you be staying?" Ardent asked. "You can stay with my wife and me, if you have nowhere else."

"I am volunteering to fight with the new army I hear so much about."

"Good, then I will show you to your quartering area, but first we must get you signed up," Ardent said, and then with his hand on Adroit's shoulder he led him through the garrison wall gate.

⌒×⌒×⌒×

On his way back to his villa after leaving Adroit, Ardent stopped on the training area to watch the men playing games. Stoic's team and Onus's team were playing tug of war. The rope was stretched out long and in the middle was a large puddle of muddy water awaiting the losers. At the present Stoic's team seemed to have the edge.

At the front of his team leaning back, almost lying on the ground, was Onus, his feet not far from the mud puddle. They were no match for the bull-like Stoic.

All thirteen kept sliding forward, until a few other bystanders grabbed on to help Onus's team. The slide slowed, but still Onus got nearer and nearer a drenching in mud.

Ardent approached the three at the end of Stoic's rope.

"Let go," he whispered. And they did just as Ardent asked, and with a big smile on their faces.

Suddenly, the event changed. First, Stoic rose upward. Then, he dug his feet in deep, but to no avail. The large gap between Stoic and the mud shortened quickly. One of his men right behind him fell to the ground, and the one behind him fell right over him letting go of the rope. Almost instantly, Stoic slid into the black puddle.

The fool had the rope wrapped around his wrist, so naturally Onus's team kept pulling, dragging Stoic across the muddied puddle and onto the dry land on the other side.

Everyone started laughing at the all muddied up Stoic, even his own team. It made Stoic mad, so mad that he threw the rope down and started yelling at his team. That is until he noticed that Ardent was standing amongst his team and laughing at him, laughing hard and loud … a falling down kind of laughter. It only got Stoic madder. His face turned beet red.

"If you weren't my commander I would throw you, right now, into that mud, I surely would."

"Well then, I dare you," Ardent, still laughing said.

"And I dare you," yelled Onus to Stoic.

Stoic stomped right through the puddle, the straightest line to Ardent. A roar of laughter arose from the gathering, now much larger since anyone that was in hearing distance had come to see what all the noise was about.

Ardent suddenly was off his feet, a mighty bear hug from Stoic lifting him high. Then the splash, as Ardent hit the puddle still laughing.

"There, how's that?" Stoic yelled out, as if it gave him much satisfaction.

"Here, help me out," Ardent asked, his hand outreached.

"Oh no, you're not going to pull me in, no sir!"

Onus approached the puddle's edge reaching for Ardent's hand and helped him out.

"It's not fair, you helped them," Stoic complained, still upset having lost.

"Life sometimes isn't fair, so let that be a lesson to always watch your back. The enemy may outflank you if you don't."

The tug of war put everyone in a good frame of mind, but now it was over with and a lesson learned, thought Ardent, as he walked into the villa where Bandy and Droll were waiting for him.

"What ever happened to you?"

The mud, now dried a bit, covered Ardent. It was a sight to be seen.

"I was just having some fun with the recruits."

"It looks like you were on the losing end," Bandy remarked, a beautiful smile on her face, as it always was when she smiled. "Now, go outside to wash off."

The day Ardent and his soldiers left brought rain and the sea was choppy, a white cap choppy. The Solders of Christ filed into the shore boats that were heading the Halcyon's way, fully supplied and readied for the sailing. The soldiers that left wives and children behind had sad looks on their faces as they sang a poem of the Lord.

Each of the Solders of Christ, men and women alike, was dressed in a new uniform. The tunic and pants were a tan color with spots of green, as was the foliage at that time of the year. The belt was also tan and had attached to it pouches for the extra cartridges of ammo, a sharp six inch knife, a water pouch and a compass. The boots and hats were also of a tan color, however, each of the hats were of a hardened and thickened cow's hide, metal like, with a chin strap. A small red cross was painted on the back of each hat. The hardened hat was Bandy's idea. The painted, red cross on the rear of the hat, of course, was Abstruse's idea. Each team leader had a dark green ribbon sewed around the right shoulder flap of the tunics, another one of Bandy's ideas.

The rifles were brand new and each butt stock was of hard wood. Although the rifles were heavy because of the hard wood, they were accurate. Since the side arms were only effective at close range only the team leader carried one in addition to his rifle.

If they were to meet up with troopers while on Yeshiva Island, the uniforms suited Ardent's plan of battle. It was a much-wooded island with plenty of trees to hide among, so the tan and green colors would hide them well.

Instead of battling head to head against a frontal attack if the school ground area was overrun, Ardent's plan was to hide in among the trees, hopefully catching the troopers by surprise. It was an idea he got from how the zealots fought. "Hit them, and then run, then hit them again," he told his team leaders.

In spite of the choppy waters and its heavy load the Halcyon made good time, arriving early the very next morning.

That first day on the island was pretty much uneventful. Only one day since leaving Harbinger and already Ardent missed Bandy and having Droll at his side. He thought it best that Droll stayed with Bandy to comfort her during her loneliness.

The Halcyon, the supplies unloaded, was on its way back and an encampment area had already been set up. So Ardent let his men rest the remainder of the day. It would be an early start in the morning and the first thing to do was to clean up the burnt out structures, a hard and dirty task, so a good rest was needed.

The island's bay had high cliffs at the ocean's edge except for a wooded area that led to a hill, and then eventually to the school. It would be impossible for the troopers to approach the school any other way if they were to come, so Ardent posted lookout sentries on the hill.

When Ardent, with Onus at his side, was checking out the burnt structures he noticed that the other four team leaders were throwing dice. Most likely, he thought, the loser's team would have to dig and maintain the waste area. A smile came over his face when he saw Jewel walk away mad, apparently the loser.

"This isn't what I thought soldiers like us would be doing," commented Onus.

"What? Digging a waste area is a necessity," answered Ardent.

"No, I mean reconstructing this school."

"It's the Lord Jesus Christ's bidding," Ardent replied back.

"In the morning I think Stoic's and your team should cut trees for the structures. The others can do the cleaning up. After the cleaning up is finished we will rebuild the mealing area structure, and then the copier structure. The quartering area structures will be last," Ardent suggested to Onus, mostly his thoughts out loud.

"Sounds like a plan to me." Onus knew that a suggestion from Ardent was a command.

◇◇◇

So far things had gone well. Only one week had gone by since leaving Harbinger and already the mealing area and copier area were completed, except for the furnishings, which Abstruse would be bringing soon.

For the time being Ardent was using the copier area structure as his bedding area and a meeting area. Each morning, first light, he and the team leaders went over what was to be done that day. Time was also spent going over what would be done if they came under attack, and Ardent was careful to cover all the possibilities he thought of. Ardent tried to keep as busy as he could. The thought of Bandy being alone, and the wondering if she had their child was often on his mind.

Chapter Twenty~Five

As the sun began its rise to the beginning of a new day, the first appearance of light, a ship silhouetted against it was entering the harbor. The banner of the United American Union of Communes was waving high above its sails. It was running before the wind, broached and its sails full. Surprise was its goal, victory its purpose, the Merrimack was its name.

Aboard the Merrimack were Commander Tome and a detachment of fifty troopers, newly trained and yet to be battle proven.

Tome was to check out what was the Pacifist School. To make sure it wasn't being rebuilt and to search for the copies of the Holy Scroll Writings that a tortured, captured student named Mundane confessed were hidden in caves on the island.

"Seethe!" Tome yelled crisply, and from mid-ship Seethe ran to his side.

"Sir." He snapped his feet together, a closed right fist to his heart in salute.

"Bring the Pariah student, Mundane, top deck."

"Yes, sir!" and again he saluted.

"And find Jejune, I want to see him right away."

"Yes sir," Seethe turned and ran off.

Below deck and in his bedding, Jejune slept. He did not feel well, and had not since departing the capital's seaport almost a month earlier. A seaman, for sure, he could never be. The ship's motion was why he was sick to his stomach, and the remembrance of his last voyage haunted him.

"Wake up, Jejune, wake up," Seethe kept saying until finally he woke Jejune.

"What is it?" Jejune asked, his stomach empty and all his bones sore, yet he still managed to sit up. "What is it you want?"

"Tome wants to see you right away. He's top deck," and then Seethe, his head shaking side to side in disgust, left Jejune sitting up in his bedding still sleepy eyed.

Jejune arrived top deck and waiting were Tome, Seethe and the student Mundane.

"I want the two of you to keep the student at your side, and protect him with your lives. After we check out the school ground area you are to take thirty troopers and go with the student to where the caves are that the Pariahs hid their propaganda writings in, and then burn them all," after which Tome gave a turn of the head motioning for Seethe to leave him alone with Jejune.

"Yes sir, we'll burn everything," and after another salute from Seethe, he grabbed Mundane by the tunic and led him away.

"Do you want me to stay, sir?" Jejune asked.

"You look awful."

"Yes sir, it's the motion, sir."

"Rumor is that Seethe has been a bit rough with you," a serious look showed on Tome's face as he spoke. "In fact, I hear that you have been beaten, and more than once."

"No sir, just an argument on occasion."

"Than what is that bruise doing on your arm, trooper?"

"Sir, I bumped into the rail. It was the motion of the ship, sir. I guess I lost my footing," a lie and Tome sensed it to be. Since Jejune was protecting Seethe Tome was going to let the matter be, for now. But when they got back to the Capital Commune he would have to do something about the matter.

"You must miss your friend Ardent," Tome asked, catching Jejune off guard.

"Yes, he was my best friend, sir."

"I miss him too, and Dank."

"May I go, sir?"

"Yes, and get your teams ready. We will be going ashore as soon as we anchor."

Chapter Twenty-Six

The lookout sentries that were posted on the hill overlooking the bay were running into the school ground area in panic, all excited and yelling, "A ship is entering the harbor."

Ardent, who was helping with the building of one of the student quartering areas heard the details' yells and rushed out onto the grounds.

Ardent waved his arm motioning for Stoic. Not to panic the others he kept calm by acting as though he had been expecting the ships arrival. Stoic was only twenty feet away working outside the copying area when he saw Ardent motioning for him.

"Yes, sir," Stoic was quickly at Ardent's side with a small saw he was using still in his hand. He looked anxious.

"Call everyone to arms. We have company."

"Yes, sir!"

And before Stoic could run off, "Don't panic, you must show calmness in front of the others."

Ardent first thought was that the soldiers might not be ready for their first engagement. Trained, yes, but were they ready to die defending the school, a day's sail from their families and villas? Were they ready for the sounds of battle, the sight of blood?

"The element of surprise is on our side. Never before has the Revolutionary Vanguard encountered a trained and well armed force as we are. Surely they won't be expecting this large a resistance," Ardent told Stoic, to calm his anxiety down.

"If you're worried about the men, and of how they will perform, then believe me when I say they're as ready as they will ever be," Stoic tried assuring Ardent.

"Yes they are Stoic. Yes they are."

Stoic returned to Ardent's side after getting the teams into a formation, their rifles shouldered. Then Ardent called out for his team leaders to quickly gather around him, after which he knelt, putting only one knee onto the ground. With a small, thin stick that he found nearby on the ground he drew a plan of battle into the dirt.

"Are there any questions?" he asked when done. It stayed quiet. There were no inquiries.

"I will be with Sully's team at the forward-most position, in the school ground area," Ardent hesitated for a moment. "Now, all that is left to do is too wait, so take up your positions."

The plan was for the remaining four teams of thirteen each to take up positions in the woods, hiding in the cover of the trees. Two teams to the north of the school ground area, Stoic and Onus's teams. And two teams to the south of the school ground area, Osmo's and Jewel's teams.

The Revolutionary Vanguard will have to come in from the east end, it being the only way into the grounds from the harbor. When they see Sully's team, and not expecting a well trained and armed resistance, they will engage them. Sully's team, to draw the troopers into the trap, will withdraw to the west of the grounds, as if in retreat. The other teams then, and only after the troopers give chase, will fire at the troopers trapping them in a cross fire.

"What if they split up, some coming in from the woods?" Osmo inquired.

"Then, have every other man turn around," Ardent said cheerfully, but loud enough that all of the team leaders heard him. He really didn't know if that was a good idea, but it was the only answer he could think of at the moment.

"How will they react when they see blood?" he whispered to himself. "I wonder how?"

Tome jumped out of the first shore boat knee deep into the water. Right behind him were the other three shore boats full of troopers. He helped drag the boat up onto dry land then waited for the other shore boats. After all his troopers disembarked and formed ranks, column of two, he headed for the woods and the pathway leading to the hill. All fifty of the force and Mundane were there with him. He felt there would be no need to leave any of his troopers behind with the ship. All he expected were unarmed teachers and students, at best maybe a few armed Pariahs. His main concern was could he trust Mundane to show them where the caves with the propaganda writings were? He had to find every last copy. He had to burn them all. As was what the government council had wanted bad enough to waste the time of fifty of his troopers, and a newly built ship and crew.

There was a lot of territory on the island to cover if Mundane wasn't helpful, and since most of his troopers were rookies he would need all fifty of his troopers to help in the search and to watch over the captives, if any.

The school was only about ten minutes away when the column of troopers reached the end of the field leading to the wooded area that surrounded the school. Tome stopped the column's advance and called for his Tertiaries.

"Jejune, take the last ten in the ranks and enter the school ground area from the woods to the left of me. Seethe, take ten also and enter from the woods to the right. It's too quiet, so we better do this by the book. And leave Mundane with me for now, he'll only be in your way."

Tome, with Mundane at his side, and the twenty-eight remaining troopers started running down the pathway and into the school ground area, their weapons ready. Tome, his revolver still holstered, saw what he thought were students running. Then he noticed the uniforms, and that those running were armed with rifles. They're retreating for cover of the structures across the way, his first thought.

"They're armed and in uniform," he yelled out trying to stop the advance. "It's a trap. Run for cover," another yell just as a volley of shots rang out from the woods on each side of the school ground area. It was too late! Two of the troopers in front of him fell to the ground, a spray of red exiting out the upper back of one and the head of the other. He looked back at his column, instinctively, and he saw three more falling hard to the ground. His troopers had yet to fire a shot. It was raining bullets. "You must get to shelter!" he yelled again. "Take cover, it's a trap," and then he pointed to the structures ahead and to his left. After grabbing Mundane by the arm, he headed straight to the structures.

When he looked back again, stopping as he approached the corner of the structure, he saw that his rookie troopers were still out in the open. The fools are down on one knee returning fire. It's going to be a blood bath, his disappointing thought.

'Where did the trained troopers come from, and how did they get armed?' Tome asked. But when he turned for an answer from Mundane, as if he would know, he was no longer there. The doorway at the other side of the structure was open. Mundane's apparent escape way.

"Where's Seethe and Jejune?" mumbling to himself. Then bullets started hitting the structure, "Ouch," he ducked around the corner. Wood splinters stung his face as a spraying of bullets danced up the corner of the structure. The noise of the battle was annoying, confusing matters. He finally drew his revolver.

Seethe saw the rising smoke puffs from the firearms. They were rising from behind the trees, and there were many.

"Tome must be pinned down," Seethe said to the troopers nearest him. "Fire at will, Tome and the others are trapped," he yelled out.

But before any of Seethe's troopers got a shot off, a volley came their way. The first to fall was Seethe, a bullet through the head and instant death. Looking on was Osmo. It was his bullet that found its mark. He had seen them coming through the woods and did just as Ardent had suggested, turned every other man around.

"Good shot," Jewel yelled. Her rifle aimed straight ahead, an eye on the sight. "Watch out!" and she fired the rifle, its bullet hitting a trooper with Osmo in his sight. The trooper fell back, rising his arms, the rifle barrel aimed upward when it fired aimlessly into the sky.

"Thanks, I owe you one," and Osmo knelt back down behind a tree.

By the time the useless, un-battle proven troopers, realizing their tertiary was dead, dropped their rifles and raised their arms in surrender, Jewel had already pulled the trigger. The trooper in her sight fell to the ground. The others, panicking, started to run. Osmo immediately sent three from his team after the retreating unarmed troopers.

Stoic's and Onus's teams didn't fare as well. Neither team leader saw Jejune's advancing troopers until they were fired upon. Several of their soldiers were hit, and in the confusion that followed all of them turned to fire at Jejune's troopers, who now were hiding amongst the trees as well. Both Jejune's troopers and Stoics and Onus's teams had one another pinned down, so a long battle entailed.

"Keep your team here. Tell half of them to turn around and fire at the troopers in the school ground area and tell the others to cover us. I'll try to advance with my team. Maybe we can hold them back," and as soon as Stoic's team re-positioned themselves Onus's team started their advance, rapid firing their weapons.

Ardent's plan was working, so far, but while Sully's team was pulling back the return, fire from the troopers hit two of the soldiers. One, on the ground near Ardent, was wounded and yelling out for help. Ardent ran over to help him. It was Elver, one of the youngest of the group, and he was bleeding from high up on his right leg.

Ardent placed Elver's right arm on his shoulder and around his neck. Then, reaching around, he put his left arm around Elver's lower back and started running for the woods nearby, pulling Elver along as he hopped on his left foot, dragging his right leg.

Tome, with a Pariah that was helping one of the wounded in the sights of his revolver had yet to fire a shot. Then, just as he was about to squeeze the trigger ... "Ardent?" Tome shrugged, staring at him. A look as if he saw a ghost. Then he turned the revolver sight to the wounded one Ardent was helping ... *BANG* ... The bullet penetrated the head and went out the other side, followed by a spraying of blood, some of which landed on Ardent's face and neck. The force from the bullet hit knocked both down, with Elver landing on top of Ardent.

Ardent struggled getting up, and then started running for the cover of the woods nearby, as bullets hit the ground near his feet, bits of dirt exploding upward trailed his every move.

Seeing Ardent on the run, Sully and the soldiers with him started firing at Tome forcing him to duck back behind the structure's wall again for cover. Tome, with his back leaning against the wall and a hailstorm of bullets coming his way, knew now, that he and his

THE LOST CHRIST

troopers were trapped and about to be defeated, and that it was a well trained resistance force he was facing. Not the ordinary zealots he'd faced in the past. No! It was a well trained resistance force trained by his student, his Tertiary Ardent. Now his only hope was Seethe and Jejune. Or were they trapped also? he wondered. "They should have been here by now. They must be trapped," he softly spoke to himself.

Tome came out from behind the wall running for the doorway to get inside for better cover, when "Ouch!" He felt a stinging pain and reached for his left shoulder. "Oh!" Another sting, and this time it was up in the chest, the force of the bullet flipping him over and to the ground, then rolling through the doorway and into the structure where he laid face down, his right foot shaking, uncontrollably.

Ardent, having made it to the woods, watched Sully and his team advance from the west woods, their rifle barrels stuttering out bullets as quick as they could cock the levers. Advancing from the south woods were Osmos and Jewel's teams their rifle barrels smoking.

The remaining troopers stood up, their weapons on the ground and their hands in the air. But still, and coming from the north woods was gunfire.

After gathering those that surrendered three soldiers from Sully's team guarded over them. Then Ardent, his hand pointing to the north woods where he had heard the gunfire: "Sully, take the rest of your team and give Stoic and Onus a hand."

"Yes sir."

"Jewel," Ardent's loud shout as his hand moved, circling high above his head. He got Jewel's attention. "Take your team and set up a perimeter around the school ground area."

"Yes sir," running as she spoke.

"Where's Osmo?" Ardent asked a soldier from his team, having noticed he wasn't with them.

"He went to check on the three he sent after retreating troopers," he himself nervous that Osmo hadn't returned yet, "Do you want us to find him?"

"No, I'm sure he's fine. But let me know if he returns without the troopers. We don't need armed troopers roaming the woods taking pop-shots at us," and he paused for a minute in an attempt to think things over. Then, still unsettled, he headed toward the mealing area structure where it would be quieter to think.

On his way there Ardent noticed that lying dead on the trailway in front of the mealing area structure was Plaudit. No longer would he be the smallest, or his hand shake, Ardent thought.

When Ardent got inside the mealing area structure, on the floor lying face down was a trooper of rank. A puddle of blood was slowly seeping into the ground right next to him, a revolver nearby.

Ardent was about to get someone to remove the body. But then he heard the trooper moan softly, apparently in pain. Ardent kicked the pistol away, and then knelt down to turn the trooper over onto his back.

"Tome, oh my God it's Tome!" A look of surprise crossed his face. He was completely surprised, because, Tome usually didn't accompany his troopers when they went on patrols. This is unusual, he thought, rushing to the open doorway.

"Come over here!" Ardent yelled, pointing at two soldiers that were standing nearby. "Stand guard over this trooper and don't leave his side. And, don't let anyone put another bullet in him!"

Suddenly Ardent, with Tome a captive and his troopers away from their ship, got an idea. But first he had to get a couple of the teams together.

Ardent started back across the school ground area. Osmo was heading his way, and with him were three soldiers from his team and four captured troopers.

"Osmo, over here," Ardent commanded. "Build a big fire and put plenty of green bushes on it. I want lots of smoke for those still on the ship to see. We must make them think the troopers are still here and burning the structures."

"I'll get right on it, sir."

"Where is Onus? I need his team!"

"He didn't make it," Ardent heard Jewel say as she approached, having just returned from the north sector of the woods. The words "He didn't make it" kept exploding in his ears. Onus dead? No, it can't be, it just can't be, his thoughts.

Ardent turned to the direction of Jewel's voice. "What do you mean?"

"Stoic said that Onus was killed advancing against the troopers that outflanked them from the rear," then she was suddenly interrupted by one of the captives.

"Ardent, Jewel, it's me, Jejune!"

"Jejune, by the goodness of the Lord Jesus Christ, you're alive!" a look of surprise on Ardent's face.

"Jejune!" was the loud shout that followed from Jewel. "We thought you were dead."

"Yes, it's me and I'm alive. But I'm not doing very well right now," his silly looking smile followed. A smile Ardent and Jewel were happy to see, thrilled! It took Ardent's mind off the news of Onus's death, for the moment.

"I saw the two ships collide, breakup and sink."

"Seethe and I were trapped on deck near the stern of the ship and were thrown overboard when the ships collided. I was knocked unconscious and Seethe saved my life. He put me on top of a piece of debris, and held onto me until the tempest ended and another ship, somewhat destroyed itself, picked us and others out of the water." Jejune had a grin on his face, as he stepped away from the other captives and started to advance to greet Ardent.

Sully quickly stepped in front of Jejune, jamming his rifle's barrel into Jejune's chest, stopping his advance.

"No!" shouted Ardent as he grabbed Sully by the shoulder. "He is a friend and unarmed."

"He was among those that flanked Onus and he deserves to die," Sully shouted out.

"We cannot be like the government forces. We must show mercy to our enemies, otherwise we are no better than them," Ardent answered, removing his hand from Sully's shoulder and placing it on the barrel of the rifle, slowly removing the rifle's barrel away from Jejune's chest. "Take them and the other captives to the mealing area and post guards to watch over them."

Sully lowered his rifle the rest of the way to his side. "I too am saddened by my friend Onus's death and for Pristine's loss, but all this revengeful killing of the unarmed must stop."

Ardent watched, as Sully gathered the captives and brought them all to the mealing area. Then he walked away looking for Stoic.

"Stoic!" yelled Ardent when he saw him entering the school ground area with a wounded soldier at his side. The soldiers left arm was limply hanging, two bullet holes in it and blood dripping off his finger tips leaving a trail of drops behind them.

"Go to the shore to where the troopers left their shore boats. Take what is left of Onus's team with you and wait for the cover of darkness. Then row quietly to the anchored ship. The ship's crew will be expecting the returning troopers and should be caught by surprise.

Tome made the mistake of not expecting the well armed and trained resistance that was waiting for him, so maybe he left only a small attachment of troopers, if any, behind with the crew. A captured ship could be put to good use transporting arms and supplies to the settlements," Ardent stopped talking for a moment to gather his thoughts.

Still deep in his thoughts, he was interrupted when he heard from behind him two soldiers talking of the battle: "I killed at least four. I just kept firing. It was awful. If I had stopped firing, I believe I wouldn't have fired again. I was that scared," said one as he held his hands together, trying hard to keep them from shaking.

The second soldier, in trying to comfort him: "You did well. I am proud of you. I don't think I killed any of them. I was scared. I hardly fired my rifle."

"What should we do with Onus's body?" and when Ardent turned Stoic was still standing there. Coming out from the woods were three soldiers. They were carrying Onus's body. "Sir, what should we do with his body?" again Stoic asked.

"We will have to bury him here with the others," Ardent answered. He didn't want to think of his friend's death or what he would have to say to Pristine when he got back to Harbinger. He didn't want the soldiers to see his sadness, so he turned his head away. He would have to be strong, for they too, lost friends and family. There was no time for moaning the dead. Their souls are with God now. For that we should be rejoicing, Ardent thought. "Yes, God has a special place for Onus," whispered Ardent.

"Soon," looking at Stoic, "Abstruse and the Halcyon will be returning with the food and supplies we will need to finish. If Abstruse was to see the ship in the harbor he would not enter. So, after you have captured the ship you are to send half your soldiers back here. With the other half you are to stand guard over the captured crew while they sail the ship to Harbinger." Ardent thought that if he kept Stoic busy it would keep his, so concerned, mind off the dead and wounded. "Stoic you have proven to be a good man. A giant you are, but with just as big a heart. Bring the good news of our victory to Harbinger. Then go to my wife Bandy. Tell her that I love her," and he put his hand out to Stoic. It was a firm grip, the handshake.

Ardent walked to where the captives were being kept. He wanted to talk more with Jejune, to tell him of his love for Bandy, and of the child that would soon be born. He also wanted to check into the health of Tome. It would keep his mind off Onus's death. Like Stoic, he needed to keep busy.

"Sir … Commander," the yell from Jewel was loud and got Ardent's attention, so he stopped walking and turned his head, just as he was about to enter the mealing area where they were keeping the captives. "We found a captive student in the woods hiding. His name is Mundane. He was brought here with the troopers to show them where the copied Holy Scroll parchments were hidden, so that they could burn them."

Ardent looked briefly at the student. He looked young and very afraid, his leg shaking.

"Take him to Salient and Pathos. The two should know him."

When Mundane heard the names of his fellow students he repeated their names, and then he started to cry; a joyous cry. "Salient and Pathos are alive?" Mundane mumbled softly.

"Yes, Commander … It appears he knows Salient and Pathos," Jewel said.

Abstruse returned to Yeshiva Island with the furnishings, supplies, the Pacifist Sect teachers and the new students, just as Ardent and his Soldiers of Christ finished reconstructing the school.

After retrieving all the parchments of the Holy Scholl Writings, and once things were back to normal, although it was a smaller group of students, Ardent and his troopers left with Abstruse to go back to Harbinger where his love Bandy was waiting for him. Salient, Pathos and Mundane stayed behind with the students to continue their education.

A boy, as Ardent had said the child would be, awaited his eyes and love. Bandy and he had decided before he left for Yeshiva Island that the child was to be named Michael, after the Archangel.

Chapter Twenty-Seven

Serpentine was pacing the floor of his office area, the thoughts racing through his mind. The Merrimack was gone over three months and he now realized that it would probably not be back for when he was to sail. He needed that ship.

A waste of a ship and fifty good troopers, Serpentine thought, experienced troopers that could have sailed with him. And the more he thought about it, the more upset he got. Yeshiva Island should have been checked out by my legion forces, and the island's bay used as a casting off point to the settlements. I could have sent a force of just five hundred legionnaires to two settlements at once. The settlement citizens are not soldiers. Surely, five hundred trained legionnaires were enough to capture a settlement. Instead, the council wants a show of force. They want me to attack the settlements one at a time, his continued thoughts. He got up from his desk, walked to the window and then looked out onto the parade area. I will issue a kill-all order to my legionnaires. Starting with those at the settlement named Harbinger. Why Harbinger? Because it was the first of its kind, so hence it should be the first destroyed.

What did the council know? They never fought a battle in their whole life, again continuing his thoughts. The fools even put my legionnaires in ridiculous bright red uniforms, as if that would scare the enemy.

"Sir, the cannons have been mounted on the last of the ships," and when Commander Serpentine looked over his shoulder his aid Rapport was standing by his desk.

"Good, then soon we will be sailing. My legionnaires are getting anxious with too much wasted time on their hands."

"Yes," answered Rapport. He too, was anxious … anxious because he had to go with Serpentine. He feared sailing almost as much as he did Serpentine.

"Tell all of the Centurions that I want them at the meeting area tomorrow at noon.

"Yes sir!" and he left.

Serpentine continued his thoughts as he walked back to his desk, a smile on his face. Now finally the waiting will be over. In just a few days my legionnaires and I will be on our way, at sea. All that is left to do now is the daily briefing with my officers tomorrow and the loading of the supplies. Then, stopping his thoughts for a moment, he looked up. The smile on his face got larger. Soon, continuing his thought … right after my sure to be victory, I will be back here to a parade through the streets of the capital, a hero. These believers of God wiped off the face of the earth once and for all. Then, he said aloud, "I shall have the souls of all mankind," a smile turned to laughter, a voluptuous, demonical laughter.

On the wall beside Serpentine, right next to his desk, a mirror reflected an image; a body of a dragon, horns of a ram and eyes full of fire.

⊂✕⊃ ⊂✕⊃ ⊂✕⊃

A day came and gone, and then another, and another and the ships to take Serpentine's legion were still anchored, their sails reefed.

In the Capital Commune was much disorder. Not only with the Pariahs, but also with the many new sects that had come into existence; the idol and sun worshipers, some of which gave human sacrifices to their false gods. Some even worshiped the devil.

Because of Regent Querulous and the council's decision to send Tome and fifty of his troopers to Yeshiva Island the Revolutionary Vanguard was too short handed to quell the disorder. Because of that decision Serpentine was told that his sailing would be postponed until later, and that his legionnaires would have to help, news Rapport hated bringing.

Serpentine rolled the message up into a ball, then threw it onto the floor.

He was in a rage. So much so, that he then picked up the container of ink that was on his desk and threw it at Rapport. He felt like strangling Rapport.

"Idiots, how could they possibly delay by months our departure?" he yelled out at Rapport, who was on his hands and knees wiping as best he could the ink up off the floor.

"Get your ugly face out of here," Serpentine yelled, the veins popping out of his neck.

Rapport quickly left before Serpentine threw something else at him, and while sitting at his desk Rapport could hear Serpentine still yelling to himself. He hated Serpentine. He hated being near him. He feared him. He wished he could run away, but that would only mean certain death. He was no fool. Maybe, however, just maybe someday the right time would come so that he could make a run for it, he thought. He hoped.

"Now they want me to do the Revolutionary Vanguard's duties," Serpentine yelled aloud, as he grabbed his chair, and then threw it through the air. Rapport sat up from his chair when he heard the crashing sound. "You are to hunt down the dissentients within the capital and end their resistance, they said, and until the resistance is put down there will be no ships leaving the harbor, the fools said … the idiots!"

Serpentine, his face reddened, and the blood vessels bulging from his neck, walked over to the thrown chair and kicked it. "The idiots want my legionnaires to be policemen," he yelled again.

The thoughts that were running through Serpentine's mind made his blood come to a boil. "I'll show the believers of God the full might of my wrath. They will all know the name Serpentine when I'm done. Those that are lucky enough to live," and there was more loud demonical-like laughter before Serpentine stormed out of the office area, walking right past Rapport without saying a word. His kicking of the entrance door was mighty, and right after came the sound of the door crashing against the wall, the door left hanging by only one hinge. Left standing, his hands shaking, was Rapport.

The torture quartering area was quiet. That was until Commander Serpentine stormed in getting the guards' attention, jumping up from their chairs. The look on his face was enough to make them worry, and they were.

"Bring me one of the captives, and I mean right now!" Serpentine yelled, startling the guards even more.

Within five minutes one of the guards returned with an old man that could hardly walk upright from the torture he had withstood, his face thin from starvation, a look of near death.

"You fool!" Serpentine yelled, stomping a foot down onto the floor. The same foot that had just moments ago kicked the chair and the door. "Bring me the youngest one you have, you idiot!"

Confused, the guard rushed away, dragging the dying old man with him.

"Can't you idiots do anything right?" Serpentine yelled over at a guard standing nearest him. The guard stood there, his mouth locked with fear, unable to speak.

"Now that's much better," Serpentine said when the guard brought back a youngster, not much older than ten or twelve years old.

Serpentine walked right over to the boy, not a hesitation in his stride, and grabbed him with his left hand by the hair, snapping the youngster's head back. Then, and in one swift motion he withdrew his knife with his right hand, stopping the blades advance only after its sharpness crossed the boy's throat and like an erupting geyser the blood rushed out and upward. Much of it landing back onto the knife and the hand Serpentine after put to his mouth to lick the child's blood.

As if an empty pair of pants the boy fell to the floor, his hand around his throat. And only a brief moment later he lay dead. The puddle of blood that was spilling out of the innocent youth slowly drained into the dirt floor as Serpentine laughed.

Serpentine quickly turned to leave, his anger relieved. Between him and the door was the guard he had just yelled at with one knee on the floor, and from his mouth was exiting his previous meal. Another guard standing just across the way was stunned, his feet unable to move, the fear so great.

"Clean up this mess," he commanded, and then he lifted his right foot jamming it into the kneeled over guard's shoulder, kicking him over onto the floor as he continued walking to the door, leaving the guard lying in the puddle of his just-exited stomach's remains. A sardonic laugh echoed throughout the torture quarters, furthering the guard's fright.

⌒⨯ ⌒⨯ ⌒⨯

Rapport stood up from his seat when Commander Serpentine entered. A smile was on the commander's face, so Rapport knew he had gotten satisfaction somehow. Then he watched him go into his office area, noticing the blood on his hand and tunic. "I wonder who paid for his anger this time," Rapport said to himself, a whisper, as he sat back down hoping he would not be called into the office area.

Serpentine's wrath was mighty and swift. His legionnaires went door to door throughout the Capital Commune, killing anyone they thought might be a believer of a god — any god. Non-believers at the wrong place at the wrong time were slaughtered as well.

Vast numbers of the citizens were gathered and assembled on the hillsides to watch the ethnic cleansing of the Pariahs, usually bomb-fired in large groups after having been tied together, wrist to wrist, and then put atop the piles of timber as the onlookers cheered the fire's inferno. The fires burnt everywhere, leaving behind the smell of death's burning flesh consuming the capital.

Those gathered that cried out were considered one in the same. Some, made examples of, were nailed to crosses, as Serpentine knew Jesus was. Then left for weeks at a time on the hillside for all to see as a reminder, this was a favorite of Serpentine's.

Serpentine's legionnaires were so engulfed with the madness that they stripped to only their pants and boots, painted their bodies and wore helmets adorning the horns of rams when going out on the raids; some even drank the blood of the damned that were slaughtered by their hand. Stanchions with the heads of victims replaced the legionnaire's team banners.

Farming communes located miles from the capital felt the killing wrath the worst, most Pariahs being farmers. Eventually, without enough farmers the crops went uncared for endangering the harvest. The capital's citizens would die without food stored for the cold winter and this worried the council.

Serpentine had gone too far. It would be best to send the legion on its way to the Pariah's settlements, the councilors thought, and meanwhile give control of policing the capital back to the Revolutionary Vanguard.

Supreme Commander Serpentine, Rapport to his disliking at his side, finally got his way. His legion, increased from one thousand to two thousand legionnaires, were on their way to the settlements and back to wearing their red uniforms.

Much to Serpentine's disliking Councilor Plethora was ordered to go with them to see to it that the killings didn't get out of control, as they did at the capital.

"A council spy will be amongst us," Serpentine told his Centurions.

Chapter Twenty-Eight

When the Halcyon arrived back at Harbinger bay the Merrimack, with its cannons removed, was the only ship anchored there. Its crew and captain, contented to remain with their ship were still under close watch.

Stoic had the two cannons that were mounted on the Merrimac taken to the caves on the cliffs, one on each side overlooking the gateway to the garrison wall. A crew was being trained to fire each of the cannons. So a surprise was in store for the legionnaires should they arrive.

Ardent ran from the docks to the villa, his backpack and rifle still with him. At the villa the first one he saw was Droll in the field nearby, and when Droll saw Ardent he ran straight to him, almost knocking him over when he leaped up resting his front two legs on Ardent's chest, his long tongue pressing hard onto Ardent's chin and cheek, soaking them with his love.

"Careful Droll," Ardent said, as he rubbed Droll's back. It only got Droll more excited. His tail wagged a mile a minute, his tongue pressed harder.

"Down Droll, I must hurry. Bandy awaits my arrival."

Once inside the villa Ardent saw Bandy by the stove heating water. He went straight to her and held her in his arms. His cheek against hers he whispering softly into her ear, telling her that he loved and missed her very much.

He felt the warmness of her cheek and the wetness of the tear that was running down and onto his cheek. Then, his eyes glancing over her shoulder, he saw the child, his child, lying asleep in a woven basket placed next to the warmness of the stove. He was wrapped tightly in a small blanket, only his face showing. Ardent could not take his eyes off his child, with golden hair and eyes a bright blue. He was his father's son for sure. Ardent started to cry, and tears of happiness flowed from his eyes.

"Here," said Bandy, as she handed Ardent the child Michael. Then, she too, started to cry while Ardent held Michael for the first time.

"Imagine Bandy, this beautiful child is a part of us both, and not from a test tube," Ardent whispered, afraid to startle his likeness, Michael.

"He looks like you," Bandy said. "He even has your golden hair, what there is of it."

A smile emerged on Ardent's face after he removed the blanket from around Michael. "He's the most beautiful thing I've ever seen."

"I put a hot stone in our bedding to make it warm for us," as she took the child Michael from Ardent's arms. "It'll be cool and damp tonight."

"It has been a long day, and I'm tired and wanting your warmth beside me," and Ardent kissed her, a long kiss.

Ardent awoke late. The sun had already risen. He could hear Bandy in the meal preparing area firing up the stove, and coming from outside he could hear Droll barking, probably at a small animal that he was most likely chasing.

When he got out of his bedding he stood tall, raising his arms high stretching them. His mouth opened wide he took a long deep breath, a yawn, a long just awakening yawn.

Then he remembered that he hadn't told Bandy, yet, of Onus's death. He had thought it better that he waited until today to tell her.

Sully and Jewel wanted to be the ones to tell Pristine of her husband's death. So this day, he knew, was going to be a sad one. Others, too, would have been told of the death of a loved one.

The day was as Ardent expected. But by the next day the settlement's citizens went on with their day to day chores, everyone still aware of the sacrifices made and worried of those yet to be made. They knew that someday, and maybe soon, a bigger battle would come. Many more would die.

On the third day of his return and right after a lengthily meeting with the settlement's council, Ardent went to the captive holding area to check on Tome and his old friend Jejune.

As Ardent approached the embankment to the grinding mill area that was being used as a captive holding area, he stared at the rotating paddle wheel. The stream water that fell upon the wheel's paddles was loud, a squeaking sound with each flow downward that rushed over the paddles.

In the trees nearby and from on the roof of the mill area structure could be heard the singing of the bird animals and the whistling of the wind through the branches of the trees, the branches dancing to the wind's tune. Ardent stopped walking, a pause to enjoy nature's pleasant moment he was being given.

The loud creaking noise from the doors opening startled the bird animals. Their wings fluttering sound echoed past him, and it reminded him of Dank and the day by the statue of Regent Querulous.

A dusting of the loosened dirt from the roof fell down onto his shoulder as he passed through the doors opening, a swift brush of his hand followed.

"Sir, may I help you?" the guard at the door asked, after jumping out from the chair when he saw the commander's rank ribbon on Ardent's shoulder.

"I just stopped by to check on the captives," and again, there was a brushing from his hand to remove the rest of the dust off the shoulder area of his tunic.

In the middle of the grinding mill were two citizens tending to the grinding of the corn into meal. At the rear, in one of the empty storage bins were Jejune and the other five captives.

"Are you comfortable, and have the guards fed you?" Ardent asked, after awaking Jejune from a nap. His thin body was stretched out along the cold dirt floor. The sight of the chains cuffed to his wrist and to the wall disturbed Ardent.

"Yes," answered Jejune. He was rubbing the sleep from his eyes, and at first did not realize it was Ardent that was standing over him.

"I am going to check on Commander Tome. Do you want to come with me?"

"Yes," answered Jejune, as he slowly rose up into a sitting position. Looking up, done with rubbing his eyes, he saw that Ardent looked saddened. Sadness, too, was in his heart. Not just for Tome's ills, but having to be in the position he now was in. Ashamed for having to face his once best friend Ardent, his once thought dead friend.

Jejune knew he didn't have the heart for all the killing. Seethe was always the strong one. But, Seethe was dead, like so many he had known, killed by Ardent's soldiers. How strange things had become, he thought.

"Guard!" yelled Ardent, and quickly at his side were two of the guards. "Unchain this man. He'll be coming with me."

"Yes, sir," answered the first of the guards to reach where Ardent was standing, placing his closed right fist against his chest over his heart in salute, then back to his side.

The second of the guards was down on one knee unchaining Jejune. The chains' rattling was loud, and louder the noise as they hit upon the ground.

"I'm putting a lot of trust in you," Ardent said. The firmness in the sound of his voice almost drowned out by the rattle of the heavy chains, as the guard lifted them from the ground.

"I'll do whatever you ask of me," Jejune answered, while rubbing his right wrist. The blood already scabbed over the cuts and bruise left by the chains tight hold. Bruised also were his feelings and hurt was his self esteem.

"Good, now let's go see our friend."

The guards, puzzled, watched the two as their commander, with his hand on the captive's shoulder, walked out of the captive holding area like the best of friends.

⊂✕ ⊂✕ ⊂✕

The medical quartering area was cold and damp. There, six of Ardent's wounded Soldiers of Christ lay in their beddings, only two able to sit up, their eyes on Ardent and Jejune.

Ardent made sure he took the time to stop and chat with his own wounded, brave soldiers before going to where Tome and six wounded troopers were being cared for.

One such moribund, grim-visage warrior lay still, unable to move. The bandage around his head was soaked of blood. His reddened eyes were wide open and staring straight up at the ceiling. And, from the corner of each his tears fell down onto his bedding's headrest. "Commander, please tell my wife that I love her," the lips barely moved. The sound but a mumbling was meant for Ardent's ears only.

"What is your name?" a bending over Ardent asked, just as he felt the soldier's grip on his arm. The hand pulled Ardent even closer.

"Bucko," his eye's glance moved off the ceiling and stared directly into Ardent's, his grip even tighter. "Husband of Harmony," and then his eyes slowly closed shut. The teardrop that hung in one's corner started drifting down his cheek. He was hanging onto life by only a prayer and a thread, and only for his wife.

"May the Lord always be with you," his heart skipping a beat, the sadness so deep, he removed Bucko's cold hand from his wrist.

Ardent soon caught up to Jejune who was standing near Tome's bedding. The thought of the dying soldier was still on his mind. "I will have to find where he lives and give his message to his wife, Harmony," Ardent said to himself.

"Tome does not look well," Jejune said to Ardent who was looking down at Tome. The bandages on Tome showed much blood, his coloring white as the winter's snow. His body, covered to the neck in the bedding, lay still.

"Is he alive?" Ardent asked of the woman that was caring for the wounded legionnaires when she approached to check on Tome.

"Yes, but barely," she answered. "He's unconscious, and if he comes out of it soon, he may live."

"Ardent, are we all going to die or end up like him someday?" Jejune asked, and then started to cry. The events of the past few days had finally caught up to him.

"Can I get you some water?" the woman asked of Jejune, but there was no reply from him.

"Thank you," replied Ardent instead, as Jejune walked away toward the door leading outside. The sight of Tome lying still on his death bedding was just too much for him.

Ardent went to Jejune who was still in tears and standing alone by the opened doorway. "Come, you must join Bandy and me for a meal." Ardent said, trying to comfort him.

"It might have been one of my bullets that killed your friend Onus," Jejune cried out, unable to control his sorrow.

"Come, old friend, Bandy await us. You must not wallow in your own sorrow. Besides, I'm hungry enough to eat a horse."

A smile of sorts came on Jejune's face, soon followed by laughter from Ardent.

"I wonder," said Jejune. "What would a horse taste like?"

⋈ ⋈ ⋈

While walking to his villa Ardent filled Jejune in on everything that happened to him since their ship sank.

"You have a young child named Michael, one not of a test tube?"

"Yes," a smile emerged. He knew Jejune didn't understand their ways, having been government brainwashed like he had once been.

When they got near the villa, Jejune stopped Ardent to tell him what Ardent already knew, of the two thousand legionnaires that would soon be departing the capital, and of the cannons with the power to kill many at once. What he did tell Ardent that he hadn't already known but suspected, was that Supreme Commander Serpentine gave kill-all orders to his legionnaires; "a kill-all order" — Jejune said it twice, "a kill-all order."

Ardent knew of Serpentine well and witnessed his brutality once in the past. He had no doubt in his mind that the stories being told of his onslaught at the Capital Commune were true. If there was an Antichrist sent by the devil? Serpentine surely was he, Ardent thought.

"Bandy awaits us, so let's not bother with what might be."

"Sir," the voice came from behind Ardent. When he turned he saw running slowly toward him the woman from the medical area that was watching over Tome and the wounded troopers.

"Yes?" he asked, an empty feeling suddenly came from deep within his stomach. He was fearful of what she was about to say.

"It's your friend. The one called Tome." She paused for a moment, as if searching for the right words to say. "I'm sorry, he didn't make it."

And there they were again. The words he heard so often the past few weeks, "He didn't make it." He lowered his head and to himself he said a prayer.

"Ardent, why are so many dying?" asked Jejune, the shock of the suddenness of Tome's death overcame him. "Our friends!" his voice, wimpy, as he fought in vain to prevent the tears. "Why?"

"It is God's will," Ardent said. He too, was fighting back the tears. "Thank you and, May the Lord always be with you," he said to the helpful woman.

Chapter Twenty-Nine

A fleet of ships was *running before the wind*, sails full. To its starboard side was Yeshiva Island. In the lead was the command ship Mount Washington. Commander Serpentine was standing on the aft deck of the command ship and Rapport, as usual, was at his side.

Serpentine could not see the Merrimack in the harbor, where it was expected to be. "Do you suppose Commander Tome is on the way back to the capital?" he asked Rapport. But before Rapport could give an answer: "It's too late anyway. We don't have the time to waste coming about to check the island out," and then he paced, his hands behind his back. When he finally stopped he yelled out: "Captain, will we soon reach Harbinger?" The demanding tone of voice rang out across the ship, getting everyone's attention.

A sailor nearby looked over at Rapport, a smile on his lips. He better hope Serpentine doesn't see that smile, thought Rapport, or else.

"It's about a day's sail from where we are," answered the captain, who was close by at the helm steering the ship on its course, a course to death and destruction.

The captain, named Albatross because he was birthed having only one ear, was fed up with Commander Serpentine and all his demands. Usually he directed his only ear away from wherever Serpentine was standing, just so he wouldn't have to listen to him.

"Captain," yelled Serpentine again. "Can you get this tub to go any faster? A full day's sail will get us to Harbinger's harbor too late in the day. It not being a deep water harbor would mean not being able to disembark my forces and supplies until the next morning, and that would give the Pariahs time to get ready for our onslaught."

"Not unless the wind blows harder," a giggle emerged under his breath.

Fed up with all the delays Serpentine went to his quarters, which he commandeered from the captain who had to bed below with his crew and he didn't like it, and he didn't like Serpentine either. Not at all.

As Serpentine expected, the fleet arrived at Harbinger's harbor just before sunset. In the harbor was but one ship, its sails reefed it would be easy target practice for his cannon crew. He gave the order to fire the cannons.

Captain Abstruse saw the fleet approaching, and knowing he wouldn't be able to set sail in time, and that the fleet's ships had cannons onboard, he would have to order his crew to abandon the Halcyon. His voice stuttered when he gave the command, the hardest he ever had to give. His heart saddened, more-so as the words "Abandon ship" exited his shaky voice.

The Mount Washington and the first two ships right behind it, the Mississippi and the Appalachian came about, then the volley, six cannons fired at almost the same time. A likening to a cascade of thunder was the sound from the guns. Ear deafening whistles followed, as the destructive balls of metal streamed across the sky. Standing by were the Concord, Mt. Rushmore, New Brunswick, Mt. Olympus and the Mt. Ouachita.

Abstruse, being the last to exit his ship and with as many of the parchments of the Holy Scroll Writings that he could carry in his arms, was just jumping into the shore boat awaiting him when the water exploded all around his Halcyon. Six misses, but he knew that the gun crews were just getting bearings. Some from the next six rounds fired, he knew, would be the beginning of the end of his Halcyon, a true friend she had been.

Three of the next six rounds fired hit his Halcyon. Splinters of planking and decking flew upward high over the water, some of the splinters landing in and around his shore boat.

One of the wood splinters penetrated into the thigh of one of his crew, a young lad named Sleek. He was also soaked with the salt water from a near miss that landed in the water short of the Halcyon.

The sea's water flowed from his face, as the sailor screamed out in pain: "Oh God! I'm going to die." His hands were wrapped around the splinter at where it entered his thigh. Blood was oozing out between his fingers.

"This is going to hurt," Abstruse yelled out after he knelt next to the about to go into shock sailor.

The Holy Scroll's parchments, soaked, left lying on the shore boats decking. The words written, disappearing slowly, were being erased by the salted water. But never would they be erased from Abstruse's mind or heart.

"Oh God — No…o…o…o!" was the lad's screams. Abstruse, standing tall in the rocking, unsteadied craft held the splintered planking in his hand, the blood dripping from its pointed end. It had cut through a vein and a pulsating gusher of blood was exiting upward from the lad's leg, a lad that was shaking with fear; the fear that the nearness to death brings.

"Pray for me," his lips trembling, the lad cried out again. "Pray for me."

Abstruse threw the bloodied splinter into the sea and knelt again next to the lad and pressed his hand down onto the wound, but all in vain. Sleek lay quiet, his eyes still open.

"Row quickly," Abstruse yelled out. "Row quickly, or like him we will all die." Then, he prayed for the soul of the lad too young to die.

Another six whistles made all aboard the shore boats duck, quickly forgetting about Sleek and what just happened. Fear for themselves were the only thoughts.

"This can't be happening. They can't take my Halcyon away. They won't, not from my heart. No never!" Loud was the scream a straightened-up Abstruse yelled out, his fist closed, as he shook it at the fleet of hostile ships. From deep in his heart the screams came, his eyes red and swollen.

But in vain were the screams. Three more destructive balls of metal crashed down onto his Halcyon, one of which hit hard the center mast. It snapped, the upper half crashing to the deck and ripping apart all that it hit on its way downward.

Another six whistles sent everyone in the shore boats ducking down for cover again, all but the oarsmen. The water from the explosions was splashing all around the smaller crafts.

⸺ ⸺ ⸺

Darkness was blanketing the harbor and the moon's reflection wavered about the oscillating ocean, as the shore boats reached the docks crowded with onlookers. The young lad Sleek, whitened with death, was carried and put down on the damp, cold sand of the shore.

Abstruse, his crew and the crowded onlookers watched as the next volley from the cannons set the Halcyon afire and on its voyage to a watery grave, the lookout nest the last of his Halcyon to disappear.

"A fine ship she was," Abstruse said, with a smile of remembrances on his face. "Salt is in my heart, the same salt that will forever stain my Halcyon."

Chapter Thirty

The cascading thunder like sounds and whistles that followed them echoed through the valley's gateway and on past the meeting area structure. Inside was the usual Sunday evening gathering for the reading of the Holy Scroll Writings. Cavil stopped his reading as soon as he heard the sounds.

Ardent, sitting next to Bandy with Michael in her arms, knew what the sounds were from. The same sound that was made when his two cannon crews learned to fire the two they now have. So did the rest of those gathered there, all of whom were now rushing out of the meeting hall.

Those chosen to fight went to gather their firearms. Some went to ready for the wounded-to-be. The women with young children were to go to the shelters deep within the caves stocked with provisions. Ardent refused to let those women with children bear arms in battle, for the sake of the children.

The alarm bell was being sounded, as Ardent reached the main trailway. The bells ring was loud and could be heard throughout the island settlement.

Ardent rushed to the villa with Bandy right next to him. The child Michael in her arms, and Droll was running in circles just ahead of them, an occasional bark of excitement. A look of panic covered Bandy's face. The thought of Ardent doing battle was on her mind as she fought off the tears.

He would get his firearms and put his uniform on as soon as they got to the villa, leaving Bandy to worry and care for Michael, and like the other woman with children she would be going to the caves.

"Take Droll with you to the caves. He will watch over you and Michael," Ardent said, both now at a quick trot, the villa just ahead.

"Please be careful," said Bandy just as they approached the villa. She was still struggling to hold back the tears, like the strong woman she was would.

"I love you."

The words "I love you" sank deep into Ardent's mind, a mind that was racing with the thoughts of having to leave her and Michael alone to fend for themselves, and of the thoughts of the battle soon to be, of the many that would die.

Ardent held the door open and watched Bandy as she set Michael down in his basket, then as she walked back to him. They stood at the doorway embraced in one another's arms. Ardent slowly stepped back and out of her arms, left extended out to him. "I love you," again she said, as she brought her hands to her heart. Unable to hold back any longer, her eyes filled with tears that spilled over and then ran down her cheeks.

Bandy watched as Ardent put on his uniform. When he shouldered his rifle she knew he was ready to go. Then Ardent took her in his arms again, as though he sensed her anxiety, but quickly he let go of her. He had to go.

Ardent took another moment and looked on as Bandy took Michael out of the basket and cradled him in her arms, bouncing him up and down upon her chest to settle him down.

"It's time, I must go," Ardent's voice cracked as he spoke. He could not delay any longer.

"I love you," and she started to cry.

"I will return to your arms soon," Ardent answered. "To you and Michael I must return."

Waiting for him when he got outside were Jejune and Jewel, a reminder of times past. Of a long, long time ago.

Ardent was standing on the garrison wall walkway trying to get the best look he could at the ships, now anchored. The thought of having to leave Bandy alone with Michael was still on his mind. At least Droll was there to watch over them both.

"Where is the Halcyon?" Ardent asked.

"They sank it. The cannons you heard," Sully, standing nearby answered. "But, at least the Merrimack wasn't. It had already sailed to Newfoundland with the sixty-five reinforcements that were here. We really could use them now."

Ardent looked down toward the dock area and well off into the distance. As yet, there was no damage along the shoreline, and the cannons on the ships quiet.

Stoic, Sully, Osmo, and Jewel were at his side awaiting his orders, as was also Jejune. He asked to be with him and Jewel when Serpentine and his two thousand legionnaires came. He got his wish, a wish that might bring his death.

Ardent asked the signal man to signal the caves on the cliffs and tell those manning the cannons to hold their fire until the government forces were in shore boats. Then he asked the signal man to stay at his side.

Using a candle lantern that was designed for signaling, he started sending the code, a little known code used by smugglers, a code Abstruse taught them.

The ships, except for their lanterns, barely could be seen, what with the clouded sky covering the moon. If the legionnaires embarked there would have been many lanterns approaching the docks, lanterns that would have been on the bows of the shore boats to light the way.

This delay, thought Ardent, would give him the rest of the night to prepare his Soldiers of Christ. It would also give most of his soldiers some time to rest before the battle that would be.

"Stoic, take your team to the docks and set them afire."

"I'm right on it," Stoic answered his commander, turning quickly and running down the stairway. He trusted Ardent's decisions. After all, Ardent was chosen by God to lead them in battle, he thought, and this battle was to be the battle of all battles. It would be a battle that they had to win, and if not, the rest of the settlements would fall to Serpentine's wrath. One at a time they would fall, until there were none left. Innocent Pariahs would die, a countless number of God's believers, if they didn't drive the Antichrist from the land.

"Sully and Osmo, you both are to take your teams and put yourselves at the villas behind the docks and spread yourselves out. When the government forces approach and while still in their shore boats, kill as many as you can before they reach the shore. Then you are to retreat back to the garrison wall before the first of their boats reach the shore."

"We'll get many and that's for sure!" Osmo answered, a grin from ear to ear crossed his face. He was ready to fight, ready to kill.

"But wait, there is one more thing."

"What?" Sully asked, he too grinning and anxious to battle.

"You must torch all the villas while retreating, so be sure to retreat soon enough to do so."

"But those villas are domicile to many," Sully questioned Ardent's decision.

"They are made of just wood and stone. The structures will make good cover for the legionnaires to hide amongst. They can be rebuilt later. Serpentine's butchers will burn them anyway and this whole settlement if they were to get past this garrison wall; let alone kill every man, woman and child." Ardent fell short of telling them of the "kill-all order."

"What about their cannons?" Jewel asked.

"The guns are useless mounted to the ships. They may reach the shoreline, but not the garrison wall." Ardent laughed at Serpentine's stupidity, and then continued. "Because the harbor is not of deep water the ships are anchored too far out for the cannon's might to reach."

"Ardent, you are so smart. That is why you have been chosen to lead us," Jewel interrupted. What she didn't know was that Ardent really didn't know the range of the cannons. He had only hoped Abstruse was right, that they would not be able to reach the garrison wall.

"Our two cannons will reach anywhere within the gateway. At least, until they run out of ammo."

"May the Lord always be with you," Jewel said.

"And also with you," Ardent answered.

Chapter Thirty-One

An explosion and then gunfire that sounded like it was coming from nearby woke Serpentine from his light sleep. Sitting up so quickly from the sudden loudness he almost fell out of his bedding.

"What in the New World is going on?" he shouted, but no one was there to hear him.

Then, and suddenly, there was another loud explosion that got him out of his bedding in a hurry and the Mt. Washington rocking from one side to the other and back again. He rushed out of his quarters, half dressed.

Starboard and close by was the Mississippi and it was in flames, its sternpost laid across its deck and a large hole aft. The legionnaires aboard and the crew of the Mississippi were jumping overboard into the dark and cold water, tunics in flames, and the screams heard a deafening cry.

At the bow area, away from the flaming inferno, were legionnaires firing their rifles at a small shore boat heading for the docks which were also on fire. The flames ashore were reflecting off the low ceiling of clouds, lighting up the sky over the docks.

"What in the New World is going on?" Serpentine yelled over to Rapport, who was standing by the rail watching the confusion and chaos that was going on aboard the Mississippi.

"I don't know, sir," Rapport, turning to face his commander, yelled back and then once again turned away to watch ahead.

Captain Albatross, having heard Serpentine's yells, walked up to him. "Captain Tenet, known to us all as a man of principals, and some of his crew set the powder kegs stored aft in the binge on fire. Apparently he and some from his crew must be recent converts."

"They're all idiots! The council gave me all the idiots there are in the world," Serpentine yelled. "Look over there, by the rail is the biggest idiot of them all … my aid. They gave me him too!"

"What is going on, and why is one of our ships in flames?" It was Plethora, her voice irritating Serpentine. "It scared me to death."

Her hair was a mess. Her large nose was spread across her fat, round face as usual. The sight of her standing there suddenly made Serpentine start laughing, a roaring laugh that got the others there laughing as well.

"Can't you keep things under control?" she said as she wobbled toward him, upset with his insulting laughter.

Serpentine, just as suddenly as he started, stopped laughing and a look of madness came upon his face. Albatross noticed the look and stepped back, just as Serpentine headed toward her. And when they met at the sternpost he grabbed her by the back of her neck and pushed her face into the sternpost hard, so hard he grunted.

Blood immediately squirted out from her enormous beak of a nose onto the sternpost. Then after grabbing a fist full of her hair, the blood left upon the sternpost trickling down, he walked her over to the rail.

She was moving awkwardly and in a dizzy state, her legs bowed outward the stiffness and rigidity gone. Then, and with a big smile on his face, he pushed her over the rail and into the water.

The waters wake from the impact of her giant body rose all the way up onto the decking, some onto Serpentine. Then like a giant stone her oversized body quickly sank out of sight, and all that was left were the bubbles floating where she had entered.

Albatross and the rest that witnessed Serpentine's audacious, beastly behavior stood still, their feet glued to the decking. Then suddenly, when Serpentine turned away from the railing and looked their way, they found their footing and quickly walked away, each thinking that they could be next.

Serpentine, the Antichrist of the era for sure, was left there alone, a roar of laughter bellowing out of his mouth. Behind him the bow of the Mississippi stood straight up out of the water, and its final sail would soon be to the ocean bottom.

Atop the up-righted bow and its decking were the legionnaires that didn't jump from the ship in time, each hanging from whatever each could grab, their legs kicking in search of something to hold them up longer; but in vain, as the Mississippi disappeared the suction from its draft took them as well.

Most of the legionnaires that were aboard the Mississippi perished. Only twenty-three of the more than two hundred legionnaires and six from the crew were plucked from the water, many of them with burn wounds.

Each of the fleet's ship captains would not forget that on that night Serpentine had refused to help or let any of the survivors aboard the Mount Washington. "We lost two cannons," was all he had to say.

Captain Tenet and his retinue arrived safely to the shore amongst the burning docks, after almost being shot at by Stoic's team. After arriving at the garrison wall, sent to Ardent by Stoic, Captain Tenet and those that came with him volunteered to fight. Since they totaled twelve men Ardent kept them together and promoted Sanguine, a young sixteen year old with a positive attitude and followed orders well, as their team leader. Soon after, Captain Tenet met for the first time Abstruse, who also just arrived and given rifles to use for the battle to come.

The early morning brought a light rain and choppy seas. It was just bad enough to make it difficult for the legionnaires to embark the shore boats. Much time had been lost, enough so that it would be daylight when the shore boats reached the now burnt-down dock area. Concerned, Serpentine had his fleet of nine ships, only nine now that the Mississippi was lost, position their cannons to the shoreline to cover his landing force, if a resistance from the Pariahs. He didn't expect much however.

The first wave of 36 shore boats, each with 12 legionnaires and 4 oarsmen on board, departed for the shore. The light rain was now just a mist. It would take five waves, at least, to get all the legionnaires to the shore and at least another two for the supplies and DIPS.

Both Osmo and Sully were ready and watching the shore boats approaching, not yet in range of their team's rifles. Twenty-six soldiers spread out amongst the dozen or so villas, their fingers on the trigger waiting for Osmo to fire the go-ahead first shot.

Osmo, by the villa closest to the water took aim at one of the oarsmen in the lead shore boat; a hit oarsman would surely slow the boat down. But the body of the oarsman kept moving as he rolled, making his aim difficult. He held the rifle steady, timing the rower's motion. Slow and with his breath held, he pulled the trigger.

The bullet found its mark. The oarsman fell forward onto the oar and its paddle end extended upward over the water. By the time he fired again the rest of the soldier's fingers had already squeezed their triggers and the bullets hitting the targets aimed at. Four, then three more legionnaires fell over the sides of their boats.

Osmo's third shot hit a legionnaire that had stood up to get to the oar left extended upward. A forehead hit flipped him backward, blood first exploding out the back of his head.

Sully, after several good clean hits, moved his rifle sideward across the water toward another shore boat. He fired three shots before his target, an oarsman, fell forward.

Some of the soldiers were getting the most pleasure from shooting at the legionnaires holding a vexillum or long colorful banner.

Osmo, his magazine now emptied was reaching for a hand full of cartridges to reload when he heard the cascade of loud thundering noises, then the whistles. His eyes blinked, instinctively, when he saw the shores water plummet skyward, as most of the projectiles landed short of the shore and in front of the advancing legionnaires.

With the next volley from the cannons the small villa next to him broke apart. Michael, the young stranger that spoke at the meeting, flew through the air with the splinters of wood and rock fragments from the villa, as Osmo watched his body land on the ground in a tangled mess. Landing all around him were the splinters and stones. Lastly, rolling on the ground was his shrapnel-severed arm.

Sully, leaning against another villa that was hit, was knocked through the air. Landing on and all around him was what was left of the roof, and not more than ten arms lengths away was a chair from inside the villa.

Osmo started running toward Sully when the next barrage arrived. The scattered projectiles, two landing in the water and sixteen in amongst the villas, were deadly. Wood splinters, rock fragments and body parts lay in the trailways. Three giant craters were all that was left of where a small villa once stood.

Osmo, having leaped to the ground at the whistling sound got up and while the damage was still falling he continued running to Sully.

Sully, dazed and confused, was trying to get up from the ground. In his right leg was a large open wound, the tan and green of his pant leg soaked red.

"Over here, take my hand," Osmo yelled.

Sully reached for Osmo's arm, extended out to him, letting Osmo pull him up. Once Sully was upright Osmo bent down and put the left shoulder against Sully's stomach and lifted him, while wrapping both his arms around Sully's legs.

Osmo, now running with Sully atop his shoulder, heard the sound of the cannons again, only this time there were only two, then the whistles. It was coming from the caves on the cliffs, and in the water amongst the legionnaires shore boats the two friendly-fired projectiles landed. Both were misses, but the gusher of water sprayed wide and the waters turbulence rocked several of the advancing shore boats, slowing them down.

"Hang in there, my friend. Hang in there," Osmo tried comforting Sully, as he reached the rear edge of the seafarer's commune area.

Running and tossing torches into the villas were six soldiers, total, and all that was left of the two teams. Still, a couple of the villas remained un-torched. There wasn't time. The first wave of legionnaire forces were now on the shore and the undamaged shore boats on the way back to embark the second wave.

"Hurry, we must get back. There is no time left to torch the rest of the villas," Osmo yelled out to the others.

"What about our wounded?" the soldier nearest him yelled back.

"Forget it. They're all dead. There are no wounded," Osmo answered, and just as he finished he heard the sound of cannons, again only two.

"They're covering us, so hurry," Osmo yelled out, already on the run and still with Sully on his back.

The noise from the cannons was loud enough that the Seer Josef heard it from his cave and left his cave dwelling for the first time since arriving at Harbinger. In his hand was a wooden staff. On his face was a look of concern. The time he saw coming had come! Ardent would need him at his side. It was the Lord's wish he be with Ardent.

Chapter Thirty-Two

"Rapport!" was the third angry-like scream that came from Serpentine, but again there was no answer. "Rapport!" a fourth time and still there was no answer. "Captain Albatross!"

"Yes," answered Albatross, from the top of the stairs leading to the aft deck.

"Where is Rapport, my aide?"

"His bedding below is empty," Albatross answered, having already checked below for Rapport, right after the second outrageously loud scream from Serpentine.

Albatross stayed standing at the top step. Serpentine's heinous nature scared him. So much so, he feared getting any closer to Serpentine. The thought of what had happened to Plethora was still on his mind.

"Well, where is he then, if not in his bedding?" As soon as he got the words out of his mouth, the two cannons from within the cliffs caves roared out their thunder. Turning to look, he saw the projectiles land amongst his legionnaires ashore. Then the noise of the cannons aboard the Mt. Washington sounded their loud thunder.

The smoke from the just-fired cannons aboard the Mt. Washington rose up into the sky, as one legionnaire from the cannon's crew swabbed the muzzle. Another from the crew loaded the black powder and a third put the ball of metal, with a cavity packed with a high explosive bursting charge of black powder, down the cannon's barrel. Its fuse, measured in seconds, was cut to length by the cannon crew co-leader. The other co-leader set the degree angle to aim the gun.

Albatross waited for the just-readied cannons to finish firing before telling Serpentine where Rapport might be.

"I believe Rapport jumped overboard and swam to shore," and right after the words exited his mouth Albatross stepped back a step at a time, never taking his eyes off Serpentine.

Fortunately for Albatross the shore boats had just returned and the second wave of legionnaires were embarking, taking Serpentine's mind off Rapport.

"I'll be going ashore with the third wave to see for myself why the resistance is so strong," Serpentine said to Albatross. "But first, I must find me another aid to replace that idiot Rapport."

On Serpentine's mind, was that the Merrimack must have been captured. That would explain where they got the two cannons. Maybe he under estimated the Pariahs' strength, after all. And who, he wondered, was good enough of a strategist to lead them?

⌒⌒⌒

After finding a new aid and ordering the captains of two of the ships to disassemble their cannons and have them brought to the shore's landing area, Serpentine embarked for the shore. Albatross was glad to be rid of him. Hopefully, a Pariah's bullet would find his heart, if he had one. He wished.

Confusion and disarray was what Serpentine found when he reached the shore. The waterlogged bodies of the dead left unattended to, were being pushed up against the shore's sand by the harbor's small rippling waves, the sand at the shore's edge reddened with blood.

"Get your legionnaires organized," Serpentine commanded a confused centurion that was just standing around with his rifle shouldered. Immediately after, an explosion rocked the ground. The sand under the centurion's feet erupted upward falling down upon Serpentine and the legionnaires close by, his severed body parts scattering about the ground, and his armless, legless torso came crashing down into the crater left from the explosion, the head still attached, and the mouth and eyes still open.

Serpentine brushed away the sand and wiped away the blood of the centurion from his arm and face, never yielding to the explosion's might.

Another centurion standing nearby looking useless jumped when Serpentine repeated the command to him, "Get the legionnaires organized," and hastily the officer ran, either to do as asked or to hide from Serpentine.

Upset with the discipline of his centurions Serpentine started gathering the legionnaires himself. Those that didn't move fast enough he grabbed by their arms, tossing them together into, somewhat, a formation. Still the projectiles from the cannons in the caves were exploding amongst them.

When a legionnaire's body was tossed upward, and landed back onto the ground at Serpentine's feet, he kicked what there was left of it out of the way, and then continued gathering his legionnaires.

The next wave of legionnaires arrived when, finally, Serpentine got them organized. And with the arrival of the shore boats were the four disassembled cannons and their battery crews.

It was nearing the evening and still the legionnaires were bogged down in the field before the garrison wall. Serpentine, upset at the lack of advancement, went to the front lines to find out why. To his surprise, the gateway was littered with the bodies of legionnaires, the earth about them drinking their blood.

The advancing legionnaires of the second wave were jumping over the dead in their eagerness to advance up the gateway, only to be cut down. It was becoming a slaughter, he thought.

From the top of the garrison wall shots rang out. Behind the rifles' sights were the blurry eyes from thickened smoke that surrounded the defenders, from fires lit in the field of grass, where legionnaires were hidden behind the dead bodies. Their rifles resting on the backs of the dead they were returning fire, as more of death's lead from the caves rained down amongst them.

Serpentine yelled over at one of his centurions: "Tell your legionnaires to retreat." But the centurion, too scared to get up from the ground ignored the command.

You could not hear the shots fired from the revolver above the noise of the battle, but you could see the centurion's body fall to the ground from the bullets that went into his back. Serpentine, his revolver still smoking, yelled the command out again and loud enough for those near to hear it.

Serpentine stood tall, waving the hand with the revolver in it toward the rear lines, "Retreat … I said to retreat!" as the bullets fired from the caves hit the ground all around him.

Not until the last legionnaire that evaded the oncoming volley of gunfire passed by did Serpentine follow.

"What about the wounded?" a retreating centurion asked.

"The wounded will have to fend for themselves," the answer from Serpentine.

--- ✦ ✦ ✦ ---

When Serpentine returned to the shore area the cannons from the ships were assembled and ready to fire.

"Fire at the caves you idiots," immediately ordered Serpentine, upset that they hadn't already been fired.

"Fire!" yelled the #1 gun officer, and quickly he bent over and away, his hands over his ears.

"Fire!" yelled the #2 gun officer.

"Fire!" yelled the #3 gun officer.

"Fire!" yelled the #4 gun officer.

The explosive sound out of the cannons echoed through the gateway valley, and soon after, the cliff to the cannon batteries right took four explosions, the caves unharmed as rocks and dirt collapsed downward into a stream below that flowed to the harbor.

Another four explosive projectiles, this time the bearings changed, bellowed out from the exit holes of the cannons' barrels, a burst of smoke following.

Two projectiles hit just under one of the caves, collapsing the stone and dirt under the sand bagged wall used to shield the team of soldiers within. Broken fragments of stone mixed with dirt, slid outward then down the cliff's side, taking with it the sandbags and three of the soldiers.

Gunfire from the legionnaires in the field struck two more that were left standing in the now unshielded cave. One fell forward following the other four to the water and rocks below.

Serpentine held back the legionnaires from advancing again, all of which were anxious too, now that the cannons were pounding the Pariahs.

"We'll pound them from here with our cannons for awhile," he told his new aid Supine, a passive person, but he was not a fool. He just couldn't run and hide fast enough from Serpentine's search for a new aide.

Chapter Thirty-Three

It was loud, very loud the sound of battle. The constant thundering of the cannon fire that echoed throughout the caves that the women and children were hiding in was deafening, the rat-tar-tar-tar of the gunfire sending chills up the women's spines.

Cuddled together in different groups some of the women were crying, some too busy to cry.

"I can't take this much longer," Myopia cried out. Standing with one of the groupings of women and children, her one-week-old newborn son in her arms she started to walk toward the cave's opening.

"No," Pristine said, grabbing Myopia's arm. "We must be brave for the children's sake."

Myopia sat back down, but still her hands shook uncontrollably, and from the corners of her eyes she glanced toward the cave's opening before resting her infant's body close to hers.

A cascade of screams and crying from one child to another rippled through the cave when the next blast from the cannons echoed off the walls. The ground shook right after, loosening the dirt and stone particles. Some of which fell down onto the ground, the dust rising from where they fell.

"We must pray for our loved ones," Bandy asked of the others sheltered from the battle, trying her best to maintain calm.

"My husband Paul is out there," Mary, only fifteen years of age and born a Pariah said softly. She was trying hard to hold back the tears. Her hand, too, was shaking.

"I want my papa, I want my papa," one of the children cried out and others soon followed. A cascade of cries, again, echoed loudly off the walls of the cave.

"I can't stand this," Myopia yelled out, standing up quickly.

"We must all kneel and pray," insisted Pristine, both her hands extended out, palms down motioning downward, as she started to bend her knees to get to the ground to lead everyone in prayer.

"Yes, we must all ...." and before Bandy could finish agreeing, Myopia started running as fast as she could out of the cave and then down the hillside toward the battle sounds heard off in the distance.

Bandy paused ... stunned. She handed Michael to Pristine and ran out after Myopia. Then Droll ran out after her, barking, as though calling her back. Back out of harm's way. Back to be with her son Michael.

"Wait up, Myopia wait up," she yelled as loud as she could, but to no avail. Myopia, running insanely and with her newborn son still held tightly in her arms was too far away to possibly catch up with.

On her way back up the hillside to the cave Bandy thought of Ardent. She too, like the others for their loved ones, was worried for his safety. She looked down at Droll, "We were meant to be together, Ardent and me. God put us on the same path. He drew us together to Harbinger, our starting place to a new life," she said, and a bark from Droll was all that she got back, then a wag of his tail.

A fire was warming the cave when Bandy and Droll got back. None of the woman asked Bandy about Myopia, instead they gathered the vegetables stored in the cave to cook over the fire. They all knew that they would never see Myopia or, most likely, the child she had only just given the precious gift of life to ... a shame, such a shame.

Bandy, after getting Michael back from Pristine, found an isolated spot at the far end of the cave. She sat upon the cold, dampened ground cuddled up with Michael in her arms.

Droll approached, his tail wagging slowly. After licking her cheek he laid down next to her, his legs stretched out, his back resting tightly against her thighs.

Bandy put Michael down between Droll's legs, resting Michael's head on the softness of the animal's stomach, and then she started to pray.

"God — Please bring Ardent back to me," she asked, and then wept at the sudden thought of ending up like Pristine — Losing the one person most important to you. "How does she do it? It's been such a short time since Onus was killed, yet she handles it so well. God, you must bring Ardent back to me," Bandy whispered to herself, and then she cried.

Chapter Thirty-Four

The darkness of night came, the moon lost behind a cover of clouds. Still Serpentine's cannons, blindly, kept pounding the fortifications. The dead were still scattered along the garrison wall walkway, a walkway and its wall that were beginning to fall apart, the projectile hits so many.

The body count paid in legionnaires lost or badly wounded numbered over a thousand, their bodies laid out from the shore to before the garrison wall.

A heavy count of dead already and this only the first of many settlements he would have to encounter, Serpentine was thinking. At best, a victory now would be pyrrhic. There would be no parade of honor now. The price in legionnaires lost was too great. Now a victory is a matter of pride. I have a surprise for those at that garrison wall, and he smiled.

"Supine," Serpentine yelled out.

"Yes," a quick answer, and there had better been.

"Tell troops 6 and 7 to find as many work carts as possible and to fill them with anything that will burn. There should be plenty of wood from the villas or what's left of the villas."

"Sir, there isn't much left of troops 6 and 7, or any of the others for that matter," Oops, he thought. He knew what he had just said didn't make Serpentine happy.

"Then use the wounded!"

"Yes, sir," and he ran off out of sight. Finding any of the wounded would be difficult, he thought. Most were left to die on the battlefield.

"Keep those cannons firing," Serpentine yelled toward the positions of the gun batteries. "I don't hear them firing!"

"But the men need to rest and to sleep, sir," questioned a gun crew co-leader.

"They can rest when this battle is over," the angered look on his face was enough to chase the young co-leader off and quickly after the guns roared again, their fire and smoke filling the air nearby. They were firing blindly through the camouflage of smoke before the wall, at a glow of red smothering ambers.

"Idiots," Serpentine said out loud to himself. "Why do they keep giving me all the idiots?"

Because of the darkness the cannon crews were unable to see the destruction caused to reset the bearings proper. The rounds previously fired were usually misses leaving only craters in the ground. But the whistles of the incoming cannon fire and the explosions that followed kept Ardent's Soldiers of Christ awake, the anxiety overwhelming. The garrison wall, however, weakened even more when it was hit, and eventually there wasn't much left. So Ardent's soldiers took up new positions on the roof of their quartering structures.

Rifle fire from the soldiers in the caves on the cliffs, and the darkness of the night was all that was keeping the legionnaires pinned down, all that was postponing the final assault.

Now that the only remaining cannon was out of ammo and the deteriorating garrison wall becoming useless, the remaining soldiers were all that was left to stop Serpentine's advances when they come, and they would come, thought Ardent.

The fires at the garrison wall footings had been put out, but weakened badly. The tree trunks were still hot with red ashes, charred badly and portions of the wall had collapsed.

Ardent ordered Sanguine's team to fortify the wall as best they could. Captain Tenet was the first to start, and the darkness of the night didn't seem to stop the legionnaires from firing at him, and the others when they came to help. The task became too difficult and several crewmen and women paid with their lives trying, lives Captain Tenet or Ardent didn't want to lose, lives wasted. Sanguine's team was called back.

It was midnight when Ardent headed for what was left of the garrison wall walkway to check on the soldiers. Near the wall's end were several soldiers standing by a fire to keep themselves warm.

"Do you mind if I catch some of your fire's warmth?" Ardent asked of them.

"No, Commander. Go ahead and help yourself," said one of the soldiers.

"Oh, that's nice and warm," Ardent said, rubbing his hands together capturing some of the fire's heat. "Thank you."

"You're welcome, sir," said each there, as Ardent walked away toward the garrison wall stairway nearby. He glanced back when he neared the top of the stairway. There weren't many of his soldiers left, he thought. A lot of families would be saddened by the news of the loss of their loved ones.

Once atop he crouched down behind the stacked sandbags and walked, stopping for a brief moment at each soldier still awake to give a comforting word. He almost fell when climbing down to one of the quartering structure's roof at one of the collapsed sections of the walkway.

When he reached the end of the walkway he turned and walked crouched down back to the other end from which he started. Then he sat down, a couple quick winks would do him good, he thought.

It was getting chilly so he slipped a bedding woolen over his body, up tight to his neck. Then the wall shook when a projectile landed nearby, and right after another even closer. Eventually, even with all the noise, he fell asleep snuggled-up to the woolen … a dreamy sleep, dreams of him, Bandy and Michael together.

"Wake up, Ardent," and when he looked up Obtuse was crouching behind the sand bags next to him.

"What is it?"

"Out there in the gateway are a lot of small fires," said Obtuse, pointing his finger over the sand bags.

"What time is it?"

"Four o'clock."

Ardent lifted his head and peeked over the sand bags. Stretched across the gateway the length of the garrison wall were at least twenty large fires moving toward the wall.

"Get everyone to gather as many barrels of water as they can carry, quickly." When he turned to look again the fires were still moving toward the wall.

"Burning carts," he yelled, looking down to the soldiers below. Then, just as he got the words out of his mouth two shots rang out from below amongst the hiding legionnaires.

Obtuse fell up against Ardent, blood flowing from the side of his face, his ear missing and a hole through the side of his head. Then, rolling off Ardent he fell to the walkway before Ardent could grab him. Then he rolled off the walkway, falling to the ground ten feet below and landing onto a fire the others had lit to keep warm. The very same fire Ardent stopped at earlier to warm his hands.

The sparks were still in the air as two of the soldiers that were almost hit by the falling Obtuse, lifted him from the fire, burning their hands when his tunic suddenly exploded into flames. By the time someone brought a barrel filled with water, his body was burnt black and his face unrecognizable.

Before Ardent could run down to Obtuse, gunfire at the approaching burning work carts rang out all along the walkway. Several of the legionnaires pushing the work carts fell to the ground, victims.

Ardent watched as the remaining legionnaires behind the carts retreated to safer ground. The carts, however, continued downward and hit hard up against the remaining wall of tree trunks, the sparks snapping as they rose high up into the night's sky. Immediately the barrels of water were being tossed onto the flames, but to no avail. The fire started burning out of control.

The legionnaires started firing at those trying to put out the fires hitting three of them, one soldier his body flipped over backwards, and then rolled off the roof of a quartering structure that was burning.

"Stop," Ardent yelled out. "Let the fires burn," and while running along the walkway he kept yelling the command. He wanted to make sure everyone heard him.

Bullets fired from the field were hitting the sand bags near Ardent as he ran. *Puff ... Puff ... Puff ...* the sound, followed by a spray of sand from the bags, the bullets lodging deep within. Ducking lower, he continued and wasn't going to stop until everyone was back under cover and safe from the sights of the legionnaires' rifles.

Stoic and others watched with disbelief. "Get down, get down!" Stoic yelled, "Get down!" And Ardent leapt forward onto the walkway flooring just as a projectile from a cannon slammed into the section of wall from which he just leaped.

The wall broke apart, first upward with the explosion's plume, and then collapsing downward. A loud thumping sound followed as the tree trunks tumbled down onto the roof of one of the quartering area structures. Right behind fell the sandbags, their once filled sand raining off the roof's edge.

Ardent got up and brushed the dirt and bark chippings from his torn and dirty tunic. Then he glanced along the garrison wall, what there was left of it. He realized then that it would be a hell's inferno soon, and that the burning garrison wall and the area around it would be an easy target for the cannons now, lit up as it was.

"Stoic!" a yell, and within moments he was at Ardent's side. "Tell everyone to fall back to the wooded areas near the commune."

"But the garrison wall," Stoic asked.

"It's lost, Stoic, its lost." And just then Stoic grabbed Ardent, taking him to the ground with him as a projectile hit the wall.

"I didn't hear that one coming. There have been so many that I'm getting use to the sound," Ardent said, standing up and brushing himself off, leaving Stoic on one knee. "Are you all right," he asked, glancing down at the big man.

"Yes, but that was close!"

"Serpentine's plan is to kill as many of us as possible before he sends his legionnaires in for the final kill." Ardent started telling Stoic. "But we will be ready for them," and as he finished speaking, the whistles from the projectiles sang out their warnings again. And they kept coming and coming.

Three rounds of four shots each from the cannons landed before everyone retreated to the woods, gathering then near Ardent. At least six of the soldiers died and several were wounded running for the woods. Surely, many more of his soldiers would have joined those dead had he kept them at the garrison wall, now a burning death trap, thought Ardent.

"Serpentine is wasting the might of his cannons. With the garrison wall abandoned his explosive projectiles are falling to no avail," Ardent told Stoic and the others gathered nearby. Then, after a long look at Stoic, Ardent noticed how exhausted, bloodied and disgusted he looked.

"Did your friend Osmo make it?" Ardent asked.

"I'm right here, sir," and when Ardent turned around standing there was Osmo, and he looked as bad as Stoic did. All three started laughing at each other. It did all three good to laugh. It was needed.

"Sir, what will we do now?" It was a sad looking Sully limping his way, a "Why are you laughing?" look on his face. Right behind Sully was Jejune. Ardent didn't see Jewel anywhere. He didn't want to ask where she was. He feared they would say "She didn't make it" so he didn't ask.

"We will spread out in the forest and hide under the cover of the trees and then wait for their advance to the settlement," he continued. "When they come we will hit them hard with rifle fire and then run, hide again, hit them again and run again. We must keep them off guard and nervous, wondering where the next bullet is going to come from. If Serpentine is as bold as he has been so far, he will see many more of his legionnaires die before getting to the settlement," Ardent told his soldiers. His plan was imbued with the methods the zealots often used, and used effectively.

"Go in the name of the Lord Jesus Christ. And, May the Lord always be with you," were Ardent's instructions.

"And also with you," each of the soldiers answered, one at a time and with a salute to the heart, an expression of their love for their brave commander.

Seer Josef, with the staff in his hand, approached from out of nowhere just as Ardent was finishing his instructions to the soldiers that remained. The Seer didn't say a word. He just stood there and stared at Ardent, a sad look on his face.

Chapter Thirty-Five

The garrison wall and quartering area structures were still burning, most having already collapsed before the remaining legionnaires, 500 at best, made their way toward it. The screams and loud bursts of gunfire from the on-rushing legionnaires could be heard from the forest where Ardent's remaining soldiers hid and waited.

The new uniforms blended in well with the foliage, hiding the soldiers where they waited to make their last stand for their loved ones, for their freedom and for their beliefs in the one God, and of His son, Jesus Christ.

><><><

Serpentine, having found the garrison wall deserted had the battery of horse drawn cannons brought forward. On his face was a look of surprise, beneath was the hate. The hate he had for all mankind.

"The cowards ran away to hide in their settlements like little children. They will get no mercy from me," Serpentine said to his aid, Supine. Then, after pacing in a small circle while thinking the situation over, his hands behind his back: "Tell the centurions to form their legionnaires in a column of four. Then tell the cannon crews to single file. We'll let the cannons go ahead with a team of legionnaires as escorts while we regroup. When they get to the other side of the woods to where they can see the settlement, blow the Pariahs precious little villas to pieces. I want nothing left standing when we arrive."

"Sir, what if the Pariahs are hiding in the woods waiting for us?"

"Just do as I told you," his voice got louder.

After Supine left his side Serpentine ruminated over what he had just said to Supine. Then he went to where his senior centurion Sycophant was standing.

Sycophant looked nervous, sweat beaded on his forehead. Then from his mouth the flattering flowed:

"Commander Sir! You had the right idea bringing the cannons to shore." The beads of sweat started running down his forehead, which he quickly wiped off. "Soon we will have the taste of victory because of your brilliant leadership, sir!"

Sycophant's usual flattering remarks didn't exactly impress Serpentine, as he watched him wiggle like the worm Serpentine thought he was.

"Stay behind with sixty legionnaires. After the cannon crews leave you are to enter the woods, thirty legionnaires on each side of the trailway. Just in case some of the cowards stayed behind and are hiding in the woods waiting for us to advance, with hopes of picking us off one by one."

"Yes sir, Commander, sir!" Turning about, he left to prepare his legionnaires for the order he was given. Then, having noticed that the cannon crews and their escort had already started their advance, he started to run. It would take a few minutes to ready his legionnaires.

"Fools, they send me all the fools," a whisper, as Serpentine shook his head in disgust while watching Sycophant run off. "Hurry," he yelled out, laughing at his fool.

Chapter Thirty-Six

Aboard the Mt. Washington, still with its cannons aimed to the shore, Albatross was signaling the other captains. A smile was on his face, as he said the instructions to his signalman.

"The Mt. Washington is unguarded. All the legionnaires are still ashore. How goes you?" He waited for the replies. They were all the same, all without legionnaires. Only the ship's crew and cannon battery crews were on board.

"I request permission to leave the harbor unharmed." The words to his signalman came slowly out from his mouth. His crew was in agreement, no matter the consequences.

There was no reply, not from any of the other captains. Albatross waited a bit longer before giving his next command to his crew. A command he had hoped not to have to give. But his mind was made up.

"Man the cannons," he yelled out. He watched as the cannon crews positioned themselves. "Ready for sail," was the next command he shouted out, and soon after he heard the sound of the anchor rising, and then the sound of the sheets and halyards lifting the sails upward. *Bang, Bang, Bang* ... the sails caught the wind. The Mt. Washington was moving.

The first of the other ships that the Mt. Washington must pass would be the Appalachian. Its cannons were removed and brought to shore, so Albatross did not fear her.

Anchored near the Appalachian was the Mt. Rushmore, which was armed with its two cannons. The other ships anchored were not in cannon range of the Mt. Washington. If he got by the Mt. Rushmore's cannons, he thought he could outrun the others having set sail well before them.

The cannons of the Mt. Washington were trained dead onto the Mt. Rushmore as it passed. Albatross held back the fire command, waiting for the captain, a friend, to make the first move. There was none, the Mt. Washington passed without incident. It was on its way out of the harbor and *running before the wind.*

A sigh of relief crossed Albatross's face when he entered the open sea. And when he glanced back aft, following the Mt. Washington in single file was the rest of the fleet, all at full sail and, *running before the wind*, running as far away as they could from Serpentine's cruelty — a memorial to those that Serpentine abandoned and let die aboard the Mississippi.

To his portside off in the distance he saw another ship and it was heading toward Harbinger's harbor. The sails full of wind and a large red cross was painted upon them. It was the Merrimac. It would continue unopposed.

Chapter Thirty-Seven

Ardent was lying in a ditch behind a fallen tree amongst the bushes, well hidden. The unarmed Seer Josef was at his side. The Seer just would not leave him alone. While he waited Ardent inserted more cartridges into the magazine of his rifle, carefully sliding each in until it was re-loaded.

"Go to the caves with the women and children," he whispered.

"I must stay with you."

"It's not safe for you," but still the Seer would not leave.

The rest of the soldiers, sixty at best and many of which were wounded, kept spread out and hidden on both sides of the trailway to Harbinger. They were all on their own now, most the team leaders dead. "Hit and run," Ardent had told them earlier. "Hit and run."

"Over there," Seer Josef whispered, his finger pointed ahead at the first of the cannons advancing along the trailway.

"If we kill as many of the gun crew as possible the guns will be useless," Ardent whispered. "Serpentine must be sure of his victory to send them ahead, and with so small an escort."

Ardent glanced to his right side. Just ahead were Stoic and Osmo, lying side by side. Friends, they would finish the battle together. To his left behind a large willow tree, on one knee, was Sully. Ardent wondered if Sully's mind was still on Jewel. He wished Jewel was there.

Lowering his head, pressing his cheek firmly against the butt of his rifle, he inserted his finger onto the trigger. He aimed, one eye closed. His rifle sight was on one of the legionnaires escorting the cannon batteries. The bright red uniform would be an easy target.

Ardent slowly squeezed the trigger, and as he cocked his rifle to reload he watched his target fall backward, then to the ground under the cannon in the lead cart. Ardent, the first to fire was the signal for the others.

Quickly, one by one the escorting legionnaires fell as the bullets rained on them from within the woods. Only a couple returned fire before they were cut down in the crossfire. Now the unarmed gun crews would be easy pickings. And they were.

The cannon battery crews, the few left standing, started running away only to be cut down in their tracks. The few that did not run managed to hide behind the wheels away from Ardent's gun sight, but to no avail. The soldiers on the other side of the trailway finished them off, their bodies twisting and flipping to the ground.

Then the horses, at one time man's friend, fell, crashing to the ground. Ardent again squeezed the trigger, his sight on the horse pulling the leading cart. Then he watched it fall. It was the last of the horses there. In all, only a couple minutes of battle passed.

Ardent heard bullets hitting the leaves and tree trunks all around him. He turned. Behind him he saw red tunics. Sycophant and his legionnaires were closing in on them. It was time to run!

Unable to run a few of the soldiers stood their ground, delaying the advancing legionnaires. They took with them to death gathering place some of the advancing legionnaires. The self sacrificial delay gave Ardent and the others the time needed to reposition themselves.

Ardent stood up to run, to his right he saw Sully. He was lying on the ground with a pool of blood next to his head and on the ground near his side was his rifle. He would join Jewel, his love, thought Ardent.

Ardent and others did manage to run and reposition themselves, but some had paired up or gathered in groups of three or four and only by chance. That wasn't good.

"Split up," Ardent yelled. "Hit and run."

Sycophant and his remaining legionnaires were closing in fast on Ardent's soldiers. Advancing from the trailway to Ardent's right and from where the cannons stood quiet was Serpentine's column of legionnaires. It would be difficult for Ardent and his soldiers to retreat again and reposition themselves.

Even above the sounds of the rifle battle you could hear Serpentine yell out commands to his centurions.

"Advance these cannons to the settlement," he yelled to the team of legionnaires nearby, as if there were crews to fire the now-useless battery of cannons, or as if there were horses to draw the carts to the settlement.

Ardent, from behind a clump of dense bushes, saw Serpentine, his real image — that of a dragon with a human-like head, horns of a ram, and fire in his eyes.

He raised his rifle, his hand shaking. The fear was from the sight he saw. Then he tried to steady his hand, the Antichrist in his rifle's sight, the barrel shaking, yet still his finger squeezed the trigger.

Suddenly two bullets hit the ground near him, then another hit the tree trunk next to him, the shots coming from advancing legionnaires heading his way. He turned and fired at them until the magazine emptied. Then he stood, ready to run. With a quick glance back where he saw Serpentine, he saw him still standing there.

Two more bullets hit the tree trunk next to him. He blinked, as pieces of bark separated from the tree, left were the two markings from the bullets. "Run," he said to himself, "Run!"

Ardent retreated toward the villas, running fast and moving side to side. He could hear the passing bullets sound, all near-misses. The thought of what he saw....Serpentine, the Antichrist, was still on his mind. He shivered, and then thought: Killing Serpentine would have to wait for another time, another place.

Ardent stopped running to fire at the legionnaires chasing him. His rifle's magazine emptied, so he started running again, and once he got a long lead, and after getting down on one knee behind a tree he inserted another hand full of cartridges into the magazine, fired until it emptied, reloaded and continued firing again.

The rifle barrel got hot, smoking. The sound of continuous gunfire was everywhere ... Pop ... Pop ... a-rat-a-tar ... Pop ... Pop ... a-rat-a-tar.

Soon his backpack would be empty of cartridges, he thought, and if so he was ready to fight with his bare hands. Then he looked ahead and he could see the sunlight peeking in at the woods edge. Off in the distance, across an open field of small yellow flowers, was the settlement.

Seer Josef appeared again, suddenly standing near him like he was immune to the bullets, his staff still in his hand. The fool, Ardent thought, and then he reached grabbing the Seer by the tunic pulling him to the ground. Ahead also, were Stoic and Osmo. They were running out of the woods toward the settlement's edge, and not far behind them were Jejune and the others. He saw that there were not many left.

Now he was alone with the helpless Seer, and why was the Seer there and not at the safety of the caves, he wondered. He stood up quickly.

"We got to make a run for the settlement," Ardent yelled to the Seer. Then, before running, he looked back to see where the legionnaires were, and he saw Jewel running, being chased by legionnaires.

Jewel is alive, his immediate thought, she's not dead after all, and a big smile broadened his face. Then suddenly, "Ouch!" he yelled. "Ouch!" Again he yelled out. He was hit, once in the hip and the other, more deadly, in the chest.

Up close in front of Ardent was the legionnaire that shot him, his face painted red with the blood of his kills. About to add Ardent's blood, the legionnaire hesitated at first, then fired a third and fourth shot, just as Jewel jumped in front of Ardent. Jewel's rifle fired in return, an instinctive squeeze of the finger as the two bullets from the legionnaire's rifle hit her in the stomach.

The ground came quick for all three. Ardent stopping when his knees hit the ground. Before him lay the other two, his would be killer and Jewel, who gave her life for him. Still standing, looking down at him, was the Seer.

Ardent leaned over backward resting on his heels. Sitting still, unable to move, bound toward death, moribund. He thought of Bandy, and of Michael.

"Bandy!" he yelled out. "Bandy, my love!" Then his head fell forward resting on his chest.

⊂✕ ⊂✕ ⊂✕

Seer Josef, having seen and expecting it to be, was right there ready to pick up Ardent from the ground. The moment he saw before had come. He quickly got down on one knee, and with the strength of a youngster, coming from deep within his old body, he lifted up the quiet Ardent.

The staff was still in the Seer's hand and dragging along the ground as he ran out from the woods with Ardent draped across his arms, Ardent's arms hanging free, dangling back and forth with each short step the Seer took. He stopped running only when they got on top of the hill overlooking the settlement.

It was the very same hill that the Archangel appeared over and the very same hill that the animals and birdlife came forth from, God's gift to mankind for the rebirth of His Son. The Lost Christ that will once again preach the word of Thy Father.

After sitting Ardent down the Seer Josef knelt down, putting his right leg behind Ardent's back and his left hand on the back of Ardent's neck holding him steady so he could watch the battle. Watch the forces he commanded.

A loud barking sound awoke Ardent from his unconsciousness. He slowly lifted his head. He saw Droll running up the hill. A small smile appeared on his face as a tear fell from his eye. Droll sat right next to him, a guardian to the first of a bloodline, of many to come, a bloodline that was chosen by God to lead His children to His Kingdom.

The Soldiers of Christ, after retreating to the settlement's edge took up positions in amongst the outer perimeter villas. There were only thirty soldiers at best left, against at least three hundred legionnaires … ten to one, a last stand.

Stoic and Osmo looked around, quick glances in search for Ardent. Unable to see him they took command.

"Fire at will," Stoic yelled. The concern for Ardent lingered on his face. He could not be dead. He was sent by God. But then, so was Jesus sent by God and He died on a cross, he thought.

"I'm almost out of ammo," Jejune yelled back.

"Then we'll fight them with our bare hands," Osmo yelled, he too, down to the last of his ammo.

"Pray for our souls," Abstruse cried out, down on one knee, his rifle's butt hard against his shoulder. Aside of him with a bullet through his neck lying dead was a fellow captain, Tenet, whom Abstruse had never met before this day. "May God have mercy on us all," he was ready to meet Jesus, in man's image, the son of God.

Faces all painted, the legionnaires stormed out of the woods, all crazy. The heads of some they killed displayed at their stanchion's tops, screaming and yelling "Death to the Pariahs," the kill-crazed legionnaires kept running wildly across the field of yellow. Serpentine was leading the way, his face also painted with the blood of the dead.

Their rifles spat out bullet after bullet in the settlement's direction. A couple of Ardent's soldiers fell to the ground either dead or wounded, while others wildly returned fire into the wall of red tunics coming their way.

"What are you doing here?" Stoic said when he saw Cavil, Sordid and Stymie standing near, each with a rifle in their hands neither knew how to use very well.

"We've come to help," Cavil answered.

"May the Lord always be with you," Stoic said.

"And also with you," Cavil answered.

Suddenly, the legionnaires started falling dead or wounded, the shots fired coming from the rear of the advancement. Ardent watched as ten, twenty, no, at least sixty men and women dressed as Soldiers of Christ came running out of the woods onto the field of yellow, their rifles raised. In their lead was Yenta. It was reinforcements from Newfoundland. The harbor having been left unguarded by the government's departing fleet they sailed in aboard the Merrimac, unopposed.

Ardent's remaining brave soldiers ran out from the perimeter villas and advanced toward the legionnaires when they saw the reinforcements. All three groups merged.

A hand to hand, gun to gun and blood to blood battle had begun, one like never seen before, a to-the-death encounter. Stopping only when there were no tunics of red to battle, only Serpentine remained. Like General Custer's last stand, alone and last he stood. Surrounded by his enemies, their rifles aimed at him, he raised the hand his revolver was in.

Chapter Thirty-Eight

Ardent was getting weak. The death gatherer was coming, and the Seer could see it to be soon. His gifted eyes were of a golden glow and sparkling deep within. He lifted his right hand, with his staff still in it he pointed upward into the darkening, clouding up sky.

⌒⌒⌒

As the battle on Earth was coming to an end, above in the sky, seen only by Ardent and the Seer Josef, was yet another battle being waged.

Perched in the sky with their wings spread open, some with spears and others with swords, the Archangels had taken up their positions to defend the Kingdom of God.

Ascending were the serpents and dragons, both with six wings and breathing out fire. The dragons, their heads human-like with horns like those of rams, all adorned spears, the blood of the souls of sinners past dripped from the three-prong, fork-like tips.

A dragon, among many that were sent, its mouth open, fangs sharpened and puffs of smoke flowing from his nostrils lead the charging sinners. From the bowels of all hell the devil unleashed all his might against God's defenders.

⌒⌒⌒

Bolts of lightning streaked across the darkened sky, as good and evil converged. The thunderous noise echoed across the land, battle drums calling the charge.

In the lead and the first to do battle was the Archangel Michael, field commander of God and highest messenger, the Advocate of the Jews. A helmet and vest of steel adorned his body. In his left hand was a shield with the inscription "Quis ut Deus" (Standing over the dragon) and in his right hand was a lance readied to launch.

His lance streaked across the sky and pierced the advancing, leading dragon just below its head. Then jumping onto its back with his wings spread opened wide, St. Michael withdrew his sword and with one mighty swing he beheaded the devil's beast. Its life's blood, the screams of sinner's souls, bellowed out from its neck, as its misguided soul fell toward the earth disappearing into the evening sun's setting glow.

All of God's guardians of his Kingdom followed St. Michael into battle; St. George, St Theodore, St. Demetrius, St. Sergius, St. Procopius, St. Mercurius and many others. The Sons of the Light, to battle with the Sons of the Darkness, and for the winner was the souls of all mankind and God's Kingdom.

While still lying against the Seer Josef's knee and as both the battles raged on, death, God's call to his Kingdom of Heaven, arrived for Ardent. The Seer, sadly, lowered Ardent's head to the ground, before him he knew laid the guardian of the new republic, a new nation.

Through his gifted eyes the Seer Josef watched as Ardent's soul rose up from his body. In his outstretched hand was a sword pointed to the battle in the sky. Opening wide his new wings, a glance down at the Seer, he ascended to the battlefield, an Archangel, guardian of the new republic, he ascended.

Swiftly he flew across the sky, his wings guiding the way, until upon the back of a serpent he leaped, his sword buried deep into its throat.

Serpentine's screams were heard all over the land *as Saint Ardent buried the sword the second time*. As the soldiers fired their rifles as a flaming inferno, a killer of mankind no more, a charred dusting, he fell to the earth as the Soldiers of Christ looked on, their rifles still smoking *as Saint Ardent ascended to the Kingdom of God, a sword in his hand.*

Chapter Thirty-Nine

Abstruse, now skippering the Merrimack was waiting in the harbor for the shore boats to arrive with his passengers, while his crew readied the anchored Merrimac for its sail. He missed the Halcyon, but the Merrimack was a newer, larger ship. He would get used to her.

The destination was unknown. "A search for an uninhabited island far away, and for the safety of the child," was all that he was told.

Stored in the cargo hold of the Merrimac were the food supplies, seed, farming tools, and livestock that would be needed.

Dawn had just appeared and the mist-like fog was lifting when the shore boats approached the Merrimac. Aboard, the first to arrive, were Stoic and Osmo with their rifles shouldered, Jejune and Pristine (married before having departed), Bandy with the blessed child Michael in her arms, the Seer Josef with a staff in his hand, and there was Droll, a guardian still, sitting tall next to the child Michael. The second shore boat was right behind and in it were six cohorts of Ardent's best-trained, battle proven, armed Soldiers of Christ. Like Templar's, and generations of them thereafter, they would be the guardians of a bloodline. At the rear of the shore boat was a water-proofed box containing a copy of the Holy Scroll Writings.

Abstruse's eyes were on the third shore boat lagging well behind the other two. In it was the casket carrying Ardent, to be rested eventually somewhere on a newfound island, well hidden from the government's forces.

Abstruse's right hand went to his chest, a salute to the bravest of soldiers. Tears were in his eyes, the short memory of Ardent in his heart. "May the Lord always be with you," he whispered.

The Merrimac sails were full and she was *running before the wind*.

Mike Difeo

What God wanted of Michael, the Blessed One, the future of a new government of the United Settlements of the Americas and the destiny of the Pariahs was unknown to its passengers.

Ending Narration

The seven New World countries would strengthen their forces and coalesce to restore government rule. The ethnic cleansing of Pariahs throughout the seven countries would soon follow, unlike any the world had ever seen before.

In masses and from all over the world the surviving Pariahs would exodus to the United Settlements of America, where they hoped to live and worship freely.

After having found an un-inhabited island to hide the gifted Michael and the others from the New World governments, Abstruse would return to Harbinger. Ten years later the freedom ship Merrimack, while sailing back from the European Union of Communes with fleeing Pariahs, would sink to the ocean floor. With it Abstruse and all the fleeing Pariahs aboard would perish. The victims of the united forces of the New World governments' newly formed Naval Battle Fleet.

Michael, born in the likeness of his father, would become a man and with Stoic and Osmo as his teachers, he was well trained in the art of combat and as a leader. Bandy, with fever, died before Michael's tenth birthday, although it is also said that she died of a broken heart. Jejune and Pristine, she not being able to bear a child of her own, continued raising Michael as if he were their son.

Other than a once-a-year visit from Abstruse and his crew to bring news and needed supplies not found on the island, no other person would set foot on the island hideaway.

The Seer Josef, having found a cave on the island to reside in, went blind right after arriving to the island. Since Ardent's death, he lost his given power of seeing all that was to be. Seer Josef lived long enough to teach Michael from the writings of the Holy Scrolls.

Jesus the child, the rebirthed son of God, would become a student at the pacifist school on Yeshiva Island with Pathos and Salient. After years of difficult studies He would, with a retinue of disciples, set forth upon the land to spread the word of His Father. So would begin mankind's next test in the search for the Kingdom of God — **The Suffering Christ: The Dark Reprisal**.

"And, May the Lord always be with you."